AWAKENING

The Maiyochi Chronicles

PHILLIP L. JOHNSON

Black Rose Writing | Texas

ISBN: 978-1-68433-782-8
PUBLISHED BY BLACK ROSE WRITING
www.blackrosewriting.com

Printed in the United States of America
Suggested Retail Price (SRP) $18.95

Awakening is printed in Book Antiqua

To Henry Lee 'Pete' Peterson, a true friend when a friend was truly needed, and to William 'Bill' Barnwell, who was always willing to share his knowledge and wisdom between sets in the gym.

AWAKENING

The Maiyochi Chronicles

"You are as a young child, lacking in knowledge, and so must be taught the ways of the world. But unlike a child, you are unaware of your ignorance. Of your world and your place in it, I know nothing. But in this world - my world - you are helpless. And as with the young of all creatures born helpless into the bounty of our Mother, you will learn or you will die."

–Hanshee of Clan Dula

PROLOGUE

The lush green jungle appeared to stretch on forever, encompassing all of existence. The birds could take flight and soar above the canopy to catch glimpses of the cloud-covered peaks far to the west. But to a man, saddled by anatomy and gravity to an earthbound existence, the jungle closed in until all thoughts of other environments were pushed aside. It was the only reality.

He sat, as he had for the past three days, on his heels with only his feet making contact with the fine sand of the riverbank. Occasionally he would stand, stretch, and quietly pace the shoreline, making sure his legs did not succumb to the sleep the rest of his body had been fighting since his arrival. He would not pace for long. More often, he would simply wiggle his toes, or slowly shift his weight from one side to the other, always careful to make no other movements. Most times, but for the rhythmic expansion of his chest, he was as still as death.

Except for his eyes.

Moving slowly from one object to another, his eyes took in everything. Never darting wildly as would those of a frightened animal, they were a window to the sense of purpose and strength of will that fueled his vigil. If his lids began to droop, his hand would slide into the leather pouch he wore on his left hip and emerge with a clump of a moist, leafy substance that he would chew until the fatigue passed. In this way he fought off the sleep which threatened to close his eyes and cut short his watch.

His ears were also alert, taking in all the varied jungle sounds, from the tranquil melody of the flowing water, to the piercing shriek of a raptor. Sounds of life were everywhere, from the buzzing of insects, to the warbling call of something unknown on the opposite bank, to the soft hiss of the foliage blown by intermittent cooling breezes. On the second night there was the sound of something large, maybe something fierce, and he had the feeling that he was being watched and weighed. Minutes passed before he heard the careful retreat of padded footsteps. Relaxing his grip on his knife, he again turned his attention to the river.

His mind, like his knife, was sharp, but its edge was dulled by every hour he kept watch. He wondered how often he could go to the well of the tabba plant that temporarily renewed his strength. As he chewed rhythmically on the potent leaves he let his mind wander over the last six seasons and the long, hard journey that had brought him to this spot on the riverbank at this particular time. In his current state of exhaustion the small details were lost to him, but the words of the High Elder rang as clearly in his mind as if they had just been spoken:

"You have prepared well. Your mind, your body, and your spirit are now focused so that the three are forged into one. Surely The One Spirit will watch over you and guide you. You have nothing to fear, for you are Maiyochi."

Maiyochi, The Chosen, is both a badge of the highest honor and a portent of the darkest dread. *Maiyochi is* the one called upon to serve their people in times of their greatest peril, likely against threats unknown and unseen.

The call would come down from the Elder Priests of the Mountain. At their word all clans, from all tribes, would begin The Test.

The purpose of the testing is to choose the finest warrior from among the People of the Earth. It is open to all men and women of an age. Only the very young and the very old are denied. Still, only a few ever answer the call. Though they are warriors and hunters in their prime, only a small fraction of men, and fewer women, could hope to endure even the initial testing.

Each tribe would choose from among its best, but so rigorous was the testing that not every tribe put forth a champion. Most fell short. Strength and skill, speed and stamina, knowledge, wit, and will, were all pushed to their limits and pushed again even further, for there could be no mistake in the choosing.

The testing was brutal.

Some did not survive. For those that remained, survival came with no guarantees.

The Elders considered *how* a candidate survived, the reasons behind the choices that led to survival. What were the different paths, and was the candidate thoughtful in their choosing? Though pushed to their physical limits, were they able to fully grasp their situation? Though almost delirious from hunger and thirst, injury and illness, exhaustion and pain, were they able to think clearly and well, so as to ensure survival and the completion of their task? And when the physical burdens became so great that rational thought was swept away by doubt, confusion, and fear, could they then trust in the favor of The One Spirit to guide their steps and see them through?

Having survived this ordeal, how could they be sure that they truly held the favor of The One? How did they know that survival was not a matter of fortune? If faced with similar obstacles, their body and spirit again beaten down, could they triumph again, and again, and yet again?

Yes, the testing was brutal. First the clan, then the tribe, and finally the Elders themselves, ensured that only the very best would undergo the cleansing and the prayers that marked the final stage of rebirth as *Maiyochi*.

As difficult as the testing was, those few who had knowledge of themselves and were secure in their ability strove for the honor. With the title came the chance for glory to rival the legends of old. And though cryptic knowledge of undefined disaster is what fueled the call, for a certain type of man or woman the chance to meet the challenge - to strive, to prevail or perish in the attempt - caused their blood to race and their spirit to soar.

So he sat at the river's edge, keeping watch and reflecting on his position, his blessing, his curse. At that moment it came into view.

Without hesitation he slipped into the water.

CHAPTER 1

Classic rock wafted from the speakers as the sport utility vehicle wound its way along two-lane county roads bathed in alternating sunlight and shadow. It was a clear and beautiful midweek morning in August, and Raymond Covington was at the wheel. His longtime friend Frank Bishop rode shotgun.

"About time you played something I like," Frank rasped while sipping coffee and gazing out of the window as the rural scenery sped by. "Hell, it's about time you played something I recognized. What was that last song you made me listen to?"

Ray cut a sideway glance at Frank but kept quiet. He knew the routine. Frank was just getting started.

"Remind me," Frank continued. "What's that word you use to describe your weird taste in music? 'Electric'?"

Ray cut his eyes at Frank again, taking in his sly grin and look of anticipation. Allowing himself a small smile and shaking his head in mock frustration, he gave Frank what he had been waiting for.

"Eclectic," he said.

"That's the word!" Frank crowed as he rocked back and forth in the passenger seat. "Man, I like that word! What's it mean again?" He raised his left eyebrow questioningly.

"It means that my musical tastes are varied and that I appreciate offerings from many different genres," Ray said, already knowing what kind of response he would trigger.

"Damn! There goes another one!" Frank exclaimed with a happy, teasing smile. "'John-rahs'? What does 'john-rahs' mean?"

"It means you need to go back to school," Ray replied, sending Frank into a fit of laughter.

"But seriously," Frank said, still chuckling from his tease. "I was groovin' to that last song. Who was it?"

"Pat Metheny" Ray replied. "He plays a style of jazz called 'fusion'."

"See," Frank chuckled. "I don't need to go back to school. I learn so much just hangin' around with you."

"Well," Ray replied with mock gravity, "I was always taught that it was my duty to set a good example for those less fortunate than myself."

"Oh, it's like that now?" Frank said as he leaned back, giving Ray the once-over.

"Oh, it's always been like that!" Ray countered, to the delight of both.

"So, how's married life?" Ray asked, settling into the drive. "How's the new job going? Tell me everything. You taking care of yourself? You look a little light," Ray reached over and grabbed Frank by the upper arm.

"I still got it" Frank said, flexing the arm Ray had grabbed, before looking over at Ray's bicep. "Not like you, though. You look like you haven't missed a day in the gym since I left."

"I haven't missed a meal since you left," Ray laughed. "If I'm going to eat like I do I have to burn some of those calories off."

"What do you weigh now?" Frank asked.

"About two-forty," Ray replied. "It's a bit much. I need to start trimming some of this fat off my gut before it gets out of control."

"You still carry it well, brother," Frank assured him. "As I recall, there was a young lady in the bridal party who seemed to think you were damn near perfect."

"Hell, I thought I was too!" Ray smiled at the memory. "But that was a year and a half and about fifteen pounds ago. Since then it's been hard to stay out of a rut. Too much sitting behind a desk at work mixed with too much food and too much TV." He patted his midsection. "This is the result."

"What ever happened to her?" Frank pressed. "What was her name again?"

"Traci, Frank, with an 'I.' She's your wife's cousin, man. How could you forget your own family?"

"New family," Frank corrected him. "Traci's not even a close cousin. Grace only included her in the wedding party because her stepmother, Grace's aunt, is her father's favorite sister."

Ray laughed. "Family politics from the start."

"That's right," nodded Frank. "So when it's your turn to jump the broom, go in with your eyes wide open, brother. So back to Traci, what happened to her? Didn't you two start dating after the wedding?"

"Briefly," Ray said. "It was good until we got to know each other."

"The usual," Frank said.

"Yeah," said Ray. "Luckily she got a job out of town. It saved us from an awkward and potentially ugly breakup."

"So that's why you're gaining weight?" Frank chuckled. "After a long, hard day at work you struggle home to the lonely couch where you spend your evenings, pining for Traci and eating tubs of ice cream while bingeing on Netflix. Man, you really needed me to come home and pull you off this path of self-destruction."

That got a chuckle out of both of them.

The laughter died down and Ray shifted in the driver's seat, getting comfortable, adjusting it so that it reclined a bit more. He was enjoying the cool morning air, the music, and his friend's company as the truck cruised down the road. He had taken the day off from his job as an insurance analyst to spend a day on the river with a group of guys he grew up with. He and Frank were in the tail car. Joining them were Wendell and Doug, who were riding together in the truck just ahead. The four of them had been friends since seventh grade. They'd managed to keep it going through college and beyond. Now in their mid-twenties, they were beginning to feel the stresses that life eventually brought to everyone's doorstep.

Since finishing college a few years back, their lives had changed. Fledgling careers now needed to be nurtured. Other relationships, both personal and professional, sometimes took precedence over their friendship. Along with the different directions that people naturally move in over time, the flames of friendship now seemed reduced to slow-burning embers, kept barely alive by brief phone calls or texts. Time and distance made it almost impossible for them to casually hang out the way they used to. Now there had to be a special occasion to bring them together. What this usually boiled down to was tailgating at one or two football games in the fall, something they all loved. Still, it was unusual for all four to show up.

When Doug called with the idea of getting together for a day and canoeing down the river, the closest thing to an adventure that Ray had experienced in years, he surprised himself with how quickly he had jumped on the opportunity.

Frank lived a couple of hours away, but he must have been excited by the idea too, since he took off from work and left the house much earlier than usual for the drive back to his home town. He'd pulled up in Ray's driveway just as Ray was setting his backpack, with binoculars, a change of clothes, his phone charger and other essentials, down in the back seat.

Remembering how Frank had arrived gave Ray the chance to get in some ribbing.

"I'm surprised Gracie let you out the house," he began. "I talked to Doug and Dell and they said nobody's seen you since the wedding." Ray made a pretense of carefully examining Frank's neck. "She even took your collar off," he said with a grin.

"That's because she knows who the man is," Frank said with feigned macho authority. "She knows what's what," he quipped, tightening his jaw and slowly nodding his head before shooting a quick glance at Ray to see if his bravado was working.

Ray let that comment hang in the air before he spoke up.

"She thinks you went to work today, doesn't she?"

Both men burst into laughter, Frank slapping his thigh while Ray tried to focus on the road, a death grip on the steering wheel, rocking back and forth with mirth.

The laughter had almost subsided when Ray took his eyes off the road to glance at his friend.

"This chicken-shit sitting beside me," he said between breaths, "had to sneak out the house this morning..." This triggered a new round of laughter, their bodies bouncing around in the truck while they fought back tears, "…and left so quick his balls are still sitting in a jar on the night stand!"

An old-timer walking on the shoulder of the road turned his head in surprise at their raucous laughter as the truck barreled down the road.

CHAPTER 2

They had decided that Ray and Doug would start off in one canoe, with Frank and Wendell in the other. This pairing included carrying the canoes to the water's edge. Ray and Doug were well onto the trail which led down to the river when they heard the shout ring out.

"You gonna help me get this canoe off the truck?"

It was Wendell yelling at Frank who, as usual, was dragging his feet at the idea of doing anything remotely strenuous. Of the four of them, Frank and Dell had the most contentious relationship.

Frank had wandered over to the edge of the clearing and was looking out over the small canyon that had been formed over the last several hundred thousand years by the DeFrance River.

The river took its name from Leighton DeFrance. He was the first white man to explore its course, if you could call it that. DeFrance was one of an expedition of pioneers who, in the early 1700s, had been pushing their way southwest. Their leader had asked for volunteers to cross the river, which had begun to swell due both to recent rains and the spring thaw. One man was to pole a raft across and tie off a rope on the opposite bank. The others would then use the rope and larger rafts to haul themselves and their equipment across the treacherous expanse.

Being strong and vigorous men of the woods, and wanting to stay that way, none of them volunteered. This left their leader with only one option: order the man least likely to argue to get across that river. Leighton was sent off on a hastily assembled raft with a long stick for poling, one end of a three-hundred-foot length of rope, and a hearty pat on the back. Three minutes later the remaining group hauled in the slack rope and made camp, waiting two weeks before crossing the newly christened DeFrance River.

Frank stretched his arms overhead as he let his gaze trail off to the bend of the river a couple of miles downstream. Reluctantly turning away from the picturesque view, he slowly made his way toward the four-wheel drive where Dell waited with fire in his eyes.

"Look, man," Dell said, "it's a long way to the river and I can't carry this canoe by myself!"

"Hey, don't I always pull my weight?" Frank asked.

"Hell no!" shot Dell.

"Tell you what then, since it's a quarter-mile downhill to the river, and your momma was a mountain goat, you take the front and I'll take the back."

Dell ignored the jab.

"First we've got to strap these on," he said, pointing toward two medium-sized coolers equipped with shoulder straps which sat on the tailgate.

"What'cha got here?" asked Frank, reaching for what appeared to be the smaller of the two.

"We've got beer and cold cuts with all the fixings on ice in one, and bread, napkins, and a few towels in the other," Dell said with a smile, lifting the larger of the two. "Guess which one you're carrying?"

Frank's arm was dragged down by the weight of the cooler he'd reached for and he realized he'd been suckered.

"Well, we've got to have the necessities," he said philosophically, as he swung the strap over his head and took his position at the rear of the canoe. On a signal from Dell they hoisted it overhead and started down the path toward the river.

The trail was steep but well-worn and they had little difficulty making their way down. At the bottom Ray and Doug were loading the other provisions for the day's journey into their canoe, which lay partially grounded on a small patch of sand next to an outcropping of rock that served as a natural pier. As Dell was the only one present with any experience in canoeing, he immediately assumed the leader's role, barking orders on the placement of provisions, the seating arrangements, and safety techniques.

"How many times have you done this before?" Ray asked, a little peeved by Dell's authoritative attitude.

"Many times, my friend. Eight or nine in the past couple of years," Dell lied. Actually, this would make his third trip down a river, none in the lead, and none on this particular river.

"Eight or nine canoeing trips? Doesn't seem like much to me," Frank said, more to rib his friend than from any sense of concern. "Don't you have to be certified to do this type of thing?" He winked in the direction of Ray and Doug.

"Look, just do what I tell you, keep your life vests on, and if you capsize and can't get clear of the rapids, be sure to go downstream feet first."

Dell eyed the two canoes with his best critical gaze before turning his attention to the expanse of river immediately before them. Though the water was dark, it was calm, with not many swirls or eddies disturbing the surface. The rocks they were launching from, and this stretch of river, was sometimes used by high school and college kids for sunbathing and swimming during the hottest days of the summer. There was no doubt that the water in the main channel was deep enough for the canoes and there should be no obstructions near the surface. This part of the river was wide, making for slower currents and easy canoeing. Smiling to himself in anticipation of a leisurely late-summer trip down the DeFrance, Dell turned to his three companions with an air of self-satisfaction.

"Let's take 'em out!" he said.

CHAPTER 3

They had been on the river for a couple of hours and the cool morning was beginning to give way to the heat of midday. So far the going had been easy, the scenery nothing short of inspiring. Everyone had settled into the relaxed frame of mind that nature induced in the unwary.

"Dudes, this is truly beautiful," Frank commented from his position in the front of the lead canoe. Dell was handling the steering from the rear, with the canoe carrying Ray and Doug positioned close behind them and a little to the right. Doug was steering. Dell glanced back occasionally to check their distances, shouting instructions to Doug and obviously relishing his role as fearless leader.

"Doug, you want to keep that boat right in line with mine," Dell said. "I'll take us around any obstacles. You just stay in tight behind me."

This was the third version of the same instructions and Doug, to his credit, just nodded his head as if taking in the Wisdom of Solomon.

"Don't encourage him," Ray chuckled in a half-whisper.

"Everybody wants to feel important," Doug smiled. "And he *has* done this before."

"So far it hasn't exactly been quantum physics," observed Ray.

"True," Doug replied.

They proceeded down the river at a leisurely pace, paddling when necessary but usually allowing the current to dictate their speed. Here and there they spotted signs of wildlife. In places there were what looked to be borrows dug into the bank, signs of otters or muskrats. There were all sorts of birds that came to the water's edge to hunt, drink, or bathe. There were turtles that had emerged from the dark water to sun themselves on the rocks and logs that were always convenient. They kept careful watch with stretched necks and wide eyes, plunging back into the depths if the travelers came too close to their chosen patch of sun.

And there were snakes.

Both chilling and fascinating, their presence was felt even when they weren't seen. Over one stretch of river there was what seemed to be a serpent convention. Two large black snakes were curled up on the few feet of a log which the river had yet to claim, while a few yards away a snake of a different variety clung precariously between two branches that overhung the water. Farther down, they spied a thick-bodied serpent as it swam through the comparatively calm waters of an eddy.

Beyond the next bend was a flat outcropping of rocks shaped like an awkward letter V. It extended about a third of the way into the river and looked like a good place for them to pause and stretch their legs. Dell guided the first canoe alongside, leaving enough room for Doug to fit his canoe in behind him.

That left them faced with finding a way to get onto the rocks while the canoes were still afloat. There was much teasing back and forth about who would fall in the water first, but with a bit of team work, they managed to do it by dropping the anchor lines into the shallow water on one side, where the current was less strong. That done, they scrambled onto the rocks, everyone managing to stay dry.

After a good stretch and few squats to regain their legs, they began exploring the rocks.

"What the…!" Ray cried out in alarm as he jumped to the side.

Startled, the others turned to where he pointed at what had to be the fastest corn snake on the face of the earth. It zipped across the rocks, its yellow-orange scales making it difficult to distinguish it against the rust-colored stone.

"Damn, did ya'll see that?" Ray asked. "I didn't know they could move like that!"

"It must 'a got a look at you," Dell said. "You've got a face that could make a snake haul ass."

Everybody laughed as Ray rolled his eyes.

This is the way the four of them had communicated ever since they were in middle school. They called it "talkin' shit." They lapsed into these juvenile insults whenever there was nothing serious on which to focus the conversation. An outsider could not join in; they wouldn't feel comfortable enough to try. You had to be a close friend to insult somebody like that.

But even close friends had secrets and Dell was trying hard to keep one now.

He turned away from the others and picked his way carefully, moving toward the downstream side of the outcropping. There he paused, closed his eyes, and allowed a chill to sweep over his body. Goose bumps rose on his arms and legs and he felt himself shudder before the feeling gradually passed and he regained his composure. He chanced a glance behind him to make sure the others hadn't noticed and was relieved to see that they had paid him no attention. He was alone with his secret: he was terrified of snakes.

Although it was among the most ancient of human fears, he was almost as embarrassed by his inability to admit it as he was by the fear itself. Hell, everybody was afraid of something, he often thought. He knew a great many people shared his particular fear. He was aware that he shouldn't be ashamed, but it didn't change how he felt.

It didn't quell the sick feeling that would rise up in his gut whenever he was exposed to one of those slick, sinister... *evil* creatures. The strange thing was, snakes had fascinated him when he was a kid. He even had one for a pet briefly. It was a common green snake he'd caught by the stream which ran through his neighborhood. He took it to school for show and tell and the teacher let him keep it in a terrarium in the back of the classroom.

Dell thought back to those times and wondered how he ever felt comfortable lifting the snake out of the tank with his bare hands. If asked, he couldn't put his finger on a time when his attitude changed and the fear emerged. It must have been at some point in his teenage years, when his body and mind began to change, he reasoned. He must have somehow tapped into a primal fear. He was sure it lay buried in everyone, but why he felt it so strongly he didn't know. He only knew that as time passed he could tolerate snakes less and less. Pictures of them in books and magazines or on the internet made his flesh crawl. If one appeared on the television he would frantically lunge for the remote to banish the slimy sum'bitch to TV purgatory. If the remote wasn't where he could quickly grab it, he would close his eyes or leave the room until he was certain the thing was gone.

The previous year, when he and a friend were vacationing in Key West, Dell had been frozen in fear after stepping out of a bar and coming face to face with a pair of the longest and thickest boa constrictors he had ever imagined. They were coiled around the neck and upper torso of two smiling tourists, having been placed there by their enterprising owner who charged a nominal fee to people who wanted their pictures taken with the monsters.

"Those are the biggest snakes I've ever seen!" exclaimed his surprised and inebriated date, before pulling him down Duval Street, toward Hog's Breath Saloon.

Dell was profoundly grateful when she pulled him away. He didn't think he could take a step under his own power and was sure he would have lost control of both his bladder and his bowels if she hadn't acted. He figured that only the warm feeling of the liquor in her system had kept her from feeling the chill that had taken over his entire body.

As they walked away Dell imagined he could feel the reptiles' eyes locked on his back. He wanted to look over his shoulder, but was sure it would only confirm that the slimy beasts had detached themselves from the tourists and were making their way toward him, intent on coiling around him. Squeezing his date's hand almost to the point of pain, he quickly moved ahead and began pulling her down the street.

Here on the riverbank these thoughts bought a chill to an otherwise beautiful setting. Dell eased himself down into a seated position on a large rock. Scanning the opposite bank, he forced himself to take deep breaths until he felt his body begin to relax.

Then, from the corner of his eye, he caught movement beside his right hand. A small, grayish brown serpent was wedging itself into a crack in the rock. It would be safe to say that the snake was as unaware of Dell's presence as he had been of it.

That didn't matter.

Although Dell found himself unable to breathe, to his credit, he didn't panic. Slowly, so as not to alarm the snake or his companions, he eased himself off the rock and away to the left. Not until he had taken five steps did he exhale. He looked in the direction of his friends, hoping not to have attracted their attention, and was gratified to hear a laugh directed at some comment unrelated to him.

He paused, taking deep breaths until he felt close to normal. A cool breeze moved over the water and gently touched him, making him aware of the perspiration beading on his forehead and threatening to run down his face. He used his palm to wipe the moisture away, gave a little shiver, and turned back toward the canoes, nearly bumping into Ray who had quietly come over to where he was standing.

"How does it look?" Ray asked. He thought Dell had been assessing the stretch of river ahead. When he didn't get a reply, Ray glanced at his friend and was shocked by his appearance. "Man, you're sweatin' like a pig. It's not even that hot yet."

"I might be coming down with something," Dell lied. "I was feeling nauseous and then these sweats hit." He shook his head to indicate his puzzlement. "It might be a bug."

"We can rest up here for a few more minutes, if you need to," Ray said.

"Naw, we better get moving," replied Dell. He was more than ready to get off of this particular piece of rock. "Let's get back to the canoes."

He let Ray lead the way. He didn't want him to notice how nervous he was and if there were any more snakes in the vicinity he wanted someone else to discover them. Frank and Doug had seen them approaching. They began moving toward the canoes, reaching them while Dell and Ray were still a little ways away.

Standing by the canoe, Frank pointed and called out, "What's that moving between those rocks?"

Ray looked in the direction Frank was pointing, toward two good-sized rocks in the river, about twenty-five feet away. The downstream rock was the largest, rising about six inches over the smaller, which was about six inches out of the water. Between them, Ray could make out something moving.

"Looks like a fish got caught between those rocks," Frank said. "Why don't you go kick it loose, Fearless?" This was directed at Dell.

"If a fish is dumb enough to get caught between two rocks, I'm not going to the trouble of freeing it," Dell replied.

Frank looked at Dell with an air of impatience. "Aw, knock the thing loose and let's get moving."

His role as leader temporarily forgotten, Dell turned toward the river. He figured he could jump from rock to rock, get there, knock the trapped fish into the water, and be back in less than a minute. Five quick jumps brought him alongside the rocks, but there he remained, frozen like a granite statue, his eyes fixed on the space between them.

Ray glanced back as he continued toward the canoes and noticed that his friend was standing there, motionless, staring downward.

"Is it a fish?" he asked.

Dell didn't answer. His eyes were locked on the fish.

It was a little less than a foot of bullhead catfish, clenched in the jaws of three and a half feet of water moccasin.

The poisonous snake had seized the grayish-brown fish behind the gills and was furiously thrashing it back and forth between the rocks. As Dell continued to watch, mesmerized with horror, the snake slipped from between the rocks and swam toward the rock where he stood, about five feet away, the fish still clutched tightly in its jaws. Halfway there it stopped, noticing its peruser for the first time.

Dell's skin seemed to take on a life of its own. Goose bumps rose on his arms as he felt his stomach lurch. He wanted to move, to do something, to get away, but he couldn't will his body into motion. For a full ten seconds he and the snake stared at each other. Then the snake, deciding Dell was no threat, slowly swam off in another direction to find a place more suitable for ingesting its meal.

"Dell...let's go!" Frank hollered. This awakened Dell to the need for movement.

Swallowing hard and tearing his eyes away from the retreating snake, Dell managed to pull himself together enough to retrace his steps back to where Ray stood, impatiently staring at him. Dell passed him by without appearing to see him, heading to the lead canoe. Frank looked at the others, puzzled, before hurrying over to help Dell launch the canoe.

Ray hurried to the other canoe, where Doug was waiting. They had decided earlier that at the first stop Ray would take his turn at guiding the craft. He was in such a hurry that he slipped on one of the damp stones and fell into the water almost up to his hips before hauling himself over the side and into the canoe.

"Damn!" Ray exclaimed as he settled himself into the rear and began to paddle toward the other canoe. "What's wrong with him?"

"It's the strain of leadership," Doug joked as he matched Ray's stroke. "Hey, you knew somebody was going into the water sooner or later," he chuckled.

"I figured it would be you," Ray replied. "Reach me a beer, would you?"

"I think what's left is in the other canoe," Doug said, "along with the sandwiches and everything else that's good. You gotta keep your eyes on Frank."

"And he's gotta keep his eyes on Dell," said Ray. "He's losing his grip, for real."

* * *

As the morning turned to midday, Dell began to feel more like himself.

The splendor of the river was working its magic again, beginning to calm his frazzled nerves. Ray pulled his canoe alongside and they passed around the refreshments. They ate, drank, and joked as they proceeded down a particularly broad and calm stretch of river.

But Dell never completely let his guard down. Although the river's beauty had calmed him to a degree, he was still slightly on edge.

He tried to focus his eyes on the water, telling himself he was checking the currents, looking for rocks and logs lurking just beneath the surface, ensuring the safety of *his* expedition. Anything to keep his eyes off of the bank because he knew *they* were there and he knew they were watching him. He didn't have to see them. He didn't want to see them. He would do almost anything to keep from seeing them. But he knew they were there, sunning beside the bank, swimming in the calm water, waiting for him, watching for him.

Dell was right. He was being watched, but not by snakes. Ray had been keeping an eye on him.

Ray was beginning to feel a little better about the situation as they progressed down the river. Maybe he was making too much out of the whole deal, or perhaps he was imagining things. After all, among the four of them Doug was the expert on the ins and outs of the human psyche. Doug was a medical doctor with a master's degree in psychology. He was currently doing a residency in neuropsychology. If he didn't feel compelled to watch Dell's every move then there was nothing to be concerned about.

It was probably his imagination, Ray concluded as he allowed himself to more fully relax and enjoy the experience. Still, he found his eyes and his thoughts straying occasionally to the other canoe.

The DeFrance had at one time been a valuable lane of commerce, used by early trappers, farmers, and settlers to move skins, furs, produce and other belongings downstream to markets and jump-off points for the continued journey west. For most of its course the DeFrance carried waters deep enough for small to medium-sized flat-bottom boats. As commerce along the river increased and larger vessels were brought into service, changes were made to accommodate their safe passage through some of the more dangerous sections of water. Along some stretches of river, canals were dug and water diverted in order to circumvent particularly rough and rocky rapids.

The canoes were approaching such a stretch now, a treacherous course with class four and five rapids, as well as some steep drops. This could be challenging for even the most experienced whitewater enthusiasts. It was certainly too much for the limited experience of the four friends who gliding along about a mile upstream. Fortunately the rapids could be avoided by steering the canoes into a canal, a stretch of calm water that veered off to the right. It ran parallel to the main river for about three miles before reattaching itself at a calmer point downstream of the last major drop-off.

Dell had brought along a guide map of the river, which showed landmarks, rest areas, and the safest routes to follow, depending on a rafter's degree of experience. He found their approximate location and looked ahead toward the fork that would be visible in a few minutes. There was a gate in place across the access point to the canal. In order to reach the canal waters, the travelers would have to bank their craft, unload, and carry everything up a slight hill and across about a hundred feet of granite and gravel that ran downhill toward the water. Once there, they could re-launch in the canal and enjoy three miles of easy, quiet drifting before repeating the procedure to get back on the main channel.

Dell saw this and recognized it for what it was: an invitation for yet another slimy reptile to cross his path. His mind flashed back to the previous encounters and his skin began to crawl anew as he remembered how close to the serpents he had been. He felt himself shudder and stole a glance at Frank to see if he noticed. Frank was reclining in the front of the canoe. Having stripped down to the waist, he lay there with his eyes closed, soaking up the sunshine and the breeze, completely relaxed from equal parts of river and beer.

Seeing Frank lying at his ease only made Dell angry. Things weren't going the way he'd planned. Though Doug had first mentioned it to Ray, this whole trip was originally Dell's idea and he seemed to be the only one unable to enjoy it. He decided there was no sense in prolonging his discomfort, even if the others were enjoying themselves.

It was at this moment that Dell made up his mind to bring the outing to an end as soon as possible.

Focusing again on the map, he noted that the end of their journey was a landing a few miles beyond the place where the canal fed back into the river. If they paddled fairly vigorously, they could make it in about two hours by canal, allotting the necessary time for crossing the short stretches of bank. But the faster route lay to the left. By taking the main channel they could avoid disembarking twice and, because of the speed of the rapids, they could cover more water in less time with less work. As a bonus they would be less likely to see any more snakes and that, for Dell, was the biggest plus of all.

His decision made, Wendell let the canoes slip silently past the junction where the canal branched off from the river with none of his companions the wiser. He figured they would be surprised when they hit the faster water and the pace picked up. For some reason, Dell found the thought of interrupting their idyllic trip strangely satisfying, and he allowed a slight smile to crease his lips.

Hell, they could use a little excitement, he thought.

CHAPTER 4

"Heads up, ladies!"

Frank jumped at the sound of Dell's shout.

"The fun's about to start!"

Frank had been lost in the tranquility of nature and beer and was a little irritated to be snatched away from peaceful inebriation. He blearily focused one eye on Dell, the other seeming to have made up its mind to stay closed. He was ready to launch into a string of curses when he heard it; not the faint, peaceful background noises of the river that had accompanied them this far, but a low roar that grew in intensity as the canoe moved forward.

And the canoe *was* moving.

Frank could tell by the tops of the trees just visible over the sides of the canoe from his reclined position that they had picked up speed. Mildly alarmed, he forced himself up to a sitting position. After first taking notice of the look of excitement on Dell's face, he turned to face the front of the canoe.

The string of curses now began, very low, inaudible to anyone but himself, but he wasn't listening because his mind was too busy processing the sight which lay before him.

The river was narrowing, funneling the water that filled the broad expanse behind them into a channel about one-third as wide. This increased the speed and power of the water many times over. By itself this would be enough to increase the danger of piloting a canoe to a level a novice might try to avoid. Add to this the fact that they appeared to be approaching a drop off, beyond which were some of the biggest rocks he'd ever seen; boulders, rising from the turmoil of the rapids.

The fear now growing in Frank's gut was real.

Doug and Ray were farther back and so had more time to prepare, but that was little consolation for two beginners to canoeing who were facing a new and completely unexpected situation.

"Didn't Dell say there weren't going to be any tough rapids?" Ray asked while taking up an oar for one of the few times since their last break.

"He said nothing above a class two," said Doug, as he began to paddle faster, "whatever that means."

"What are you doing?" Ray asked.

"We've got to get in closer to Dell."

This thought quickly ran through Ray's mind and was just as quickly discarded.

"No," he said. "We need to get to the bank."

"And do what? Walk this thing through the woods?" Doug asked as his paddle was momentarily stilled.

"Didn't we pass a canal back there a ways?" asked Ray, inclining his head in the direction from which they'd come. "We can't be too far from it. We could carry the canoe that far."

"Where does it go?" Doug asked.

"I don't know, but it's better than this. Let's do it!"

Even as he spoke, Ray knew they weren't going to make it. The current was already strong, and getting stronger by the second. Maybe if they had more experience, had worked together at paddling a few times before, they would have had a chance to ground the canoe. As it was, they found themselves being swept toward the rapids where the only way out was to go through.

"Can't do it," panted Doug at the same time the thought was running through Ray's mind. Fixing their eyes on the boat ahead, they began to paddle at a frantic pace to catch up.

In the lead canoe Dell was oblivious to the danger he had placed everyone in. He was back in charge again... he could feel it! In this moment that was all that mattered to him. Having guided the canoe to the middle of the current, he submerged his paddle and used it as a rudder to keep the canoe moving in a relatively straight line.

"Yeeee-haaaaa!"

Dell raised his paddle overhead with both hands as they shot through the center of the gap. There was a feeling of weightlessness followed by a hard thud and a splash as the bottom of the canoe met the water again, the roar of the rapids drowning out the sound of both. The canoe tilted hard to the left then back again to the right, coming level just as Dell's stomach returned from being lodged in his throat.

Quickly he glanced behind him and caught a glimpse of the boulder fifteen feet across that, due to blind luck, they had narrowly missed. The sight of that rock and the speed of the water made him realize that they were in a truly dangerous situation. But there was no time to think this through; the reality was staring them in the face.

Almost as soon as the boat righted, more trouble loomed in the form of three huge rocks. The first of the three was slightly to the right of the center of the current, with the second jutting from the right bank about twenty feet beyond. The third was in the center of the flow and created a narrow path between itself and the ledge of rock that jutted from the right bank. The safest path would have been to the left of the first rock, where the water was fast but the course was straight. In his growing state of panic, Dell thrust his oar into the water to the right of the canoe. This caused the front end to move to the right, narrowly missing the first rock and setting them up for the two quick twists that the current demanded in order to circumvent the three boulders. Fortunately the canoe was riding high out of the water as the force of the curve tilted the boat first on its right side, then on its left, and back on its right. Still it took on water each time before righting itself, shooting past the third rock, and back again into the main channel.

Wide-eyed with fear and surprise, Dell forced himself to glance down into the canoe now empty of food, beer, coolers, and map. The binoculars were also gone, as were the sunscreen and his shoes. What remained was Dell himself, his paddle, and a cringing Frank who maintained a death grip on either side of the front of the canoe. Frank had forced his body down to the point where only his head could rise and peer around the bow to take account of oncoming obstacles before ducking back to the comparative safety of the interior.

When he saw Frank's head duck down again, Dell looked up to see what caused this reaction. His eyes grew wide not at what he saw, but what he felt.

Dell felt the canoe tilt skyward, as if it were a missile preparing to launch, then came down hard into the water only to tilt skyward again. This pattern repeated itself, over and over again, until they thought the vessel would come apart. With each bone-jarring impact Dell's emotions rose. Fear had replaced surprise, with terror and panic swiftly approaching. His paddle now long gone, Dell mimicked Frank with a death grip on each side of the canoe and his body forcefully pressed down as far as it would go into the interior.

The second canoe entered the rough water at the same place as the lead canoe, but Ray and Doug were smart enough to be afraid from the very first drop. Had they been frightened to the point of inaction, the current may have taken control and carried their canoe through the dangerous stretches as it did the first craft.

That was not their fate.

Upon laying eyes on the first massive boulder, they both reacted. Without any experience, and no plan, both oars were thrust into the water. Neither was clear on what they were doing but each felt that he had to do something. What they did threw the light canoe into complete disarray.

Instead of following the lead boat around the first large rock, the uncoordinated actions of Ray and Doug caused the canoe to shift until they were heading toward the boulder sideways. The vessel struck the rock with such force that it fractured the left side, the sound of splintering fiberglass drowned out by the sound of the wildly rushing water that surrounded them. Ray was slammed into the rock, striking his left shoulder and the left side of his head, before the canoe disengaged and continued past the left side of the boulder and through more rapids.

They were again headed downstream, but now they were *backwards*.

Ray, who had been in the rear of the canoe, facing foreword and trying to guide it, was dazed and bleeding. His back was toward any danger they would quickly be approaching, in a broken canoe that was taking on more water with every passing moment.

As they went over a drop, Ray felt like his stomach was launched into his throat. This had the effect of clearing his head to some degree and, when he focused his eyes, he found himself alone in the canoe! His gaze quickly swept the water for some trace of Doug as panic gripped his heart at the thought of his friend falling into the treacherous current.

From the corner of his eye Ray caught sight of the orange life vest to his right and just below the river's surface. As he watched, the buoyancy of the vest forced Doug's head momentarily above the water. Silently thanking Dell for making them wear the vests, Ray lunged for Doug's head as it was about to disappear below the fast-moving water again. His first attempt missed, but Ray reached deeper and was thankful when he felt his hand close around the collar of the life vest. Summoning all the strength he could, Ray hauled the upper half of Doug's body into the canoe even as the vessel continued to careen downstream.

Still dazed and working on instinct, Ray struggled to pull Doug completely out of the river, not realizing the damage that the collision had caused to the canoe.

The cracked fiberglass was leaning toward the water on the left side while Ray tried to pull Doug up on the right. Only the weight of Doug's body kept the damaged left side of the craft above the waterline. As Ray pulled, trying to get Doug into the canoe, the damaged side fell closer and closer toward the wildly gushing water. They were shooting downstream at a high speed now, but with no boulders in their immediate path. With a final heave Ray pulled Doug's soaked but conscious body completely into the canoe.

As the craft again found its balance, its damaged left side dipped low and began taking on water at an incredible rate. This completely altered the course of the boat, causing it to spin in a counter-clockwise direction just as they reached another drop. As they plunged over the short waterfall, Ray was thrown from the half-submerged canoe.

There was a brief feeling of weightlessness just before the bone-numbing impact of his body striking another large rock at the bottom of the flow. He remained conscious just long enough to see the canoe, barely afloat, as it passed almost within reach of his outstretched hand. The canoe and his consciousness faded at the same time.

CHAPTER 5

Ray was not aware of his body being dragged from the shallow waters and up onto the bank, or of the quick examination that told his rescuer that maybe his life could still be saved. The manipulations that restored his breath and produced a steady heartbeat were beyond his ability to feel. Even the bitter, pungent potions which were forced into him failed to elicit a response for many days.

His first brush with consciousness was brief.

His sense of smell returned first. The faint smell of smoke drifting slowly in his direction hinted at the presence of a fire nearby. He did not recognize it for what it was but only as something different, which served to help wake up his other senses. Next the sounds of the riverbank filtered into his weak state of consciousness. He heard, or thought he heard, the sound of the water as it trickled past. He heard the rustling sounds of leaves moved by a gentle wind.

The crunch of sand underfoot brought him almost fully awake and he made a painful effort to turn his head toward the sound. He had to force his eyes open and summon the concentration to focus on his surroundings.

He recognized nothing.

In his dreamlike state he didn't know where he was or how he arrived at this place. His glazed eyes passed slowly over the small clearing, seeing everything but taking in little. A sudden unexpected motion drew what attention he had to a spot among the thick growth just on the other side of a small fire. His eyes widened, straining to make sense out of the shape that was there, blurred by the shadows, just beyond his ability to grasp. Then his eyes drifted closed and his head lolled gently back to its previous position as he left his brief brush with clarity and sank back into blissful unconsciousness.

He is a strong one, thought the young warrior watching from across the clearing.

He had just returned from foraging along the riverbank and had moved up to the clearing as silently as only one experienced in the wild can, not wanting to startle his patient. Instead, it was he who was startled. He did not expect the man he had fished from the river to regain consciousness so soon. For the first few days it had been doubtful that he would even live.

It had taken much labor just to restore his breathing. It was a miracle, considering the vast amount of river water that had to be cleared from his chest. Once started, his breathing was anything but tranquil. For a good while the young warrior was afraid to leave his patient's side for fear that the shallow, labored motions of his chest would cease and all would have been for naught. Twice this happened, and twice he was there to render aid until stable breathing was restored. By the evening of the third day the warrior decided he had done all that could be done.

The fate of this man will now be in his own hands or the hands of whatever god he believes in, the warrior thought. *I have no further time to waste with him. I must find food or I will starve here beside him. Then the maggots will feast upon two corpses, and who would complete my task?*

Now he smiled as he placed his evening meal, the hind parts of three large frogs beside the small fire. It was good to save a life, much better than taking one, unless the life taken was to right a great wrong. This thought increased the smile on his face and he settled down beside the fire to roast his meal. Once more he saw the head turn, the eyelids slowly part, and the glazed look as the man focused for the briefest of moment on the warrior as he went about his task. Then, as before, the light faded and he floated off into another deep sleep. The warrior never stopped working, but again he smiled.

He is a strong one, he thought.

• • •

It was not until close to midday of the seventh day that Ray completely awoke from his fatigued sleep. The warrior had kept him almost comatose with potions made from the herbs he carried in his pouch. For four days he had administered regular doses, at sunrise and sunset, so that his patient could find the rest he so desperately needed in order to heal. When he thought the man was ready, the warrior administered a different potion, a stimulant to help counter the sedatives' hold on him. The effects were such that the stranger was able to regain full consciousness for the first time in many days, though still with a fog over his thoughts.

And so it was that the first time he really looked at his savior he showed no emotion, not surprise or astonishment, not a bold stare, or questioning glance. It was more like a man opening his eyes for the sole purpose of making sure they worked.

He looked around the small clearing, testing his vision and trying to bring the world into focus. He saw the smoldering remains of the fire and what appeared to be an aboriginal tribesman sitting against a tree at its far side. He continued to move his head around, taking in most of his immediate surroundings before bringing his gaze once again to the figure across the clearing. He made an attempt to focus on the strange man but was thwarted by the sunlight. Even filtered through the foliage, it was too intense for eyes which had been closed for several days. He lowered his head and squeezed his eyelids tight, hoping to clear his vision.

There he froze - head down, eyes tightly shut - as the reality of what his eyes had revealed began to burn through the fog which clouded his brain. His body began to involuntarily tremble as what he saw registered on his conscious mind. His heart pounded in his chest, its sound drowning out the soft chorus of nature that had occupied the background as he was coming awake. Panic made his breath become labored and his mouth gaped open as he struggled for each one. This went on for a while before his body began to calm, but still he kept his head down and his eyes closed.

After a time he raised his head again, this time slowly, his ears now focused on the sound of the rushing water only a few yards distant. His last memories were of the river and he began to feel better after recognizing the familiar sound. His courage bolstered, he took a deep breath, opened his eyes, and looked in the direction of the thick foliage of the riverbank and the river itself, just visible through the cracks in the wall of vegetation.

This time a smile of relief spread across his face as the thought of what must have happened occurred to him. Of course! He was dreaming! Waking up from a deep sleep, and with this god-awful headache, not to mention the horrible taste in his mouth and this bright sunlight, he could imagine all kinds of things! He began to laugh at himself for his panic, his weak laughter giving way to a feeling of relief that everything appeared to be all right.

He was gathering himself for an attempt to rise when he caught the faint smell of smoke in the air and again he froze. Not willing to commit himself totally just yet, he let his eyes wander. From their corner he saw the sticks which had been arranged to feed a small fire. Recognition blossomed in his mind and without looking he knew what lay beyond that small flame in the center of the fire. A chill of fear came over him again and his mind began racing.

There's somebody over there, just past the fire. Who is he? Dressed like that, he could be a crazy man!

Though he knew there was no getting around it, still it took a supreme effort to force his eyes to once again look beyond the fire.

There he sat. What appeared to be an aboriginal tribesman, but was probably a crazy homeless person living down here by the river while the warm weather permitted. As he continued to stare, the homeless man stared back at him with no sign of hostility in his eyes. After a few moments, the homeless fellow broke into a grin, showing strong white teeth set into an angular jaw.

I don't think he wants to kill me, Ray thought, with a sense of relief.

In attempting to push himself into a sitting position, he came to realize just how weak he was. He then gathered his strength and, with great effort, rolled over onto his stomach and slowly fought his way up to his knees. There he paused as his head began to spin, the surrounding landscape whirling dizzily around him. Dropping down on all fours, he felt his saliva glands begin to secrete the thick mucus that precedes a vomit. He braced himself as his stomach heaved and knotted far in excess of the small amount of fluid that was brought up.

He continued in the same position after his stomach had settled, his breathing heavy, the residue of his saliva forming a thick string that almost reached the sand before it broke and joined the rest of the puke in a puddle between his hands.

Raising his head, he cast a timid glance toward the strange man, who had not moved from his position and had the same grin on his face.

The relief he felt, coupled with embarrassment, brought back his smile, which quickly turned into a chuckle, then a full-fledged laugh. The homeless man began laughing too, which made Ray laugh that much harder. Within moments the two of them were laughing so hard that Ray thought another spell of vomiting could commence at any second. Instead his laugh deteriorated into a fit of coughing. This had the effect of launching the homeless man into another attack of laughter.

After a while their laughter settled down. Ray again gathered his strength and attempted to stand. Now understanding his weakened state, he moved much more slowly and carefully than the first time. Seeing this, the homeless man sprang easily to his feet and stepped lightly around the fire so as to catch him if he should falter. This proved prudent because Ray, startled by the quick movement of the other, rose too fast. Instantly the dizziness was upon him again. It took the strong, steadying hand of the other on his upper arm to stop him from pitching over into the sand.

"Thanks," Ray said, as he righted himself.

A quizzical look came upon the face of the homeless man. Then he smiled, dipped his head, and said, "Dajee."

"Not from around here, huh?" said Ray. He grimaced, tasting the sour remnants of what had been ejected from his stomach.

"Ugh!" His face contorted and he swiveled his head, looking around the clearing. "Got any water?" He peered at the homeless man, wondering why he didn't respond, before remembering that he appeared to be a foreigner. He cupped his hands and brought them up to his mouth, throwing his head back to simulate drinking. This movement threw off his balance and the homeless man, still clutching his upper arm, carefully guided him back to a sitting position. Once he was sure Ray was steady, he went over to a leather pouch that lay beside the tree where he had been sitting.

Beside the pouch was a small leather flask. It was kidney-shaped, with one end fitted around a wooden tube of some sort and tied with a leather string. A wooden stopper had been inserted into the tube to keep the contents from leaking out. The strange man carefully removed the stopper and handed the flask to Ray. The first mouthful was swished around before being spat out. Then Ray took a long pull, savoring the taste of the cool water as it ran down his throat. After a few more mouthfuls he felt much better.

"That was good... just what I needed. Thank you." he said as he handed the flask back to its owner, who again replied, "Dajee," as he inserted the stopper into the mouth of the flask.

The cool water having helped to clear his head, Ray looked around, taking in the small campsite. He noted the makeshift bed made from leaves and grasses. The vegetation was flattened and the imprint of a body was clearly visible. By the color and condition of the vegetation, it appeared to have been in use for some time. It occurred to him that he must have been in a bad way and this homeless fellow had cared for him for a while. Knowing that he owed an acknowledgment of this debt, he thrust his hand toward the homeless man and spoke: "My name is Raymond."

This got no response, other than a brief, quizzical examination of the extended hand.

Ray pulled his hand back and let his gaze take in his benefactor.

He was a hair shorter than Ray, around six-one, and on the slim side. He had a medium build, as broad at the shoulder but not as wide at the hip as Ray. Though not as thickly muscled as Ray, the lack of fat made every muscle stand out, almost like those of a body builder. Ray attributed this to the sparse life the man must be living, out here on the river basin. Ray guessed that he probably left this place at night to search the surrounding trash cans, dumpsters, and other places for whatever was edible. He didn't look unhealthy, only like he could use a few home-cooked meals.

The man was dressed in the very basics. On his feet were leather sandals which laced up and tied off just above his ankles. A soft leather thong covered his groin area much like a jockstrap, and a heavier piece of leather fit somewhat like a skirt in that it ran from one hip to the other, both in the front and the back, leaving a slit on each side which allowed his legs full movement. That was all he wore. Though sparse, it appeared to be supple and of good quality.

Since he was of a dark complexion, Ray figured him to be a native of some African country, or maybe a South Pacific islander, from somewhere where they didn't speak English. His skin shone with a clean, healthy glow. *He's got good hygiene, even camping out here,* thought Ray. His head was shaved bald, except for a small braided lock that began above his right ear and ran down behind it, hanging halfway to the base of his neck. His hair was jet-black, as were his eyebrows and eyelashes.

Ray now studied his host's face.

It was a young face, or perhaps it only appeared that way due to the absence of lines. The man's smooth skin was pulled taut over high cheekbones and a strong, angular jaw. His features were full but not bulbous. His eyes reflected a competence and a confidence well beyond his perceived years. They held a gleam of curiosity as they took Ray's measure, even as he sized up the stranger.

Something about this didn't add up, Ray thought. Though this man was obviously poor (or else why would he be living in a makeshift camp in the woods at the edge of the river?) He gave the impression of being completely at ease, even thriving. He looked like he belonged there.

Well, as long as he's comfortable, thought Ray. *It was nice of him to take care of me, but now I have to find my way back to the others.*

The others!

The memories began to flood back: the ill-conceived canoeing trip and that asshole Dell leading them into water that was way beyond their ability to handle. The brief fight for control of the canoe and then... what? The next thing Ray knew he was waking up in a daze, in the care of a homeless man.

I've been here for a few days, by the looks of things. People are probably worried sick. They might be out searching for me - the police, the county sheriff - I bet this was on the news! They must think I drowned by now!

He turned to the stranger, wanting to ask if he had seen any boats, helicopters, or searchers combing the river. Then he remembered that this would fall on what essentially were deaf ears.

The stranger still stared at him, now with a puzzled expression, as if weighing whether this man was coherent enough to really communicate. He must have reached a decision, because he spoke, slowly and evenly, in what must have been the language of his homeland. Ray understood not one word of what was being said. With his new awareness of his predicament and his desire to get back to someplace familiar, he was quickly becoming impatient with the situation.

He cut the stranger off in mid-sentence.

"Hey… HEY! Look, I appreciate all you've done. Seriously, thank you," Ray said, putting his palms together and bobbing his head to indicate thanks, "but I've got to go back, to my home. Home? You know, the place where I live?" He made his hands into a triangular shape, to indicate a roof. "People are looking for me."

He wished he had something to give him, a few dollars maybe, but his pockets were empty.

"Thank you, um, Dajee?" he said with a quick bow, and turned to what he figured was northwest and the way back to the city.

Maybe I'll come back and find him after I get home, maybe take him to get some food and clothes, help him find a warm place to sleep, Ray thought, as he haltingly worked his way through the brush.

Behind him he heard the man speaking, and he smiled, imagining that he knew what he was saying this time. *"Hey, where are you going? Do you know your way around here?"*

I'm going home! Ray thought, as he started up an incline that, from the top, might give him a view of the city, at least of the tallest buildings. Then he'd know which way was the quickest route to get home.

Right down here on the DeFrance, they should have found me pretty easily if they had been out looking, Ray puzzled. *I wonder if that guy was hiding me down there. He's probably afraid of the police. He might have been given a hard time when he first got here, what with speaking a strange language and the way he's dressed. Aren't there any paths up this hill? This is killing my legs. Wonder how long I was passed out down there? It might have been days. I've got to get something to eat. I'm about to starve! Maybe a rib-eye and a loaded potato...*

It was an exhausting journey that took longer than he thought it would, due to his having to pull his weakened body up through the heavy undergrowth, and moving on shaking legs. He'd had to pause several times to rest and catch his breath. Having finally fought his way to the top, he found he needed to pause again and gather his strength just so he could stand and take in the view. When he finally did, it was nothing like he expected.

There was no skyline silhouetted against the horizon. The city that should have been only a few miles away was nowhere in sight. The railroad tracks running parallel to the river for several miles were missing too.

No wonder they didn't find me, thought Ray. *I must have drifted farther downstream than they thought.*

He eased himself down to a sitting position on the crest of the hill so as to rest and review his options for getting home. They currently consisted of a long, hard hike through what looked like some pretty tough woods. He wiped the sweat from his brow with his forearm and looked around again. Maybe he was on the wrong side of the river and needed to get to the other side before he could get his bearings. But the flow of the river was right, and the direction of the sun told him that he was indeed looking north-northwest. Unless he had drifted for miles, there should be some sign of the city nearby. There were bridges for miles up and down the river and though he had never walked the railroad tracks, it was common knowledge that they followed the course of the water all the way down to the town of Beachem, and beyond to the Lake Foster reservoir.

So according to everything I know, those tracks should be right over there, he thought, *and there should be a road around here somewhere where I can hitch a ride back to town.*

He struggled to his feet once more, still feeling weak from his ordeal, and let his gaze run full circle from his current position. He was on the highest ground he could see. Behind him, about two hundred yards downhill, was the river. Below and before him was a broad plain of untouched vegetation for as far as the eye could see, with no hint of a city, a farm, a road, or even a trail.

He heard a noise and turned quickly to find that he was being watched by his rescuer. Apparently the fellow had followed him up the hill and had been watching the whole time.

Still looking out for me, Ray thought as he turned again to search the wooded expanse for signs of other people. There were none. It didn't make sense. He frowned as the thought flashed through his mind that the stranger was looking more and more at home in these woods with every passing minute.

* * *

Ray had been crashing through the undergrowth for about six hours now.

He sensed this because the sun was well behind the trees to the west and the daylight was fading fast. He was as near to a state of complete exhaustion as he had ever been in his life. The only thing that kept him going was adrenaline, a byproduct of the panic that had overtaken him hours ago. His flesh was torn in several places along his arms and legs, and even his face. Everywhere he stepped he had to make his own path and the low branches and thorns were completely unforgiving.

And so were the insects.

Flies, mosquitoes, gnats, whatever, they obviously saw him as a walking buffet and were determined to get their fill. The fact that he had by now stopped swatting at them only illustrated how completely they had won. Their bites were expected, and almost ignored, and the constant buzzing that had driven him so close to the edge for the last hour or two had now taken on the effect of background noise.

Every time he stopped to rest, his "shadow," the man from the river, was there, speaking to him, trying to communicate in his strange foreign tongue. Ray was in such a panicked state of mind that he imagined that he was beginning to understand him. It was just a word here and there, among the constant stream that flowed from the man's lips whenever Ray paused to rest. Not enough for understanding, but enough to add to the strangeness of the situation and the feeling of fear and confusion that had seized control in the hollow of his chest.

• • •

He had been in full flight for an hour or so, just moving forward, hardly aware of where he was going, just needing to keep moving. The darkness and exhaustion were catching up to him. When he tripped over a tree root, Ray found he lacked the strength and the will to rise again.

As he knelt there in the twilight with nothing left - no hope to continue, no idea what to do - the foliage parted and the stranger again appeared. Ray turned to him with a look of complete defeat. His sweat, mingled with the blood from his many cuts, was joined by his tears as he gazed into the face of what he saw as his last hope. The stranger took a step toward him, paused, and spoke…and Ray was astounded!

"You are tired, weak, injured, and lost. Let me help you."

On the outside he appeared calm, but Ray's mind was screaming, a high-pitched scream that he thought was louder than anything his ears had ever heard. It was a loud, frantic, incoherent scream, with no recognizable phrases or sounds… just noise. Underneath it a small voice, maybe a prayer or a plea, was saying *this isn't real… you're still asleep… this is a dream… only a dream… wake up… WAKE UP!*

At this point it all became too much for him. It was too bizarre, too much of a strain to comprehend. Ray's consciousness, under assault by all that he had taken in since waking up beside the river that afternoon, simply shut off.

• • •

As Ray pitched forward, the strange man caught him. Easily lifting Ray to his shoulders, he moved deeper into the brush to what he considered a suitable place to make a camp. He propped his burden in a sitting position against an outcropping of stone and went off to gather the firewood they would need to see them through the night.

He was not concerned that anyone would see their fire. He had made a thorough sweep of the area while trailing the strange man. It had not been difficult. Unlike himself, this man was obviously 'not of our Mother'. He made such noise while trampling through the forest that there had been time to range out and scout the area, enough to determine that there were no signs of people hereabouts. A moment to listen and he could always follow the noise back to his quarry. So could other, more menacing, dwellers of this forest, but the fire, which would surely attract man, would just as surely keep wild animals at bay.

He quickly gathered the necessary kindling, twigs, and small and large sticks and brought them back to where his "burden" lay. He frowned as he considered the thought, but what else was this outsider but a burden? Based on the woodcraft he had witnessed this day, this man could not hope to survive for more than a few days on his own in this wild.

During those first days beside the river, he had considered ending the stranger's life. It would be a pity, after having worked so long and hard to save it, but he was, after all, on a quest for something of great importance. He had no time to waste in what could end up being a futile effort to keep this one alive.

But as the days passed the warrior had begun to sense an attachment between the two of them. How did this stranger get here? Upon his arrival the warrior had traversed the banks of the river for a good way in either direction and found no sign of man. For days he had felt compelled to post a vigil at the spot where he discovered the stranger floating in the river. This stranger, who appeared completely lost in the wild, who he found floating almost lifeless in a river so far from the dwellings of man that the only rational explanation for his being there was that he had fallen from the sky above.

The more he considered this, the more he was convinced that this stranger could be the reason he was here. He had been sent to find, and bring back, something that could help his people in time of great need. Who was to say that the *something* could not be some*one*? Though he had no idea how, he was beginning to believe that this stranger held the key to the future of his people.

After clearing a circle in the forest floor of anything that could burn, he made a small nest of the kindling. He pulled from his pouch the flint he always carried for starting fires. Striking it with his knife, he created the sparks needed to ignite the dry bark. He encouraged the flames with soft breaths as he added the smallest of the twigs, then the larger, and finally the small sticks. Once these were burning, he used the larger sticks to surround the fire, one end in the flames. These would burn longer. He need only push the unlit portion toward the center every so often for a flame which would hopefully last till morning.

With the fire now burning, he sat back on his heels and again took stock of his situation, as a wise man should.

He had left his people in the early warmth of the springtime. The moon had been a comfort to him those early nights away from his homeland. He had headed east, as he had been instructed. *"You must travel toward the rising sun,"* the Chief Priest had said, and he had obeyed, not knowing that his journey would be of such length. He was a warrior and was proven the best his people had produced. He was well schooled in the ways of the wild, but he could also make his way through the lands of city dwellers if the need arose.

It had.

Several times on this journey he came into contact with others, such people as he had never known existed before leaving his home. He had no idea there were civilizations this far to the east. To his knowledge he had traveled farther than any of his people ever had before, far beyond the Blue Mountains. Those peaks were so high that there was no record among his people of their having been crossed. Across deserts that had seemed as wide as the mountains were tall, through woodland and over endless plains, through farmlands and past small towns and large cities, he had journeyed. It was the dream of every man with a heart for adventure.

It was a journey that, by the rising and setting of the moon, had taken him almost five seasons.

And now the warrior must make that same journey in reverse, but this time with a stranger who would, based on his manner, serve as a heavy weight tied around the warrior's feet, a stranger who knew nothing of what lay ahead. It was as if this strange man truly had fallen from the heavens, a babe in a foreign land, who must be guided back to the place where he could grow into…what? A gift for his people?

The warrior leaned back against the stone outcropping at the base of which he had made their camp and again eyed his burden. He would do what had to be done. He would see this stranger into the hands of the priests who had sent him. Of this he had no doubt.

CHAPTER 6

Ray awoke with the midday sun.

A different kind of fog clouded his brain this time. It was a fog born of physical exhaustion coupled with the pain of muscles unused for days and then traumatized by his headlong flight to nowhere. But as bad as these feelings were, they quickly gave way to a feeling more biting, more urgent, more demanding: hunger.

This was why, despite his pain and fatigue, he nearly lunged for the remains of a rabbit that were on a spit near the fire. His weakness got the better of him when his shaking fingers dropped the roasted meat onto the still-smoking ashes. He quickly dug it out, burning his fingers in the process. Ignoring the pain, he brushed off the ashes and devoured the morsel with hardly any chewing. He licked his fingers clean and was seriously eyeing the bones, when a vision appeared before him.

By this time Ray's psyche was more prepared for the strange man who seemed able to magically appear from the surrounding woods. Sometime during the night he must have reconciled himself to the reality of his plight, as impossible as it seemed, and now he took the time to study this man who was responsible for saving his life.

What he first attributed to malnourishment, he now recognized as lean, hard muscle with no unhealthy fat. This told him that a physically powerful man stood before him. Ray knew something of this, as for the last several years he had spent many an afternoon in the gym. Pumping iron was one of his early loves, and he liked to think of himself as thoroughly fit, ready for any physical challenge. Just looking at his benefactor, his opinion of his own fitness took a significant hit.

The stranger was dressed the same as before. This seemed more in line with Ray's current assessment of his abilities. There was, however, a difference. Now the stranger wore a harness with weapons.

Strapped to his back with a three-inch-wide band of leather was a scabbard which housed a sword, its hilt visible behind and to the right of his head. The leather band ran over his right shoulder and down across his body. On the front was another scabbard. This one was much smaller, maybe seven inches long, with the leather-bound bone handle of a knife protruding from it. They were joined to another leather band of equal width which encircled his waist. The leather pouch Ray had seen soon after awaking beside the river now hung across his right shoulder, settling comfortably at his left hip.

While Ray saw his benefactor for the first time without a mind clouded with the potions that had helped him to heal, so the warrior took in the sight of Ray, hunched protectively over the remnants of the morning's kill. The juices of the meat were smeared across his mouth. He noticed that his patient's eyes reflected a calmness that was not present when he had awakened the day before. This was a good sign. Perhaps he was ready to come to terms with his situation.

The stranger approached the fire, knelt, and placed before it a large leaf filled with several long, dusty-brown roots which he had recently dug up and washed. Ray watched in silence as the stranger unsheathed his knife and used it to scrape the outer skin from the roots, careful to catch the shavings in another of the large leaves. The inner meat of the root, just below the surface, was almost blood red. This was peeled off separately from the skin and placed in yet another of the broad leaves. What remained resembled a slender peeled potato.

"You must carefully remove every trace of redness," the stranger told Ray, as if instructing a child. "If the redness is eaten it will lead to sickness, maybe death."

As he spoke, the stranger cut the "potato" into slices of about an eighth of an inch in thickness. These he spread across another leaf and placed before the fire.

"When they are thoroughly dried, they can be eaten."

This instruction was given clearly and precisely. Without realizing it, Ray was drawn into the role of the pupil.

"What is this called?" Ray heard himself ask as he pointed to the freshly prepared root.

The warrior, head held down as he sliced another of the roots, smiled at the ease with which this man was coming to terms with his situation.

"This is the root of the ochos. I thought it only of my homeland but it is not uncommon if one knows where to look. I have seen it on all of my travels. The skin and the redness make powerful medicine which can dull pain and bring sleep."

As he spoke, he placed the remainder of the sliced root beside the fire, before moving the leaf which held the red portion of the ochos off to the side.

"This must dry slowly; then it will be crushed and added to my pouch," he said, patting the bag hanging from his hip. "It is needed. It took much of the blood-powder to heal you."

"You gave me that?" Ray asked the question with a tone akin to accusation.

The stranger stopped what he was doing to glare at Ray, and his piercing stare drove any sense of indignation completely from Ray's mind. Ray dropped his eyes, then his face, unable to meet the stranger's gaze, but he could still feel it burning into the top of his head. After a period the stranger continued with the task of cleaning his knife. When he finished he re-stoked the fire and, finishing that, he spoke.

"You have much to learn."

• • •

The remainder of the morning was passed in silence.

The warrior climbed to the top of the outcropping of rock to a place bathed in sunlight for most of the day. There he placed the large leaf containing the skin of the ochos. It would take several days for it to thoroughly dry out. Only this slow process would preserve the powerful narcotic which was the basis of its medicinal powers. The meat of the root which hung by the fire was soon dried and, at the urging of the warrior, Ray made a meal of several pieces. It was starchy and bland but it relieved his hunger. In time it would provide some measure of strength.

With his stomach temporarily satisfied, thirst now moved to the front of his concerns. He looked around for his benefactor and found that he was gone, having again silently merged with the surrounding forest. Beside Ray's resting place lay the water skin he had drank from when he awoke beside the river. Ray drank deeply and greedily at first, then contented himself with smaller sips as he savored the cool water

His hunger and thirst sated, Ray again became aware of his ever-present exhaustion. As it reasserted itself, he was content to sit back against the rocks and rest his bruised body. This allowed his brain the chance to work.

He took stock of his situation, which he still recognized as bizarre and desperate, but now he was able to digest a little more information and attempt to build a more rational scenario with which to calm his fears.

Although he didn't recognize the lay of the land, he was convinced he wasn't far from the city. It was inconceivable that he could have drifted so far downstream that a city or at least a town wouldn't be within a day's reach. Then he recalled his frantic search for signs, any signs, of people nearby. He had tramped through these woods for the better part of a day and found nothing.

The proximity to the river almost guaranteed that a road of some kind should have been easy to find. As he recalled, the land southeast of the city, though rural, was crisscrossed with state highways, secondary roads, and even some dirt roads that ran through the woods. This was primarily farm country, corn and soybeans being the major crops. The farmers used the dirt roads to move their planting and harvesting equipment between the various fields that provided their livelihood.

The land southeast of the city was whitetail deer country. The hunters who flocked to these woods usually left their mark in the form of deer stands, used shell casings, and empty tobacco pouchs. Ray had found none of these things.

His heart began to beat faster as he remembered his frantic, almost hysterical, search through the woods. How could it be that there were no signs of anyone having been here before? A pristine wilderness this close to the city simply wasn't possible.

But there was one sign of man. Ray fingered the wooden plug of the water skin to remind himself that the stranger was real.

Here in the southeastern United States was what appeared to be a native tribesman, but not a Native American. The stranger was too dark of skin. He was apparently born into the wilderness and was completely at home here. This man had saved Ray's life more than once and was providing for them both from what was available from the land.

He thought back to his awakening at the river and recalled that at first, neither could understand the other's language. That had changed. At an unusually rapid pace he found himself able to translate a word or two of what the man was saying during his stops for rest. It wasn't that the man was speaking English. It was just that over the course of a few hours Ray began to understand *his language*.

This, along with everything else that was happening to him, simply made no sense. He thought back to their brief conversation. He was actually speaking with the man, and now that he thought about it, he wasn't sure that *he* had been speaking English.

All of this was extremely distressing. Confusion ruled his thoughts and his body had not yet recovered from the abuse of the past several days. Together they led to a state of mental and physical exhaustion and Ray felt himself sliding into unconsciousness. He put up a brief resistance but it was futile. He drifted off to sleep with many questions, and few answers, whirling around in his head.

• • •

When Ray awoke the next time, it was with the satisfaction of having enjoyed a good night's rest. His body was beginning to heal and even his spirits felt refreshed. This newfound satisfaction lasted only until he came fully awake and realized that nothing about his predicament had changed.

He lay on the bare ground, with only a thin layer of vegetation beneath him to provide what little comfort there was to be had. What joy there may have been on such a beautiful morning was slowly being crushed from his chest, bit by bit, as the sights and sounds that greeted him came together to remind him that this was not a dream. He was lost in the wilderness with no means to survive on his own. He was totally dependent on a stranger who had kept him alive thus far, but whose long-range intentions were unknown. The feeling of depression these thoughts brought settled onto him like a weight, causing his head and shoulders to droop as he struggled to a sitting position.

How long he sat there, his arms wrapped around his legs, chest pressed into his knees, he didn't know. He wasn't focused on the passage of time, or on much of anything, until one urgent need managed to pierce his melancholy.

Forcing himself slowly to his feet, the soreness still evidenced by the trembling in his thighs, he staggered toward the edge of the small clearing. Stepping a few feet into the forest, he paused beside a large tree and, leaning against it, he relieved himself for the first time in at least two days.

Moving back toward the clearing he saw his benefactor standing beside the fire, observing his progress as he shakily made his way back to the pile of vegetation on which he slept. Reaching his makeshift bed, Ray turned to meet the stranger's eyes. They seemed to be weighing him, examining his fitness, evaluating just how he was coping with his situation. Feeling as if he was being graded, Ray tried to draw himself up to his full height and meet the man's look with one of his own, one of confidence, to let this stranger know that, paraphrasing William Henley, his head was bloodied but unbowed.

The warrior recognized this for what it was and gave him a smile that conveyed understanding and the slightest bit of respect.

This one reminded him of the lion cub he had found on a hunting trip two snows ago. Though cornered and helpless, it had bared its tiny fangs and made the most menacing noise that it could, determined not to show the depths of its fear.

"You are feeling better," the warrior said. "Good. I know not how long we can remain here. It is best to keep on the move when in a strange land."

He noticed the look of confidence leave Ray's face. In an effort to set him at ease, he continued, "We will spend more nights here, and then follow the sun. It will be a long and difficult journey, but we will find my people at its end."

Ray was still trying to make sense of exactly what had happened to him, but the question in his eyes could not find form on his tongue. His mouth opened in a futile attempt to make the words. Finally he asked, "The city?"

The warrior paused for a moment, considering Ray's words before responding.

"There is no city," the warrior replied. "There are no sign of men within many days of this place. Perhaps the city you seek lies in another place. Here there is only our Mother, only natural things."

The confusion, the frustration, was an aching inside Raymond's chest which became a pounding in his head. He fell heavily against the rock at whose base he had slept these past what? Two nights? Or was it three? His head slumped to his chest as he slid down to a sitting position. Then he slowly lifted his head toward the stranger who had saved him, nursed him, fed him, and given him a place to rest. Now he needed something else. He needed to be understood.

"Sit down, please. I need to tell you something ... to make you understand," Ray haltingly said.

The warrior paused at these words and regarded Ray with curiosity. Maybe some of *his* questions would be answered now. He approached to within an arm's length of where Ray sat and then lowered himself to the ground, squatting with his knees on his chest and his butt on his heels.

Ray searched the warrior's eyes and held them with his gaze, hoping this would aid him in communicating his predicament.

"I'm lost," he began hesitantly. "I don't know where I am, but I know I don't belong here. There's got to be a way for me to get back to where I do belong."

Although he tried to speak slowly, his haste to be understood was causing his words to run together.

"You've got to help me! There must be something, somewhere," he pleaded. "You must have seen something that can help me."

As the warrior sat across from Ray, allowing him to hold his gaze, he could feel the frustration in his words and in his tortured expression. He wished to help this one, but all he had to offer was the truth... his truth. It would have to do.

"I am Hanshee," the warrior began, "and I come from a land far to the setting sun." As he spoke, he gestured with his arm toward what Ray deduced was the direction from which he had come.

"I am 'Maiyochi,' the first in the memory of even our oldest old ones; the first in generations. I have come far, farther than any of my people have ever come, farther than I knew it possible to come, in search of that which will help my people in a time of great need. I was sent by our Elder Priests, who dwell farther up the mountain than do we. My people are an old race, older than all others, with much knowledge. Our priests are the keepers of this knowledge. To ignore their summons is to invite evil onto your lodge. I was not told what to seek, only that I must go toward the rising sun until I found it."

Ray listened in silence, taking it in.

"Hear me," Hanshee continued, "when I tell you that I have traveled swiftly, as a warrior can, for five seasons. I have crossed high mountains that seemed to touch the heavens. I have crossed swamps so wide and fraught with peril that, truly, I marvel that I am still alive. I have crossed desert and grassland, forest and jungle. I have seen wonders that I knew not existed. I have seen strange people, and strange cities, but my charge was upon me and hardly did I linger, though the temptation was sometimes great.

"Almost a full moon had come and gone since I last saw man, and then I came to the river. There something changed. I was drawn to tarry by its banks. I knew not what I sought, but it was at the river that I needed to be... to wait for my calling to find me. I traveled its length for much distance in both directions. I found no sign of man, no sign that I should wait there, but wait I did, for the feeling was strong and grew stronger with every moment spent there."

Here Hanshee paused and stared intently into Ray's face, ensuring that he still held his attention.

"Twelve days ago I found a place to wait. For two days and a night I was as still as a rock, as alert as a hawk, knowing my destiny was upon me. Near sunset of the second day I pulled you from the water.

"Listen to my words, stranger. They are true. I know not how you came there. There was no place for you to come from. You say you are from a city and this I believe, for I have seen that you are not of our

Mother. Unless the city you seek is in the heavens," he made a gesture toward the sky, "I know not where you come from."

Finishing his tale, Hanshee realized that he too had needed to talk, to tell his truth and to be understood. He looked deeply into the stranger's face and saw that his words had some effect. The stranger was more calm now, the little that he could understand having taken the edge off of his confusion. Hanshee could see in his eyes that his mind was now working, forming questions, focusing on finding answers that would help him solve his own problem.

Hanshee did not grasp the depth of Ray's confusion. He was right to surmise that he was moving forward in his understanding of his predicament, but the reality was so far beyond anything that Raymond had experienced, likened to something he might have read in a book of science fiction or adventure fantasy, that the inescapable conclusion continued to escape him.

Not knowing this, Hanshee prodded him out of his deep thought with a question.

"Who are you?"

Raymond's head shot up as if startled, and his eyes focused again on Hanshee as the question prompted his thoughts to take on some order

"I'm Raymond Covington, but you can call me Ray." He smiled and shook his head at the absurdity of a formal introduction out here in the wilderness.

"Look, Hanshee? I don't know where we are, but I come from a big city," he spread his arms wide to indicate the size of the city. "It has many tall buildings and thousands... hundreds of thousands of people. Some friends and I were on that river, the DeFrance River. There were four of us, and there was an accident. We were within a few miles of the city. We couldn't have drifted far. Did you see any others? Was there anyone else floating in the river? Any canoes, or beer cans? Anything?"

As Ray spoke his voice began to take on a high-pitched pleading tone that hinted at the hysteria again rising to the surface. Hanshee sensed this, but he could only shake his head as every additional hope of Ray's was dashed. He had seen nothing on the river that did not belong there. Only Ray was out of place, an impossible distance from where he thought he was supposed to be, with no plausible explanation.

It was then that Ray's face lit up as a thought occurred to him.

"You said there are cities to the west?" he asked.

Hanshee seemed confused.

"Toward the setting sun... cities... that way?" Ray excitedly pointed west, or toward where he thought west was.

"To the ... *west*... are many things," said Hanshee, "lands and cities and people, and farther on, my home."

"You can take me there?" asked Ray, ignoring most of what was told him. "You can get me to a city?"

Hanshee regarded him as if looking at a small child.

"Yes," he said patiently, "we will see cities on our journey beyond the stone mountains."

"I don't know about these 'stone mountains,' but just get me to a city! If I can get to a phone I can get some help and find my way home!"

Hanshee had no idea what Ray was talking about, but the look of excitement and dumb optimism on his face, completely out of place with what Hanshee knew the immediate future held, told him that this one had not yet come to grips with his plight.

Ray's weakness was that he came from a society built upon science, technology, and rational thought. Any problem, no matter how complex, could find its solution in the application of logic and reason. He had been weaned on $A + B = C$, and it mattered little that he had no idea what the values of A, B, and C were. He knew... *knew*... that his salvation from this impossible situation lay just around the corner, at the first pay phone that they stumbled across. It had to. The alternative was to accept the conclusion that his present circumstances dictated and that his five senses told him was true.

And that would be madness.

Hanshee's world was different in that his environment, primitive by any measure that Ray might apply, was filled with many things that he did not fully understand. He relied a great deal on what his five senses told him, and sometimes on what he sensed on another level, to be true. For the answers to some of the mysteries of his world,

Hanshee turned to the elders and the priests of his people. For others he sought no explanation, simply accepting that it just is, or what will be, will be.

This was an advantage because it allowed Hanshee to bypass many of the vagaries of a situation and focus on what had to be done. In a very real sense, he had a more agile mind than Ray, able to accept and adapt to the apparent reality of a situation in a way that provided the best opportunity for survival.

While Ray was wedded to the perception that he was a day's walk from the DeFrance River and not that far from civilization, despite what his senses told him, Hanshee was quite comfortable with the concept of this stranger having fallen from the sky. It was as good an explanation as any for now, and their real concern should not be how this situation came to pass but how they would survive it.

With this in mind, Hanshee was content to know that Ray intended to willingly accompany him on the difficult journey to what he called "west." He knew that, for the sake of his survival, Ray really had no choice. And though Hanshee was lacking in a full understanding of their situation, it was enough that this part of his task was complete. He now stood a good chance, with luck and a little cooperation from 'Way-Mon', of completing his task and serving his people.

Hanshee again regarded Ray, this time with an eye toward his physical condition. He had endured considerable hardship over the past several days but seemed to be regaining his strength at a rapid pace.

Maybe this one is not as soft as he first appeared, thought Hanshee.

Always aware that he was a stranger to this land, Hanshee disliked remaining in one location for too long a time, even a location as secluded as this one appeared to be. They had camped near the crest of a hill, at the base of a large outcropping of rock that served as a shield to whatever the elements might bring, as well as from human eyes looking down from above. This was a fair amount of comfort to the warrior, but still he would prefer to be fully mobile, the better to avoid trouble before it stumbled upon them.

He looked at Ray again, concluding that he would need several days of rest and nourishment before they could begin their long journey back to his people. They would have to be very careful and leave little sign of their presence here. He knew it would be slow going at first but the pace would quicken as Ray gained more strength and became accustomed to the ways of Mother.

This was another concern, for a journey of many seasons could not be survived by one with so little knowledge. Ray would have to be educated, taught the skills of survival that had taken Hanshee years to learn and were now second nature to him. And here, where there was very little margin for mistakes of any kind, the unlearned lesson could lead to the end for both of them.

And for my people, thought Hanshee? *Will my failure mean that they cannot overcome the danger before them? No, I will not fail. Way-Mon will learn. He must learn, and learn well, for if I should fall...* This thought he left unfinished, as he was unable to conceive of Ray making his way alone to Hanshee's homeland.

Now it was Ray's turn to watch Hanshee as the young warrior reached for a bundle of leaves beside the fire. Ray had not noticed them before, but now he paid close attention as Hanshee untied the thin piece of root that held the bundle together and exposed several scaled and gutted fish, each about the length and size of his hand. As Ray continued to watch, Hanshee produced several Y-shaped sticks which he had cut to use for cooking. Hanshee stood several of these up in what he determined was the best place to capture heat from the fire. He then draped a fish over each stick in such a way that the heat and smoke from the fire could do its work without scorching the delicate flesh.

Ray felt his hunger reassert itself. His meals had been few and far between of late and the way his mouth watered as he eyed the fish told him that he was more than due for a good feeding. To help pass the time until the food was ready, he struck up a conversation.

"Hanshee, where did you get the fish?"

A better question would have been "How far is it to the water?" but Hanshee recognized an opportunity to teach and seized it.

"There is a stream." He made a motion with his hand in the direction from which he had come. "It is in this valley. It may flow into the distant river. The fish are plentiful and not difficult to catch."

He glanced up at Ray as he stoked the fire, and saw that he held his interest.

"You must prepare your kill away from your bed if you plan to sleep there many nights. The offal will draw scavengers and predators of the wild down upon you."

Hanshee cast his gaze over the fire, met Ray's eyes, and smiled.

"It is best to sleep alone in the wild," he said.

CHAPTER 7

Three more nights passed and as the setting sun signaled the onset of the fourth, Hanshee made the decision that they would abandon their campsite in the morning. He had kept a watchful eye on Ray and had determined him now fit enough to begin their journey. He did not anticipate making much progress the next day but he knew that in order to finish, one must begin.

Since they first made camp Hanshee had been providing for their eventual departure.

In the bag on his left hip was a replenished supply of the "blood-dust" made from the ochos root. It was in a small pouch inside the larger pouch. Beside it were other small pouches containing other herbs and remedies known to Hanshee's people.

In a bundle newly made from the dried and scraped skins of animals, he had managed to put together other provisions such as bits of dried meat and fish, dried fruit, nuts, and the dried centers of the ochos. This was for Ray to carry. Hanshee fully expected him to help himself to its contents during the coming journey. In this way Ray could keep up his strength, and there would be less of a need to stop and rest.

Good water had been plentiful during the journey here, and Hanshee saw no reason why that should not hold true for the journey home. Still, he kept the water skin full. It was on the small side, intended for his use alone. Hanshee knew that someone new to the trail would need plenty of fresh water on a regular basis. He intended to fashion another, larger, skin once he was able to get leather of the right quality.

Having replenished the provisions and eliminated all signs of their camp, Hanshee tilted his head back to view the sky. The sun would be rising soon. He wanted to be well away from this place before its rays struck the rock behind them. His nostrils flared as he took a deep breath, using another of his trusted senses to read his environment. Though nowhere near as keen as that of a wild animal, Hanshee's sense of smell was well trained. He could recognize many scents that would go unnoticed by someone unfamiliar with nature. On this morning as the sky began its transition from opaque to gray and then to blue, he smelled nothing that would cause them concern.

Just when Hanshee was considering waking him, he noticed Ray beginning to stir.

Slowly he rolled over on his bed of now-dry vegetation, making a crackling sound on the dead leaves and alerting all within earshot that he was here. His slow rise to a sitting position produced an equal amount of racket. By the time Ray had gained his feet and brushed the debris from his clothes, Hanshee was sure that every forest dweller within an arrow's flight had marked their position.

There really was no harm done. Spreading the dead vegetation to hide their passing would be at least as noisy. But to Hanshee's way of thinking, a warrior should arise silent and alert.

"The ears should awaken first," the lesson from his father had begun, *"so as to listen to the surroundings while the body remains motionless. The nose should awaken next, and smell the different scents that ride the winds. The skin should have already told its tale. Is it hot or cold? Damp or dry? Was the air still? Only after these senses tell their tale should the eyes open, fully alert and already having a sense of what would lie before them. The body has not moved, save for the easy breathing which has not changed and not alerted any creature watching that you are awake, ready to glide silently to a place of hiding, or spring suddenly into battle, whatever the moment demands."*

This lesson, and much more, had been drilled into Hanshee by his father and every one of his teachers, as they themselves had been taught, as it had been done for countless generations.

The training of a warrior was the most serious of the training that the young men of his people endured, for the warrior was more than a fighter. He was a protector and provider. He defended his people from outside threats, enforced their laws and customs, and kept the peace. He provided meat for the fire of his lodge, as well as for those who lacked a provider. He explored far lands, returning with wondrous stories of adventure to delight young and old, and with new knowledge to benefit his people.

Yes, Hanshee thought, *a warrior is many things.*

And as he watched Ray stagger to his feet, like a bull elk that had eaten too well of the aged fruit, Hanshee could only think the obvious: *This one is no warrior.*

* * *

For the hundredth time Ray silently cursed the heat.

This was the third day of the change which had taken them from the river basin and its deeply shadowed woods to this plateau and what he could only describe as a scrub forest. The once-towering trees had given way to stunted oaks rudely protruding from the dry, sandy soil, with thinly leaved branches extending no higher than ten or twelve feet. They were too short and their leaves too sparse to provide any real shade, and they grew so close together that passing through them was an ordeal. A painful ordeal, as the small trees seemed to produce more prickly parts than leaves. The journey through and around them was one of burning sun and misery. Add to this the fact that at about the same time that they had entered this hellish landscape a heat wave had descended on the area. Ray could only guess at the temperature, but he wouldn't have been surprised to find out that it was over one hundred degrees Fahrenheit.

He took a moment to glance ahead at Hanshee, who seemed to glide through the punishing vegetation with smooth, silent strides. His head was held high, swiveling constantly from side to side. He was always searching, not only with his eyes but with all his senses. He seemed able to *feel* his surroundings.

It had been this way, Hanshee in the lead and Ray doing his best to keep up, since the two had begun their journey almost three weeks earlier. Ray kept track of the days by making scratches with a sharp stone on the walking stick he carried. Earlier, he had counted the marks, an exercise he seemed to perform on an hourly basis for the past several days. There had been no change. There were still twenty notches in the stick.

Ray thought back to the first few days of hiking through the river basin. It was a new experience for him, which again drove home the point that there was fitness and then there was *fitness*.

After the first hour or so of hiking the uneven terrain, Ray's legs felt like they were on fire. His macho vision of matching Hanshee stride for stride through the wilderness soon dissipated into painful reality. By the time the sun was halfway to its peak he was begging Hanshee for a rest. The rest granted, Ray took a seat at the base of a large sweet gum tree, expecting to be treated to disapproving looks and comments about how soft he was, how unfit for a life in the wild. But Hanshee surprised him with his graciousness. Ray was treated to a smile and a friendly hand on the shoulder, as well as a rest far longer than he expected he would get.

Only later did he come to realize that Hanshee had intentionally set a punishing pace on that first morning.

Hanshee had pushed hard, considering the novice who followed him. He was impressed with the fact that Ray had stayed close on his heels for the better part of the morning without asking for a rest. When Ray finally did ask, Hanshee was glad to give it, having at that point covered far more ground than he had anticipated.

Having decided that he wanted to pull his weight on this journey, Ray had taken to initiating the little teaching sessions that occurred throughout the day as they made their way across the terrain. He had trained himself to become a keen observer of most everything Hanshee did, asking questions sometimes to the point that he thought must be aggravating to his companion. But this was not the case. Hanshee had taken notice of his interest and was gratified that Ray had reached this point on his own. He took the time to explain the how's and the whys behind much of his woodcraft, and Ray had learned that even the most mundane task, such as gathering firewood, had a right way and a wrong way.

Certain types of wood were needed to make a long-burning fire that produced coals right for cooking. It was also a plus to have a clean-burning fire, so as not to alert all within eyesight to your presence. And of course you must gather the wood in such a way as to leave as few scars as possible on the landscape. No hacking and sawing. If possible, use only wood that has already fallen, taken from a place where it would not be missed. This last was a precaution taken when traveling in small numbers in potentially hostile country.

Gathering wood, building fires, preparing food, these things had become a part of Ray's regular duties, along with erasing all evidence of their presence once they were ready to leave a campsite. Hanshee stood by with a watchful eye as Ray had learned the art of covering one's tracks. Ray learned fast and Hanshee nodded approval when he felt only a well-trained eye could discern their trail. With these duties Ray was now trusted, but Hanshee would not yet take him hunting.

"Capturing prey takes a practiced eye, stealth, cunning, and patience," Hanshee had explained when Ray asked why he couldn't hunt, "especially as we have no bow with which to strike game from afar. We would starve should I try to teach you the ways of the hunt as we hunted. Better that I catch the meat. I will keep watch. When I see that you move silently through the brush, then will I trust you with my appitite."

The things that Hanshee taught, from the smallest bits of information given in some offhanded way to grave warnings spoken as if his very life might someday depend on the knowledge, all of these things Ray tried to soak up like a sponge. There was so much to learn that he might never know it all, certainly not to the point of being almost a creature of nature as his rescuer/healer/protector/teacher appeared to be. But Ray hoped to retain enough so that when he returned home he could again seek out wilderness similar to the one he had experienced and feel some level of comfort there. Nature had much to offer and Ray was glad that, with Hanshee's help, he could now appreciate it. He might even be able to share his new appreciation with his friends.

His friends.

He had thought of them off and on over the past several weeks. This wilderness had encroached on his consciousness to the point that his family, his friends, his job, his whole life before the accident, was more like a dream than reality. He had been away from all of that for almost five weeks by his rough calculations. Five weeks and no search party, no airplanes flying overhead, no cultivated fields, roads, or any sign of civilization. No trace of another human besides himself and Hanshee. It was enough to make him wonder if he was still in the United States. But of course he was. Where else could he be?

Where could he be that he was lost for so long and with the friends he began the trip with nowhere to be found? Did they find their way back? Did they just forget about him? Ray knew that couldn't be the case, but he had no answers. There was nothing to keep the questions from coming back. During times of rest, when he was alone with his thoughts, he wondered how he had held together this long. Without any answers as to how he had arrived here, how he had related so quickly to this stranger, and no signs of his former life save the clothes he wore, what had kept him sane?

Maybe it was thoughts of the city they were approaching.

Hanshee had said they were moving toward a city, and although the journey was taking longer than Ray had expected, he was sure that Hanshee knew what he was talking about. Hanshee had said the city was a moon away, measuring distances in time rather than in miles or kilometers. Ray had first thought of a moon as being a night and a day. After the third night he began to understand that a moon meant a *cycle* of the moon. In the context of time, this is a little less than a month. That time had almost passed, and Ray expected to see signs of a city any day now, though it seemed Hanshee was in no particular hurry to leave the forest. Sometimes Ray wondered if Hanshee had chosen routes most likely to keep them concealed.

No matter…as long as they eventually reached the city, and help.

CHAPTER 8

With the sun just past its zenith, Ray was not surprised when Hanshee called for a stop.

This was the usual practice. They would take a brief rest, treat themselves to water and maybe a handful of their provisions and then they would push on until about an hour before dusk. If Hanshee had managed to bring down some game during the course of the day, or if he determined that conditions called for it, they would stop earlier so as to give them time before nightfall to prepare a proper camp.

This time when they stopped, Ray observed Hanshee begin going through the routine of setting up a campsite. He instructed Ray to gather what was needed to make a small fire.

"Are we staying here tonight?" Ray asked, puzzled by the break in their routine.

Hanshee looked around, surveying the area yet again.

"It is a good place," he said. "We can build a fire here. There is wood, and cover."

"But there's no water, and we're running low," said Ray.

"We will have water soon enough," Hanshee replied.

Ray looked around. The woods here were denser than those they had been traveling through. The trees were higher and there was a bit more shade. Though his body was acclimating to the constant heat, he was thankful for this apparent reprieve. As he began the preparations for making a fire, Hanshee again spoke.

"I will see what is near," he said. "You will wait here."

It was a command, but not given as such. Ray was not inclined to argue since this was the usual way they'd gone about it after a camp was made. But this time he felt something was different. He again looked around the secluded campsite, about to open his mouth in mild protest, but Hanshee was gone.

Ray could only smile. Whoever, whatever, this guy was, he was good.

* * *

The sun had traveled half of its remaining distance to the horizon before Hanshee returned. He carried with him the dressed carcasses of two meaty rabbits. The coals in the bottom of the fire pit were just right for cooking, and Ray eagerly looked forward to fresh meat after several days of dried badger, or whatever it was they had been eating. He eagerly began setting up the necessary framework of branches so the meat could be cooked.

Once the rabbits had been set to roasting over the hot coals, Hanshee produced from his pouch several varieties of roots and leaves. Some of these Ray recognized, but not all. As usual, Hanshee took the time to explain what the plants were, where they could be found, and whether they were for medicinal purposes or nourishment. Ray was relieved to learn that some of the more questionable-looking plants were mosses and fungi, not meant to be eaten, but would be dried, powdered, and stored for future use.

"It is wise to learn to use what is at hand," explained Hanshee as he separated the different flora. "One cannot be sure what lies ahead. It is best to be prepared."

"You sound like my mother," Ray joked, "or my scout master." After so much time spent with his companion Ray was feeling very much at ease.

"Before this journey's end, I may well be mother to you," Hanshee smiled.

Hanshee was referring to the relationship in his culture between an adolescent and a seasoned warrior. The process by which the boy was taken under the wing of an elder and molded into one who can serve the tribe was likened to a pregnancy and a new birth. It was often said, jokingly, among the warriors that they were "mothering" the young ones, bringing them into a new world and a new phase of their lives. Hanshee was already filling that role in his relationship with Ray, and Ray, without realizing it, had fallen into the role of an adept, though somewhat over-age, pupil.

Lessons and small talk continued until dusk, at which time Hanshee announced that they would very soon be moving toward the south. This intrigued Ray, as they had never before traveled at night and their direction until then had always been west. He set aside his walking stick, having just marked it with notch twenty-three, and listened as Hanshee explained.

"The city you seek lies to the south," Hanshee said.

"A city? With people?" Ray's excitement rushed to the surface.

Traveling for so long a time with Hanshee in the wild, Ray did not realize to what extent he had become comfortable, but the thought of a city, with technology and telephones, meant his salvation! He was ready to leap to his feet and bolt in the direction that Hanshee had indicated, but was brought back to earth by his next words, and the solemn tone with which they were spoken.

"Way-Mon," Hanshee began. "I know not from where you come. You came from nowhere, adrift in a nameless river. You clothe yourself differently. You speak a different tongue, though you now speak mine easily enough. In truth, I have not seen your like before. But I have seen this city and its people. These are not your people. You will not be welcome there."

"I will lead you to this city because it is important to you," he continued. "We go at night, to go unnoticed. We go with ears sharp and eyes wide to danger and opportunity. We do not rush in foolishly, never again to leave. You must be wary, or we will not go."

Not go? That possibility never occurred to Ray. He was shocked that Hanshee would even say it.

"Look, Hanshee," he began, trying to tamper down the spirit of rebellion now taking form within him. "I appreciate all that you've done for me. I mean, I never would have made it this far if not for you. I probably wouldn't be alive if you hadn't pulled me from the river.

But I have a home. I have a job, and friends, and a life. And this…" Ray made a sweeping gesture encompassing their surroundings "…this ain't it! It's been different. Hell, it's even been *fun* in some crazy way, but if there's a city south of here I'm going to find it and I'm going to get home!"

Hanshee met Ray's fierce stare with one of his own, and silence. He saw in his companion's unflinching gaze that he was prepared to wander off into the night, alone if need be.

Foolish man, thought Hanshee. *With his look and manners he would wander into death. My protection is his only hope. I pray I can deliver us both from this place with our lives.*

Having made up his mind, Hanshee spoke.

"You will not go alone. I will lead you there. But you must do as I say."

Ray looked at him in disbelief.

"Why? I don't need you any more. If we're that close to a city, hell, I'll find it from here!"

A slow smile spread across Hanshee face. He let a small bit of humor rise into his eyes.

"Way-Mon, my friend, it is as you say that you owe me your life. I pulled you from the river when there was only a spark of life remaining, and I nursed that spark into the roaring fire that now stands before me. I have guided you this far, providing for your needs as I have my own. I have asked for nothing in return.

"If you are a man of honor," Hanshee continued, "you will allow me this one boon. Let me lead you to the city. Let me go with you inside. We will go unnoticed, and we will see what this city holds for you. If it is the place you believe it to be and you find your home, or word of your home, I will leave you and our paths shall not cross again. But if what we find is danger, we will leave together and continue our journey to the high mountains toward the setting sun. I think this is not too much to ask of one to whom your life is owed."

Hanshee spoke these words eloquently and in a soothing voice, the half-smile never leaving his lips. His wide eyes and arched brow conveyed a message of warmth and caring. Hanshee could be very persuasive when needed.

Ray considered his words.

All that he said was true, and he had nothing to lose by allowing Hanshee to guide him to the city. Once they arrive, he might even find some way of repaying Hanshee for all of his kindness. This alone was enough of a reason to agree to his request. It was little enough to ask. Ray returned Hanshee's smile and extended his hand.

"Agreed," he said.

Hanshee looked to the outstretched hand without understanding. Ray then reached for Hanshee's hand and, after assuming a firm grasp, began to shake it while offering an explanation.

"This is a custom from my homeland. When two men agree to a bargain this is done as a gesture of goodwill."

The scene reminded him of old movies he had seen, where the white man, or the American, or the human, introduced the handshake to the naitve, or the foreigner, or the alien. He felt corny but, hell, he could afford to feel a little corny. He smiled in satisfaction. He was finally going home!

CHAPTER 9

They made their way down from the plateau where they had camped toward the denser woods surrounding the city during the twilight hours between dusk and full darkness. Once the darkness enveloped them, they moved from the concealment of the woods and followed the narrow paths that led south. As it turned out, the city lay a farther distance away than Ray had thought and he was glad he had Hanshee to show him the way.

Hanshee was just a shadow moving several yards ahead of him along a narrow, rutted road of the kind Ray had seen used by dirt bikes and four-wheelers. Though it was little more than a wide trail, it was a way to make good time unnoticed.

For his part Ray was ecstatic. This narrow dirt road was the first sign of the presence of other people that he had seen in well over a month. It required real effort to keep from bolting headlong down its length to the city he believed lay at its end. But he was true to his word, as he knew Hanshee had been, and would be regardless of what they found at the road's end. For now, Ray would go nowhere without Hanshee's guidance.

And so he stifled his excitement and kept pace with Hanshee as they proceeded under the night sky. As they carefully made their way, the cool night air and the peaceful surroundings served to calm his racing pulse. After a while Ray allowed himself to reflect on this strange experience which he felt was finally coming to an end.

He had been hesitant to allow his thoughts to wind their way into the true depth of this experience. There were, after all, several aspects of his situation that defied explanation. His current location was a good example.

Of course he had given *some* thought to this mystery. Where in the continental United States could he be that he had seen absolutely no sign of anyone other than his rescuer for this length of time? He knew there were some parts of the western mountains that were considered remote, maybe some areas in sparsely populated states like Idaho, Montana, or the Dakotas where you wouldn't see another human being for weeks if you stayed in an isolated location. But they had been moving constantly and had covered a few hundred miles without seeing another soul.

Even when there was no one around, you should be able to find *signs* of people.

Ray had often been perplexed and sickened by the amount of garbage that could be found in parks and beside lakes, rivers and streams; the "wilderness" as he knew it. But here, on this journey through this landscape, he had seen no trace of anyone; not one discarded soft drink can, not a vapor trail in the sky to mark the jet that had long since passed. There had been no cleared land, no old wooden fence posts that marked the boundaries some farmer had fleetingly imposed on the terrain many years ago. It had been both glorious and troubling at the same time.

Logic told him that he couldn't be in the western United States. You don't start down a river in the Southeast, almost drown, and then wash ashore somewhere in Oregon. And even if you did, there would be signs of others.

Okay, so I assume that I'm still in the Southeast, he thought. *Most of the plants look familiar, and the rabbits and squirrels look the same. There are no monkeys in the trees, and no rhinoceroses running about, so scratch South America, Africa, and Asia.*

It was no use. He hadn't a clue as to his whereabouts.

That's all right, Ray thought. *I'll probably get to this city or town - more likely it's a crossroads or small community of some kind - and instantly have this thing figured out. Then I'll laugh at how I should have thought of it in the first place.*

Refocusing on finding his way in the darkness, he sought out the silhouette of Hanshee, who had come to a stop up ahead. Ray continued moving forward, coming almost abreast of his companion before he saw Hanshee's outstretched hand signaling him to stop. As they stood motionless, the night breeze gently blowing into their faces, Ray wondered what it was that had caused Hanshee to stop here. He couldn't hear anything except the usual night sounds of the insects and frogs, and the soft breeze as it whispered through the treetops.

Ray thought of the water flask he carried, which he'd filled at a stream at the base of the plateau atop which they'd camped. He reached for the cord hanging across his chest, but his hand never made it. Hanshee, ever alert, had detected even that small motion. Firmly grasping his wrist, Hanshee led him off of the road and into the deeper darkness of the trees. Stopping about twenty feet off of the road, Hanshee crouched down and motioned for Ray to do the same. Though a little annoyed, Ray was still quick to obey.

"Why are we doing this?" he asked in a whisper.

Hanshee's immediate response was a finger to his lips, the universal sign for quiet. Then he leaned closer to Ray while motioning down the road in the direction from which they had come.

"Someone comes," he said.

Ray's face brightened.

"Maybe we can hitch a ride into..."

Before he could finish his sentence, he felt Hanshee's hand snake around his head and clamp down on his mouth. He was instantly silenced, and he knew by the strength of the grip that he would remain so. Hanshee pressed is lips close to Ray's ear.

"Please, my friend," he whispered. "You said we would proceed as I say. You agreed to this."

Ray acknowledged this by nodding his head as much as he could while in that powerful grip. Hanshee loosened his hold on Ray's head.

Again the quiet settled down upon them. In another moment Ray could hear the distant rhythm of hoof beats on the hardened earth. They seemed to be approaching from the same direction that he and Hanshee had come. As they waited the sound grew louder. Soon the light from a lantern could be seen creating a strobe-like flicker as it became visible between the trunks of the trees. The lantern cast a small circle of light as it moved down the road. As it came closer, it could be seen to hang from a stick that stretched out in front of a horse whose head was just visible at the edge of the circle. Not wanting to impair his night vision, Hanshee did not look directly at the light, instead focusing his gaze a few meters behind it. Thus, he was the first to identify the moving shadow that followed as a wagon.

One of the two-wheeled variety, it was balanced by the weight of the horse at one end and by a large load of wood over its axle. There were two figures seated almost atop the wood. One appeared to have its arms outstretched, as if holding the reins which steered the horse. The other sat quietly beside the driver. It was impossible to tell anything else about them, since they appeared only as dimly lit shadows moving against the equally shadowy backdrop of the forest.

As Ray and Hanshee continued to watch, the one that was driving passed something over to his companion. The passenger grasped it and raised it to his face, tilting his head back. A moment or two passed before he brought it back down, wiped his mouth on his forearm, spit, and said something to his companion in an unknown language. This was followed by the nervous laughter of the driver, which was followed by loud guffaws from both. A slap on the back from the passenger to the driver ended the interaction, and then there was silence as the wagon continued past the two hidden observers and moved down the road in the direction of the city.

Hanshee remained motionless long moments after the wagon had passed, marking its departure by the dwindling sound. When the hoof beats had passed from earshot and he was satisfied that no others were approaching, Hanshee slowly rose to a standing position. Ray had been following his lead since his earlier faux pas and slowly rose with him. Noiselessly, Hanshee made his way through the underbrush and back onto the road. Here he paused again, his mouth slightly open, listening for faint noises carried on the breeze. Hearing only the night, he motioned for Ray to follow and they resumed their journey in the direction the woodcutters had taken.

This close brush with others, the first since their journey began, prompted Ray to again consider his position.

In all of his life he had never seen a wagon like the one the two men rode in, nor had he heard a language like the one they spoke. He could recognize Spanish or French or Italian if he heard it spoken, but he couldn't place what he had just heard.

He considered that Hanshee had spoken a strange language when he had first awakened. One of the greatest mysteries of this entire adventure, if it could be called that, was how the two of them had managed to communicate.

Upon reflection, this was all very frightening. No wonder he had tried to avoid coming to grips with it earlier. There was no logical reason why he should understand Hanshee's language, yet he now spoke it without effort, occasionally throwing in a phrase or two in English when he was not sure of the equivalent in Hanshee's tongue.

Ray moved closer to Hanshee.

"Did you understand their language?" he whispered.

"No," said Hanshee. "I passed here while journeying to your river. I tarried only long enough to take what was needed before moving on."

This last was said matter-of-factly. Hanshee's people generally looked down on thievery, but a warrior was trained to do what was necessary to survive and triumph. How much more so the Maiyochi?

"I have traveled far and seen many peoples," Hanshee continued. "I know not these people or any like them."

They continued on their way as the moon climbed higher into the night sky. After a while the sky in front of them began to reflect a faint glow as if from many lights or fires. Before long they found themselves at the foot of an embankment atop which a stone wall stretched out into the darkness to either side.

"Where are we?" Ray asked, afraid of the answer he would receive.

"At the city wall," stated Hanshee.

Ray wanted to ask Hanshee if this was his idea of a joke, but he held his tongue and examined the wall in front of him. It looked to be about twelve feet high, and of a uniform height all around. It sat upon a severely sloped embankment, which gave it another six feet of height, curving gently away to the right and left. The road they had been following forked at its base before following the curve of the wall in both directions. The stones with which it was made were not smooth. They were fitted together as best they could and the spaces which were left were filled in with a mixture of straw and clay that had hardened to form a kind of cement to hold them in place.

Ray thought this might be useful to keep out wild animals or delay large groups of people, but one man could easily scale it. As if reading Ray's thoughts, Hanshee stepped forward and began climbing.

Ray watched as Hanshee carefully sought out good holds for his hands and feet. With no problem, but in no hurry, Hanshee approached the top of the wall. He found that it had purposely been fitted with the roughest and most sharp-edged rocks, most probably to discourage climbers. Near the top there was much less of the crude cement used which left gaps between the stones. This meant it was not necessary for Hanshee to look over the top and risk revealing his presence. He found a suitable hole about a foot from the top and took stock of what he could see from there. Spying no immediate danger, he climbed to the top and inched his head high enough so that he could look over the wall. Now he had an unencumbered view of what lay inside. After a short while Hanshee slowly let himself down, alighting softly beside Ray.

"We will climb the wall over there." He pointed to a spot farther down the wall to their right. "There we will have cover when we cross over. I have seen cloth with which to disguise ourselves."

Ray again took stock of the wall surrounding what Hanshee called a city. He couldn't tell what was on the other side, but it was hard for him to imagine what he would consider to be a city behind it.

It's a stone wall, he thought, feeling equally disappointed and uneasy. *It's not even fitted stone…a rock wall! Who could live behind this thing? Was this some kind of off-the-grid survivalist camp? Would they even have a phone?*

Based on the wall, and the cart, Ray felt he couldn't expect much.

That doesn't really matter now, he thought. *We've come all this way and this place, whatever it is, is the best chance I've seen to get some questions answered and find my way back home.*

Reluctantly he fell in behind Hanshee.

CHAPTER 10

The stench was terrible.

It assaulted their senses with the fury of a living thing. It was so pungent that Ray was afraid to breathe through his mouth for fear that a smell so powerful might have a taste.

The ones responsible for the disgusting odor were on both sides, curious as to who these strangers could be, and wondering if they brought with them good things to eat. They were silent, save for the occasional grunt of anticipation. Ray was thankful for the rail fence which kept them at a distance. He was sure that he and Hanshee would be overrun by now if not for that flimsy piece of protection.

Hesitantly, he looked back at the wall they had just scaled and wondered if it was too late to go back over to the clean air on the other side. When he turned back he saw Hanshee already halfway down the path created by the two rows of fencing and he hurried to catch up.

Realizing now that there would be no food from these two, the mood of the huge hogs to either side of them began to change to one of agitation. One of the larger ones threw his bulk against the fence and Ray was surprised that it held. Deciding that it wouldn't hold for long, he quickly moved to catch up with Hanshee, who had cleared the hog pens and was moving toward a small wooden building from which a dim light was visible through a cloth which covered the only window that he could see.

Straining to control the fit of coughing that threatened to reveal their presence, Ray moved up beside Hanshee who was now crouching against the shadowy side of the building. Hanshee's ear was pressed to the weathered wood as he listened intently to the goings on inside. Curious, Ray pressed the side of his face to the thin wood, closed his eyes in concentration, and listened. Almost instantly he heard sounds: the shuffle of heavy footsteps, the sound of metal scraping against metal, and a loud belch.

Someone lives here? Ray thought in astonishment. *How can they stand it?*

Feeling a light touch on his shoulder he opened his eyes and was startled to find Hanshee's face barely a foot from his own. Hanshee's gaze was intense as he held up three fingers and pointed to the house. Immediately Ray understood that there were three occupants. Cautioning him to stay where he was and to remain silent, Hanshee stealthily crept around the corner of the flimsy building to the side that had the window. Not knowing where Hanshee was going, but understanding his orders, Ray crouched down on one knee in the mud and weeds that surrounded the shack.

Again he considered just how he had gotten to this point.

Nothing made sense and yet, deep down, he was beginning to feel something. He was beginning to put the facts of his situation into a form that he could deal with. Somehow he knew that he was not yet ready to handle it, not quite ready to look the truth in the eye. If only he could... OH, SHIT!

Ray's eyes went wide as a powerful hand snaked over his shoulder and clutched his mouth, closing off the startled yell before it left his lips. Gently but steadily, the hand turned his head around until he could see that it was Hanshee. The warrior had made a circle around the building and come up behind him. Not wanting a frightened novice to give away their presence, Hanshee had opted to reveal himself only after he had guaranteed quiet. After giving Ray time to gain his composure, Hanshee leaned in and quietly relayed what information he had gathered.

"There are three inside," he said, "an old woman and two men. They must be the keepers of the swine. We have nothing to fear from them so long as we remain quiet."

He reached behind him and brought forth a rolled-up length of cloth. Opening it, he revealed two shabby robes, handing one to Ray.

"Place this over your garments. With these we will move more freely among the people who dwell here."

"Where did you get them?" whispered Ray, as he struggled to find a way to put this strange piece of clothing on. Finally he just stopped and watched Hanshee, copying his movements until he had the robe covering his clothes.

Hanshee made some final adjustments as he explained, "I saw them from the wall. The old woman was airing them out."

When Hanshee had finished, the robes covered everything but their feet. In Hanshee's case this was not a problem as he wore sandals of a kind that were worn here. Hanshee had stolen them from this city on his first passing. Ray wore Nike hiking boots. He looked up at Hanshee to find him staring at the boots with a look of disapproval.

"They must be removed," he said.

Ray's thoughts turned immediately to the mixture of waste, slop, and excrement in the hog pens responsible for the stench which threatened at any moment to drive him to his knees. Having to endure the smell was horrible. Walking in it was unthinkable.

Shaking his head with gusto, he stated flatly, "The boots stay on. I know I said I would do this your way, but this..." a sweeping gesture of his hand took in the filth of the hog pens and the surrounding area, "I can't walk barefoot in this."

Hanshee almost smiled. He was not immune to the smell, and had had to fight back the tearing in his eyes when they first crossed the wall. He came from a people who valued cleanliness and he sympathized with Ray, especially since he had nothing with which to replace the boots.

"You may keep them, but they must stay hidden." With that, he reached for the sash that held the robe tight to Ray's waist. Loosening it, he freed the material of the robe and pulled it downward so that it was almost dragging the ground. Better an unkempt robe than an open declaration that they did not belong here. Finishing that, he stood back to examine his work.

It will do, he thought. Looking up at Ray, he whispered, "Walk slowly and be careful."

The shack of the swine keepers was situated about seventy-five yards from the wall. Another seventy-five yards beyond the shack lay a cluster of buildings amid a few sparsely spaced trees. It was toward these buildings that Hanshee led Ray.

They eventually left the stench of the hog pens behind them, but as they reached the nearest row of dwellings it was replaced by others: the smell of human waste from the garbage that was piled up in narrow streets; the feces and urine that had settled into the runoff ditches; and the smell of unwashed men and women who had worked hard for days, maybe weeks, yet did not see the need to wash the perspiration from their bodies. Indeed, when he passed too close to one of the more decrepit of the citizens, Ray wondered if soap and water would be enough to remove some of the odors he smelled.

Hanshee was sure he could track some of these people over great distances on their scent alone.

In another city, this would be called a slum. The people here were the dregs of the citizenry. Most made their way through life under the employ of another, doing the type of work others would disdain. A few were craftsmen, selling baubles, carvings, woven baskets or polished stones for anything that would help them survive for another day.

Those were the more honest folk.

Others simply preyed upon whomever they could, selling their wares, or themselves, swindling and bilking the hardworking out of their wages, robbing and stealing if the opportunity presented itself.

For the most part the people were poorly dressed, wearing robes much like the ones Hanshee had stolen, many in need of varying degrees of repair. The hucksters were more brightly dressed, wearing a colorful piece of cloth, or head wrap as a means to attract the attention of those on which they depended for their daily bread.

Some of the females were actually clean and well dressed, wearing colorful shawls and skirts that hugged their curves. They stood in front of the low mud-brick houses, sometimes dancing to the music of flutes played by old men. Some could be seen to toss a coin to the musician upon emerging from the interior, usually with one of the laborers following close behind. A few smiled and spoke to the pair, but neither

Hanshee nor Ray could understand what was being said. Hanshee just continued a steady pace forward while Ray would nod his head and sometimes smile back at the insincere grins, blind to the sharp eyes that weighed him and his probable worth.

What Ray did see, with a growing sense of despair, was the lack of anything he could recognize as technology. There were no power lines running down the streets or from rooftop to rooftop. Every light that he saw was produced by a flame. Transportation was by foot, or by a dumb beast pulling a cart or wagon. Every now and again someone on a horse would ride by, but for the most part, the people who inhabited this part of the city used their legs to get wherever they had to go.

There was another sign that he would not find what he needed here: a distinct lack of anything modern.

Even in the worst parts of a town, the majority of the trash consisted of paper or paper products such as cardboard, posters, wrappers, and the like. There was none here. The garbage that he recognized was mostly rotted food and food scraps. There were bits of useless wood and badly soiled pieces of cloth among other things that were strewn in the gutters, but no paper or plastic.

As he walked through the narrow streets he observed many people eating. What he gradually noticed was that they ate from bowls made of wood or clay. There were no plastic containers, or glass for that matter, anywhere. The only metal was in the large kettle-type cooking pots that some were using over outdoor fires. A closer look confirmed for Ray that those who ate either did it with fingers, carved wooden spoons, or flat wooden sticks that resembled oversized tongue depressors more than anything else.

The total picture spoke to Ray of a level of poverty rarely seen even in third world countries. Where could he be? Some part of Southeast Asia? No, Latin America made more sense, though even in the worst conditions he had ever encountered or heard of there was some sign of Western civilization if nothing but the people wearing old, worn-out Western-style clothing. And the language he was hearing was not Spanish.

In some parts of South America they speak Portuguese, Ray thought. *Yes, that must be it! This must be the dregs of a Portuguese-speaking country! That would explain a lot.*

But it wouldn't explain enough, not nearly enough. He knew he was grasping at straws to even think such a thing. This place was nowhere on earth that he could conceive of, and the reality of this place, along with everything else he had experienced since blacking out in the river, was beginning to take its toll.

It just didn't make sense, none of it!

Things had happened to him that he had dismissed as coincidence, or bad luck, or for unexplained reasons that he didn't want to consider at the time. These things were now coming back to haunt him. That "something" he was beginning to feel deep down that he had avoided facing was beginning to assert itself, making its way to the surface and to the forefront of his thoughts.

He was afraid.

He was afraid because he knew he wasn't ready for what it would show him. He wasn't ready to face what he felt, deep down, was the impossible truth, or as much of it as he could stand.

Loud shouts brought him out of the depths of his thoughts. He looked up just in time to see a boot whiz past his head, or where his head would have been had he not been snatched out of harm's way by the ever-alert Hanshee. Stumbling and then regaining his balance, he looked not at the boot but at the man attached to it.

He was angry, that much was clearly apparent. He was angry, and large.

He wore heavy leather, from the helmet on his head, to what Ray could only describe as a smock, to the boots on his feet. The smock covered his shoulders and ran down front and back, to his waist, where it was tied with a heavy belt and split on either side to allow room for his legs to swing while riding a horse. Were he standing, the smock would probably extend almost to his knees. He wore a shirt of some kind under the leather smock but his arms were bare. Thick and hairy, tanned and scarred, they spoke of a man of physical power who knew how to handle himself and others. His legs were bare, save for the high boots he wore that protected his shins to just below the knees.

He sat atop a big gray horse and glared down at Hanshee, angrier now at having been deprived of his intended target. The stream of curses flowed, to the point where it was beginning to agitate his horse, which was prancing nervously in the mud of the street. This kept the man off balance and no doubt prevented another boot from being launched in Hanshee's direction.

For his part, Hanshee was doing all he could to defuse this potentially dangerous situation. With hands spread apart as if in submission, he maintained a steady rhythm of bows while smiling an apology. Careful not to speak and reveal themselves as foreigners, and even more careful to stay out of range of the strangers boots, Hanshee continued his act of contrition until the man seemed finally appeased. He turned his mount and moved away with a backwards glare and a surly, "...scum need to watch where you step...!"

"Scum need to watch where you step," Ray repeated as if in a trance, and immediately he realized what was happening. He turned to Hanshee who had heard and was staring at him in a quizzical way.

"That's what he said," Ray explained. "As he rode away... that's what he said."

"You speak their tongue?" Hanshee asked.

"No," said Ray, staring vacantly after the man. "I don't think so. Not yet."

Hanshee noticed that people had stopped to watch the two of them. Clutching Ray by his upper arm, he encouraged him to resume walking. They had now reached a better part of town than what they had encountered after the hog pens. Ray had been so lost in thought that he had failed to notice the transition. Still, there were none of the accoutrements of modern life that he had expected to find.

The questions rolling around in his head finally became too much for him and Ray stopped in his tracks. After a few paces Hanshee realized he was alone and whirled around, only to see Ray sweeping angry eyes around the city before resting his gaze on Hanshee.

"Where have you brought me?" Ray asked, this time not bothering to keep his voice down. "Where the hell is this place?"

Hanshee closed the gap between them in an effort to get Ray to lower his voice.

"My friend," he said quietly, "you wished to see this city. I have only brought you to where you asked to come."

"Bullshit!" said Ray. "This ain't no city. This is a pile of mud in the middle of the woods! This is a bunch of people living in the Stone Age! You promised me a city and I want one... a real city... with electricity and cars and newspapers... and a telephone!"

By now Ray's outburst, spoken in a language foreign to this place, was starting to attract attention. The many lit torches surrounding them revealed Ray's agitated state of mind as spittle ran from the corners of his mouth, his eyes bulged, and his skin started to take on a purplish hue. Hanshee could clearly see that Ray was on the verge of hysteria. He needed to be removed from this spot and calmed down before the attention they attracted became more than just curious stares.

"Please be quiet, my friend," Hanshee whispered. "We will talk of this... we will talk of this now."

Again taking Ray by the arm, Hanshee led him toward the edge of the road. Objecting at first, Ray reluctantly allowed himself to be led to an alley between two buildings. Down this alley they went, pushing their way past people who were out in the cool of the night, until they came to a doorway that was the entrance to what appeared to be a tavern.

Damn this crowded city, Hanshee thought as he led Ray through the milling people toward the door. *Damn all cities! But it is better to be off of the street and away from so many eyes.*

The inside of the tavern was dimly lit but still brighter than the torch-lit streets outside. Hanshee ran practiced eyes over the room upon entering. He was gratified to see that more people were outside in the alley than were inside drinking. Still, there were enough to make this small space seem full. He led Ray to the darkest, most private corner, and there they stood, the three rickety tables in the room having been taken. Thinking that strong drink would calm Ray down, and wanting some for himself, Hanshee motioned to a serving girl and held up two fingers. She looked them up and down and extended her hand, on which Hanshee quickly placed a coin produced as if by magic from the pouch under his robe. She turned away after examining the coin, allowing them some privacy. Hanshee used this time to engage Ray before he could again begin to lose control.

He gazed into Ray's eyes with a concern that was genuine, and spoke in measured, soothing tones.

"My friend," he began, "I see your confusion and it troubles me. I have done as you asked and brought you to this city. I did warn you of the many dangers here, and that we should not draw attention upon us. Even so, you would act as a fool and we may be in danger as we stand here speaking.

"I have traveled far," Hanshee continued, "seeking something unknown with which to save my people. I found you. Never have I seen your like in dress or manner. Truly you are not of this place. Even so, I pulled you from the river and tended to your..."

"We've been over that already," Ray interrupted testily, "how you saved my life, how you cared for me." He spoke in a voice louder than necessary. "That guilt trip got me to follow you through the woods and up a damn mountain for God knows how long and now to this dump." He waved his arms for emphasis. "You told me I could go to a city, one with a telephone where I could contact somebody who knows me and can get me home. Then you bring me to..."

"You asked to come here!"

It was Hanshee's turn to interrupt.

"You asked to see this city! My advice to you was to avoid this place, but you insisted so I led you here! Only to satisfy you! A warrior of..."

"And there you go with that 'warrior' crap again. You're on some kind of sacred quest," Ray said mockingly. "What are you after, the Holy Grail?"

Before a puzzled Hanshee could ask what that was, the serving girl had reappeared with two clay bowls, each three-quarters full of wine. Nodding curtly, Hanshee took them both and offered one to his companion. Hanshee took a small sip, as if to assure himself of what he was about to drink, then large gulps until he had drained the bowl. Ray watched him, and then looked to his own bowl.

This can't be any worse than that rot gut we drank in college, he thought, as he brought the bowl to his lips. To his surprise, the wine was rich and sweet and left a pleasant warmth trailing down his throat, prompting Ray to drain his bowl as he had seen Hanshee do. Lowering it, he felt the warmth spread throughout his stomach and chest as the wine settled in.

One good thing about this place, he thought.

After seeing Ray had finished his bowl of wine, Hanshee again sought his companion's eyes with his own.

"My friend," he said, "this is serious... as am I. I am a warrior. I am Maiyochi. I will do my duty by my people. I feel... I know… that you are a part of my duty. About you I will say no more, for I know no more. Only that you are foreign to this place. You fell from the sky into the River of Dreams. Why else was I there, if not to save you?

"I know not what you search for," Hanshee continued. "You say you wish to return to your home. So do I, but neither you nor I will see our homelands if we fail to leave this city alive."

Despite the wine, confusion was now a pounding, living thing in Ray's head. Hanshee couldn't seem to understand what he was going through. Jaws clenched tight, gritting his teeth in frustration, Ray spun on his heels and walked across the room to where a small, swarthy man was pouring the wine. The serving girl was there too, and upon seeing him approach she scooped up an urn and poured more wine into his bowl. Still gripped by frustration, Ray quickly brought the bowl to his lips and drank deep, feeling some of its contents seep out of the side of his mouth and run down his cheeks before falling from his chin to the dirt floor below. It also spilled on his boot that was partially visible from beneath his robe, as well as the sandaled foot of the man standing close on his left. Without thinking, Ray offered an apology, a curtly spoken "excuse me," and went back to his bowl of wine.

Koz was a thief by trade. He preferred to ply his craft on the edge of the slums where there was more to be had than in their bowels. This evening had not been his best and he had retired to this tavern with his two companions to await the late night. When thieving was not paying, one sometimes had to resort to the next tier of crime to make one's coin. Koz had found that the quiet darkness of the later hours was always best for violence.

But Koz was getting impatient here in this tavern. He was on edge and spending more than he had collected, and now this stranger, a foreigner by his strange words, had come to stand beside him and had spilled wine on his sandals. He looked down to assess the damage and... Oh ho! Look at those boots! Never had he seen their like! They were crafted by an artist, probably by a nobleman's cobbler! They spoke of vast wealth!

Now Koz took the time to see the face at the other end of the boots. He was tall and darker than most, and with a lean look about him for a nobleman. Maybe it had been too much travelling for his noble blood, to come here from his faraway lands. But that robe! He'd seen better in the very heart of the "swine-land." That was the name foisted on the slums of this city.

Koz readjusted his opinion of the foreigner. With a coarsely spun, worn-out robe like that, this man could not be a nobleman. Rather, a thief like himself who had the good fortune to meet the original owner of those boots one dark and quiet night. Koz smiled, for now this kinsman's good fortune was his own. He meant to have those boots!

"Pig!" Koz spat. "You spilled your sour wine on my sandals! Look at them! They are drenched! They are ruined!"

Ray was caught completely off guard by the sudden shouting in his ear and turned to see what the cause could be. He found an enraged man, shouting who-knew-what at him, and pointing at his feet! As he looked on in surprise, the man sent more growls in his direction while thrusting an accusing finger at Ray's boots just visible under the hem of the robe. Then he stood there, impatiently looking at Ray, obviously awaiting a response. When there was none, he again pointed at the boots and spoke more loudly.

"...are ruined, I say! I will have yours! Give them to me!"

This last part Ray understood. *How can I understand him*? A small voice from deep down asked, but this was no time to indulge small voices. Ray took a step back while holding up his hands, palms outward. Smiling, he shook his head in the universal sign for "no."

The blade seemed to leap into the hand of Koz.

Where it had come from, Ray couldn't say. What he planned to use it for was more than obvious. Ray was speechless. His head bobbed up and down as his eyes went first to the blade, then to the thief's face, where he saw no hesitancy, no mercy, then back to the blade. Ray's lips moved as he tried to speak, but words failed to form in his bone-dry mouth. His mind raced, but his thoughts were a jumble. Although he knew he would soon be stabbed, knew it with a certainty that was absolute, he couldn't seem to move a muscle to prevent it.

The next few moments were almost a blur, but this is what Ray believed he saw:

Just as the hand with the knife drew back, Ray felt himself go weightless as his body was thrown backward. He struck the floor awkwardly and felt pain shoot up his right arm but he didn't call out or even grimace. His attention was centered on Hanshee, standing where he had stood a second before. He was up on the balls of his feet, which were shoulder width apart. His knees were slightly bent, and there was an almost imperceptible bounce. He didn't look back to see where Ray had fallen or if he was hurt. He didn't appear to care about anything but the knife-wielding man before him.

Like a flash of lightning Koz moved the blade from his right hand to his left. Before his grip had tightened he was thrusting it into the center of Hanshee's chest... or where Hanshee's chest had been. Not rattled by the switch, Hanshee stepped back with his left foot and pivoted as he brought the palm of his right hand across his body at the level of the thrust. His palm struck the back of the thief's knife hand, sending his aim off to his right side. Having put his weight into the thrust, Koz was now leaning forward with his left arm outstretched. Hanshee was quick to close his left hand around the thrusting left wrist and pull, while at the same time viciously striking into the left side of his attacker's jaw with the heel of his right palm.

The effect was to stretch the thief's extended left arm across Hanshee's chest. The stunned attacker's fractured mandible, and indeed his entire face, was now pointing in the opposite direction. All that remained was for Hanshee to pull back on the left arm while pushing out with his chest.

Crack!

The sickening sound of Koz's dislocated left elbow seemed to hang in the air.

A scream of pain formed in the thief's throat and sprang from his broken jaw but was cut short as Hanshee, having brought his right hand back and ripped the knife away, now brought it quickly and precisely across the thief's neck, the target tantalizingly exposed due to the twisted and still outstretched head. At the same time Hanshee pivoted his body back, struck his attacker's torso with his left hand, and neatly batted him to the side and behind so that he now faced his two companions. As Koz struck the bar, the first spurt of blood from his severed jugular seemed to leap in slow motion through the air and onto the prone figure of Ray, who was transfixed by the combat and powerless to move.

Koz's two friends, unsure whether their comrade was dead or alive, produced blades of their own from the folds of their robes.

Gripping his weapon right-handed, as if for a downward stab, the nearest of the two raised it high and lunged at Hanshee. Moving smoothly forward to meet the attack, Hanshee caught the descending arm on his left forearm while it was still above his head and, sliding under and past his attacker, used the knife he still held in his right hand to slice deeply into his opponent's torso below the ribs. Without hesitation, making it all one motion, he brought the blade back toward his now gravely wounded assailant, plunging it almost to the hilt into his lower back. From his place on the floor Ray looked up and saw the second thief's eyes go wide with shock and surprise, which quickly turned into pain and defeat as he began his collapse toward the hard-packed dirt floor.

Before the fall of the second thief began, Hanshee was preparing to face the last of the three.

With his eyes locked on the blade of the third assailant, Hanshee pulled at the blade imbedded in the back of the second, but it would not come free. Seemingly without thought, Hanshee's left knee came up and his foot launched forward with the speed of a striking serpent. The kick struck solidly into the oncoming body of his attacker, just below the solar plexus, with such force as to lift him onto his toes. He settled back to earth still on his feet but now bent over, as if searching the dusty floor for a dropped coin.

The force of the kick, along with Hanshee's continued tug and the weight of the second thief's dropping body, combined to dislodge the blade from his spine. Ray watched transfixed as the blade pulled loose from the body and cut a silver arch through the air, only ending when it plunged almost to the hilt into the back of the third thief's skull!

If a stopwatch were available it would have recorded that this entire spectacle, a warrior at his most lethal, leaving one dead and two dying, took just under eleven seconds.

To Ray, it seemed like an eternity.

As he watched the third thief hit the earth at the feet of the second, he felt a tugging at his right shoulder. Tearing his gaze away from the carnage before him, he came face to face with Koz. Still alive, his quivering lips agape but his mouth making no sound, he had crawled forward until his hand had found purchase on the shoulder of Ray's robe. As the hand pulled loose and again extended toward Ray, their eyes met, and Ray thought he could see in them the realization of approaching death. The stark terror reflected in the eyes of Koz was like a current of electricity flowing from him to his intended victim and Ray remained transfixed, forced to view the blood spurting rhythmically from the gaping wound in the dying thief's neck. As the pool of blood on the hard-packed earth slowly spread toward him, Ray could see the thief's terror begin to recede, replaced by a resignation that turned ever so slowly into a vacant stare. The outstretched trembling hand slowly sank to the floor and the frantic heaving of a body trying desperately to cling to life came to an end.

The unseeing eyes stayed locked on Ray's. He could not bring himself to look away.

As suddenly as he was thrown to the floor, Ray was snatched upright again. This time Hanshee's face was inches from his own. With a voice that was calm but urgent he spoke: "We must flee!"

With this, he started for the door, leading Ray with a strong grip on his upper right arm. Not in a panic but swiftly nonetheless, they moved across the room peopled with stunned faces.

So quickly had the scenario played out that no one had the presence of mind to sound an alarm. Hanshee took full advantage of this, never hesitating as he stepped through the door and into the throng of people gathered in the alley outside. Threading their way between them, Hanshee pulled the hood of the robes over both their heads to maintain anonymity. The pair quickly made their way to the main street and, turning left, proceeded toward the slum where they would appear to be just two more of the many impoverished dwellers of that purgatory.

Raymond remained in a state of shock, not quite believing what had happened, surrendering to the guiding hand without which he would be adrift in this sea of humanity and maybe in his own madness.

Had he really just witnessed Hanshee, *his friend Hanshee*, send three men to their deaths in the time it would take to make an introduction? Did all of that really happen? He cast a sideways glance at Hanshee who was intent on evading any attempt at capture, sweeping his head to and fro with a hard gaze just visible beneath the hood pulled low over his forehead. Ray felt his own hood brush his cheek and wondered how it had gotten up over his head. He didn't recall putting it there. He also didn't recall the flight from the tavern for, in his mind, the dead man's eyes still stared.

After a short while Hanshee's ears picked up the sounds of pursuit. Behind them, men were shouting; there were the curt sounds of authority and the shrill whining of complaint. Chancing a glance behind him, Hanshee could see three mounted men pushing their way down the narrow street. Their horses sending the locals scattering for safety, the three ignored the curses in their wake. They did not move slowly, as if unsure of their quarry, but swiftly and with purpose.

Could it be that they know for whom they search? Hanshee thought.

On a whim, he guided Ray toward a torch hanging above a doorway. Once there, he pushed him to arm's length and looked him up and down. What he saw told him all he needed to know. The back of Ray's robe was soaked with the blood of the thief. He quickly glanced at his own robe and assured himself that it was bloodless.

They search for two men, one with a bloodied robe, thought Hanshee, and he swiftly considered his options.

One look at Ray was enough to tell that he was in shock. His eyes stared trancelike, locked on a place that Hanshee was not able to see.

In different circumstances Hanshee would simply melt into the surrounding crowd, leaving this one to fend for himself and provide the needed diversion for his own escape. That strategy was now unacceptable. Although having proven to be completely worthless in an emergency, Hanshee still felt that Ray had a hidden value. He had yet to discover what this value was but he knew that, if necessary, he would give his life to make sure Ray lived.

To disrobe would be the obvious move, but the clothes they wore beneath the robes, Hanshee's leather skirt and harness and Ray's strange garb - cargo shorts and a long-sleeved khaki shirt with the sleeves rolled up - would scream the presence of outsiders to all who viewed them. Find new robes? Maybe in time, but for now, *right now*, there was nothing they could do except stay hidden and hope that the riders would pass them by.

"Into the shadows!" said Hanshee, with a nod of his head toward a narrow opening that separated two buildings. Very little light found its way there and, with luck, they could await the passing of the guard unnoticed. Ray remained motionless, causing Hanshee to whirl on him with growing impatience. He was met by a curiously blank stare. Partly in frustration, partly due to necessity, Hanshee slammed Ray into the wall behind him, thrusting his face inches from Ray's. His eyes pierced the veil of confusion and startled Ray back to clarity for an instant. In that instant Hanshee spoke again, this time in a low, menacing hiss calculated to catch and hold Ray's attention.

"Fool! You would have us join the dead this night! They seek a man with a bloodied robe. Yours! Into the shadows! NOW!" As he spoke he shoved Ray toward the narrow opening. "We may still elude them and live!"

Ray looked dumbly down at his robe and everything clicked into place. He lurched toward the gap, followed closely by Hanshee. Their feet sank into the mud and a revolting stench rose up. Neither had guessed that this was a favorite urination place for the locals, and neither cared. The thought of evading their pursuers was foremost in both their minds.

•   •   •

Issica was the youngest of the three by far, this being his twenty-first summer. He was a strapping lad, much larger than the two older men with whom he had paired up to hunt down the unknown killer. He was a bully, well known for the terror he had instilled in the hearts of those unfortunate enough to cross his path while growing up. Coming from a poor family who dwelled outside the city, he never had much to speak of and took offense that others should be better dressed, have better food, and live better lives than he due simply to an accident of birth. When he first came to the city, even the dwellers in the "swine-land" had felt themselves superior to him.

But all that changed when the captain of the city garrison noticed the oversized barefoot lad as he beat a full-grown man with his bare hands and took his food. Of course the captain arrested the lad. It was his duty. But he also took an interest in the boy and, after suitable punishment was administered, began grooming him for a future with the guard.

Now Issica proudly rode a horse and wore the leather and insignia of the city garrison. No longer just a scavenger prowling the streets of Aggipoor, he now saw himself as a man worthy of admiration. He demanded respect from all about him, and woe unto any who would withhold it!

Issica counted it as the best of fortune that he now had a position that allowed him almost free rein to harass and bully. And for pay! Many of his comrades, the other soldiers of the garrison, did not seem to share his delight in inflicting misery on those unlikely or unable to defend themselves. Some had even expressed displeasure at his attitude and refused to ride with him. Their loss.

Issica thought the two he now rode with to be different.

Drannon and Old Ben had a touch of the hell-raiser in them also. He had seen it in their eyes the first time he stomped on a man who had the nerve to shoo Issica's horse from the tiny garden that fed his family. Issica had dragged the comatose body to the jailers and told them a story of an unprovoked assault. His partners had backed him up, or at least they didn't say differently, and Issica knew he had found kindred souls.

"Two men, one with a bloodied robe, aye?" Issica spoke absently, and his two companions exchanged glances.

Drannon and Old Ben had not been sure at first, but by now they knew that they rode with a madman. They also knew the most probable outcome should they find the two men or any strongly resembling them.

The serving girl had the presence of mind to describe the two. "Ragged men, but with heavy gold, one wearing a robe bloodied from the killings," she had said.

The gold had gotten her attention.

Drannon and Old Ben knew it had gotten the attention of their murderous comrade as well. He'd not be bringing these two in alive, that's for sure. The greed of the two veteran guardsmen had surfaced also. It would take only a small share of the expected loot to buy their silence while their mate had his fun. Riding with a madman had some advantages.

It was Issica, riding out front, who spied them first.

"There the bastards go!" was his overzealous shout, and the others swiveled their mounts to see where Issica's sword was pointing. "There, between those houses!"

• • •

Hanshee heard the shouts but knew not what they meant. Then Ray spoke his first words since leaving the tavern,

"They've seen us."

"How...? Hanshee began to ask.

"I know their tongue. Don't ask me how, but I do. I know it, just like I know yours."

"Quickly, to the other side!" Hanshee said, willing to save the mystery of tongues until a safer time.

• • •

"They are passing through, hoping to escape us on the other side!" said Issica. His eyes burned with a gleeful light as he turned to his fellows. "Stay here and keep them at bay. I will go 'round and meet them!"

He spurred his horse through the crowd toward the nearest corner and disappeared from view. Drannon and Old Ben were happy to stay where they were. They took no pleasure in hacking men apart, or in seeing it done. Better to let the young fool have his fun, and take the risk, alone. They would be close enough behind to share in whatever gold was found.

• • •

"Curse this narrow passage!" said Hanshee.

The walls seemed to close in more and more the farther they moved into the tight space. Along with the sticky spider webs and the odor, it made their journey of sixty feet seem to last an eternity. At least Ray had regained his mind, hopefully enough so that he could aid in his own escape. Peering around the shadowy form in front of him, Hanshee could see that they were making progress. The opening at the other end was about ten feet ahead, the inky blackness that surrounded them causing the opening to stand out.

The brightness at the end of the narrow passage was as daylight to the darkness in which they moved. *Much too bright*, was the thought that leaped unbidden into Hanshee's mind. Another glance revealed a flicker of torchlight that had not been there before. Reaching foreword, Hanshee clutched the back of Ray's hood and stopped him in his tracks.

"Wha...," started from Ray's lips, only to be shushed by a hiss from Hanshee's own. Pulling himself up closely behind Ray, Hanshee whispered in his ear.

"They wait for us."

Now Ray, too, took notice of the unnatural flickering brightness which shone at the end of the alley.

Cursing the closeness that would not allow him to change places with Ray, Hanshee's mind raced. He knew there could be as many as three armed men waiting at the opening. Those who waited there could skewer the two of them at leisure as they made their way out from between the houses. If Hanshee were to emerge first he could hope to hold one man off. More than one would be difficult. They could wait on either side of the opening and one was bound to strike the killing blow.

Could he and Ray make their way back? Not before the three riders could get back to the other side. Hanshee glanced back anyway, just to measure the distance and be sure. There, against the dim light at the other end, he could make out the silhouettes of two men. As they peered into the narrow space, Hanshee could make out the smooth outline of their helmeted heads. Once this was known, he had his plan.

Quickly, he whispered instructions into Ray's ear, and then he slowly and noiselessly freed the sword that until now had remained hidden under the robe in the scabbard he wore on his back.

CHAPTER 11

"Hold! Do not strike! I surrender myself to you!"

The voice coming from between the walls was tentative and afraid. Tentative because although Ray could somehow understand the language, he was not sure he could speak it; afraid because he couldn't be sure that his plea would stay the sword that surely waited for him in the light just outside the opening. Hearing no response, he spoke again.

"Hold your sword, I beg you!"

At first the flicker of torchlight was the only response. After a moment's silence, a voice thick with triumph and bloodlust greeted him.

"Show yourselves, dogs!"

Ray was hesitant but Hanshee's push reminded him of his role as he slowly covered the remaining few feet to the opening. Holding his hands out before him, more for instinctive protection than to show that he bore no arms, Ray emerged from the shadows and stepped into a circle of light.

The first thing he noticed was the torch held high in the left hand of the young guard. The light from the torch illuminated a giant of a man, clad in the same heavy leather tunic, boots, and helmet as the man on horseback whose kick he had earlier avoided. But his man was much larger, with a broad torso set upon thick legs. His face was contorted into a scowl that straddled the line between anger and glee, a sight which further fueled the fear growing in Ray's chest. Tearing his eyes away from the menacing face, Ray took note of thick arms and a huge right hand that engulfed the hilt of what appeared to be a broadsword, the almost four feet of iron resting easily in the giant's grip.

After stopping short upon seeing the size of the fellow, Ray regained his composure. With his hands still held out before him, he moved slowly away from the dark alley from which he had emerged. The guard glanced back toward the shadows, before hanging the torch on the wall and again focusing on Ray.

"I saw two of you enter there," Issica said. "Where is the other?"

As he spoke he raised his right arm and aimed the tip of his polished blade at the place where Ray's neck met his torso. His eyes bore into Ray, who only had eyes for the silvered death before him. His chin went to his chest as he focused on the blade less than six inches from his throat. Somehow he remained true to the plan and continued to move slowly away from the opening between the houses, even as he answered the giant.

"He saw your fire. He turned back."

A sneer parted the lips of the youth.

"My partners will take him right enough, but you belong to me!"

The plan was for Ray to circle away from the house, so as to place the guard's back to the narrow opening. His fear and the pressure of the moment caused Ray's steps to falter. The giants back was never fully to the crawlspace. Thus it was that Issica, from the corner of his eye, caught the figure that separated itself, sword in hand, from the darkness to his left. Though poised to strike the unarmed fool before him, his mind registered the threat and he whirled to face the second, and obviously more dangerous, of the two murderers.

Again Ray was witness to a life and death struggle. He seemed to go into a trancelike state as he took in the scene before him.

There stood a giant of a man, six feet, nine inches tall, at least, holding a sword that looked to be able to cleave a man in two with a single blow. His leather tunic did nothing to hide his well-muscled torso, and his helmet, also of leather, only served to frame the insane light that burned in his eyes.

Before this giant stood Hanshee, who was still dressed in the robe that, though cumbersome, had not slowed him down one bit at the tavern. He held his slender blade with both hands on the overly long hilt, his feet again spaced to his shoulders, left foot forward. From the fall of his robe Ray detected a slight bend in the knees, and there again was the almost imperceptible bounce. The flickering torchlight revealed a face devoid of expression, with only the arch of an eyebrow hinting at the focus that had taken hold of him.

"You must be the one who killed those three at the tavern," Issica said through the beginnings of a smile. "The wench spoke of you… and your gold."

Issica tilted his head slightly as he examined this stranger. "Those men back there, they were of no concern. Empty your purse, and you might yet leave," he said, grinning like a wolf.

Hanshee heard only gibberish and remained silent. Crossing with his left foot, he began moving slowly to his right, away from Ray. Issica moved to mirror Hanshee, wanting to keep both men where he could see them.

A puzzled look came over Issica's face.

"You have the gold, don't you?" he asked, surprised that these two were not pleading and bargaining for their lives. *Maybe the wench was lying,* he thought. He glanced quickly toward Ray before returning his attention to Hanshee. "Which of you has the gold?"

Hanshee glanced at Ray, a question in his eyes.

"He asks for your gold," Ray said, correctly interpreting the look.

Hanshee nodded his head and again focused on the death standing before him. Knowing they were pressed for time, that at any moment the giant's companions could come rushing to his aid, Hanshee decided to fan the flames of greed and recklessness he spied in his foe. To that end he met and held the young giant's stare, while instructing Ray on the words to speak.

Swallowing his fear, working through the dryness in his mouth, Ray summoned all the courage he possessed to repeat Hanshee's words: "What are riches to a dead man?"

The words came out high pitched and strained, barely above a whisper, but they had the desired effect.

Hanshee watched as color flooded into the behemoth's face and neck, even as his expression contorted to that of a snarling beast.

"Oh, it will be SO GOOD to kill you!" Issica spat, as he lowered himself into a crouch, and began to circle to his left, slowly closing the distance between himself and Hanshee.

Hanshee noted that the guard's footwork was sound and showed him to be a practiced swordsman. For his part Hanshee simply pivoted, keeping his opponent directly to his front, not distracted by words in a language he did not know, focusing only on the attack he knew would be coming in the next instant.

Issica saw an opening when Hanshee allowed himself to appear just a little slow in adjusting to his circling. With a speed uncharacteristic for a man of his size, Issica leapt foreword for what looked to be a thrust at Hanshee's chest. But this was only a feint. Before his blow could reach its mark, his powerful wrist swung the massive blade down and around, in a three-hundred-and-sixty-degree arc, so as to cleave his adversary's skull from above.

Coolly, Hanshee met the attack. Stepping across his body with his right foot, he brought his sword above his head for the parry. Much stronger than its slender length implied, it was equal to the task of bringing the descending death to a sudden stop. Surprised that such a thin blade could block his own, Issica again raised his sword, this time taking a two-handed grip so as to bear down with all of his power and shatter this man and his blade. No sooner than the giant's sword had left his own did Hanshee execute his next move. Stepping behind the planted right foot with his left, he spun quickly around to his left, completing a half turn and using his speed and momentum to drive the edge of his blade in a horizontal arc, through the leather tunic and into Issica's exposed midsection. Arms still extended above his head, Issica was completely unprotected. Although the tunic was of tough leather, Hanshee's blade sliced deep.

The shock of being lured into this trap, of being caught unawares by his rightful prey, showed on the giant's face. His legs went limp and he began to slump. At the same instant Hanshee took a step back, withdrawing his blade across Issica's body in such a way as to slice even deeper into the bloody midsection. At this new pain, Issica was brought out of his shock. He gave a bellow of agony and rage as his knees struck the dirt. Summoning his strength, he brought his right hand, still holding his sword, across his body and let loose with a vicious backhanded slash toward the enemy who now stood to his right.

Hanshee's front kick was a thing of beauty as it flashed out, catching Issica's sword arm just behind the elbow, stopping his blade in mid-stroke. The sword dropped from the giant's hand, his grip destroyed by his hyper-extended elbow. His quivering arm remained extended for a fraction of a second more. That was enough time for Hanshee to drop his body into a blow that bought his blade down on the outstretched arm right above the elbow, cleanly severing it from its upper third. Without a pause, Hanshee pulled his left leg and outstretched arms back, then launched forward again, extending his arms and thrusting his sword deep into the behemoth's chest, just under the right armpit. Behind this powerful motion, the slender blade was driven past muscle and bone, skewering the right lung, the heart, and then the left lung before coming to rest in the wall of the left ribcage.

With eyes glued on the spurting stump that had once been his good right arm, Issica was oblivious to the fact that he was dead. The remainder of his life, the few seconds left him, was spent in shock and disbelief.

"You… can't (cough!)… kill me (cough, cough!)... can't..."

As the giant's head turned to look at him, bloody froth flowing from his slack mouth and down his chin, his recent look of glee replaced by pain and confusion, his face was met by the sole of Hanshee's sandaled foot. Pushing roughly, Hanshee pulled his sword free from the corpse that then toppled into the dust.

Not stopping to admire his work, Hanshee raced over to the guardsman's horse and untied its reins from the post to which they were attached. Walking the beast toward the shadows that led deeper into the city, he gave a loud cry as he slashed at the horse's haunches, sending the surprised and terrified animal running into the darkness at full speed.

Quickly grabbing Ray's arm, Hanshee shoved him toward the narrow gap from which they had emerged moments before. Following him in, Hanshee bid him to keep silent and still. Almost on cue, the sound of hoof beats came from around the corner of the building as the other two guards, having mounted their steeds and forced them through the throng on the street, galloped up and surveyed the situation.

Before them lay the butchered corpse of Issica. He was sprawled in the dirt, his left arm extended above his head. A gaping wound in the side of his chest leaked blood beneath the stump of his right arm. The remainder of the arm lay on the blood-soaked earth a few feet away. There was a pile of intestines on the ground, a trail of which led to the open cavity in the dead guard's abdomen. In the dark distance beyond the circle of light the sound of receding hoof beats could be heard.

These were no squeamish men. They were hardened soldiers who had served as mercenaries before settling into comparatively easy employment as part of the city garrison. Seeing that nothing could help their young comrade, they wheeled their mounts and started out in the direction of the hoof beats, determined to capture the escaping felons on the stolen horse.

Once the sound of their hoof beats had receded, Hanshee, with Ray in tow, again emerged from the shadows. A quick glance told him they were alone and he turned to check the condition of his companion.

One thing was clear: Ray had never experienced conflict of this nature. He had never seen anything remotely like it before. His face was flushed beneath his brown skin. In another second he was doubled over, retching wine and rabbit and whatever else was in his stomach onto the dusty ground. Hanshee waited as patiently as he could, but he knew they had little time before the guardsmen caught up to the riderless horse. Then they would return. Once Ray finished, Hanshee grabbed him by the shoulders and forcibly moved him in the direction of the hog pens. Stumbling at first, Ray regained a semblance of composure as he tried to keep pace with Hanshee.

Back into the streets they went, hoods pulled over their heads, walking quickly, but not too quickly, back toward the way they had come. Hanshee had correctly guessed that the three guardsmen were the only patrol sent down this particular street. Others were probably close, no doubt waiting for a prearranged signal that would tell them that the felons had been seen. With no one left to give the signal, Hanshee hoped to walk unmolested to the wall.

Ray's head was swimming. The blood, the violence, the butchery was real. It wasn't a movie; it had really happened, right in front of him! If he doubted, he had only to look down at his bloodied robe to remind himself of that. He'd watched as Hanshee killed four people. That all four had meant to kill them was buried in the jumble of thoughts that choked off any attempt at reasoning. One thought managed to make it to the surface. They had to get out of this place...now!

Ray's pace increased as he and Hanshee rounded the last building. Before them lay approximately one-hundred fifty yards of open ground to the wall, with the swine herders shack about halfway between. Here they paused to be sure that no one had followed them, nor was waiting nearby for them to emerge into the open.

CHAPTER 12

It hadn't taken Arnia long to notice that some of her laundry was missing.

That had occurred about an hour ago, when she had stepped outside to see how much the damp robes had dried in the still-warm night air. She did laundry every night. Working with those damnable swine left such a stink that she wanted to do it twice a day. She would, too, but her boys would have none of that. It would be a waste of time, they said. "We would only get them dirty again in the half a day left," they'd told her.

If it were up to them they would wear those filthy things every day. When the time came she wouldn't wash them, she would burn them, or maybe give them to the pigs. But a day's work here was more than enough to nearly ruin any garment. Arnia had to scrub hard, much harder than her old bones should, to get them somewhat clean.

And now some damnable thief had snuck up in the darkness and stolen one of the two pairs of garments that her boys had. Well, she wasn't going to let that go unpunished! She had been sitting by the small front window ever since, the house darkened, watching the other garment that she had hung on the clothesline. Whoever was desperate enough to steal two ragged robes would not be able to resist one more. And when they showed up… she looked down at the heavy iron used to poke the fire… she would give them what they deserved for stealing an old woman's laundry!

What was that?

As she peered out into the darkness she thought she could just make out two figures approaching.

There!

The figures moved quickly toward her shack in the middle of the field of mud. The figures wore robes just like the ones that were stolen. The fools! She would jump out and surprise them and there would be no escape!

"Pathis, the thieves have come back!" Arnia whispered to the older of her sons. "Pick up your bow!"

Pathis had been sitting on the pile of dirty cloth that served as his bed. He was well into middle age. Long hours working with the swine, his job as it was his father's before him, had given him a large, strong body but had done nothing to develop his intellect. In truth, he was still a child in many ways. Although he thought his mother was crazy to wait up for the return of a thief who was probably long since gone, he had obediently stayed up with her.

Surprised by her call, he struggled to raise his hog-fed bulk from his bed before gathering up his ancient bow and the quiver with six arrows. The bow had been his father's. Before tonight it had not been strung since his father's death many years before at the hands, or rather the feet and tusks, of a particularly large and nasty boar hog. Bow in hand, Pathis glanced at his sleeping brother, Trajon, who was snoring loudly, flat on his back in his own nest of none-too-clean cloth. Reluctantly, he joined his mother at the door, ready to spring out and surprise the thieves as they approached to steal another robe.

• • • •

Hanshee and Ray waited at the side of the building for what seemed to Ray to be too long, watching for any movement that would point to a patrol lying in wait. A few minutes passed before Hanshee, satisfied that the way was unguarded, signaled to Ray and they started out across the field toward the shack and the hog pens beyond.

Ray's head was clearer now and he could appreciate not only the danger they were in but the caliber of man who walked beside him. As they approached the darkened shack, his mind replayed how

Hanshee had acquitted himself in the tavern and again behind the houses. Only in movies had he seen such combat, and then the action was choreographed and the effects digitized. What he had witnessed this night, the speed, fluidity, precision, and power, was almost enough to make him forget the gore. It had been necessary, that much he was trying to come to terms with. In this moment he was thankful that he had Hanshee at his side in this hostile place.

So that is what a warrior is capable of, thought Ray, who was frightened, awed, and humbled all at once.

He was snatched from his thoughts by the door of the shack exploding outward and the sight of a gray-haired hag, followed by a lumbering behemoth, bearing down on them. The old woman waved what appeared to be a fireplace poker above her head as she charged forward. The oaf who followed fumbled with an arrow, attempting to notch it onto a bowstring while keeping pace with the woman.

With a scream of evil intent, the hag reached them and brought the poker down with all her strength toward Hanshee's head. Hanshee neatly sidestepped the blow. Catching the now-falling woman by the arm, he spun her toward Ray. At the same time his right hand flew to the hilt of his sword, which he drew with a speed akin to magic before thrusting the tip beneath the chin of the onrushing man. Pathis pulled up sharply rather than skewer himself on the gleaming blade. The old woman had fallen into Ray's arms and, surprisingly, he had the presence of mind to grab her and hold on through the kicking and cursing that followed. Pathis simply stood there with his now-empty hands hanging by his sides. He had given up on notching an arrow in favor of drawing breath for a while longer.

"Let me go, you thieving bastards!" the woman screamed while attempting to twist free and resume her attack. Ray was surprised at her strength and was finding himself hard pressed to hold on to her. "You thieving, belly-crawling, dog-buggering, bastards! I'll get you! I'll get you...! I'll... ugh... I'll... Let me go!" she screeched.

Hanshee, still holding his attacker at bay, looked at Ray with annoyance. Ray returned the look with one of confusion. He had forgotten that, of the two of them, only he could understand what the woman was saying.

Finally Hanshee spoke.

"I do not wish to take the lives of such as these, Way-Mon. Find out what they want so that we can be away from here."

"Oh," Ray composed himself before speaking. "Old mother, we mean you no harm. If you will quiet yourself, I will release you."

The words were spoken softly and calmly and, upon hearing them, the old woman stopped struggling and let her body go limp. Ray slowly released his grip, but he knew enough by now to take the poker from her hand.

"Why have you attacked us?" he asked, turning from one to the other, and finally settling on the woman as the leader.

"You would steal from an old woman and feign ignorance?" she asked with a scowl. "Would you also kill an old woman and her son for fighting for what is their own?" She spoke these words with head held high, staring directly into the eyes of Hanshee, who continued to hold his sword at the throat of Pathis.

A light went on in Ray's eyes as he came to understand the situation.

"You mean the robes?" he asked, as he pulled on his own to show Hanshee what this was about. "It was merely a loan, old mother, for two strangers who did not want to appear out of place. Please take them back with our thanks."

With that he untied the belt and pulled the robe over his head, presenting the bloodied garment to the old woman who looked first at the bloodstains, then at Hanshee. At Ray's urging, Hanshee reluctantly lowered his sword and removed his robe. He draped it over the outstretched arms of the man before him then, again at Ray's urging, he reached in his pouch and produced a coin. Even in the moonlight Arnia recognized the glint of gold and her eyes grew wide as Hanshee gave the coin to Ray, who reached for her hand and placed the coin within.

At exactly that moment the sound of a horn pierced the night air. The four of them turned as one to see two riders appear from among the buildings some seventy yards away, spurring their horses toward them as they drew their swords.

Old Ben was the closest and he rode in low, preparing to use his horse as a shield for close combat with the two killers. Drannon, getting his mount under control after the sounding of the horn, was about ten yards behind Old Ben and drawing his sword in preparation for ending these dogs' lives.

Hanshee sprang to action.

Driving his sword into the ground beside him, he reached for the forgotten bow, scooping it and the arrow up simultaneously. Before he had fully straightened up, the arrow was notched. Less than a second later it had taken flight on a path that ended deep in the chest of the horse carrying Old Ben. The beast's momentum carried him a few more steps, but then he stumbled, and with the next step fell foreword, throwing its rider over its head and face first into the dirt with a force which may well have snapped his neck. It was lucky for Old Ben that his neck stayed intact but, because of the blow to his head, he was out cold. This caused Drannon, following close behind Old Ben, to pull up, lest he, too, be thrown from his horse. Violently he jerked back on the reins to keep his mount from stumbling into its fallen brethren. Not liking it one bit, the horse reared on his hind legs, forcing the guardsman's attention to shift from running down the killers to regaining control of his mount.

As soon as he fired the arrow, Hanshee turned to Ray and shouted, "The wall!"

Without waiting to see if Ray was following, Hanshee pulled his sword free from the dirt. Still carrying the bow and quiver, he sprinted for the hog pens and the city wall beyond. He need not have doubted Ray's instincts, as his ears told him that Ray was matching him stride for stride.

It was over eighty yards to the wall, and he knew that the second rider could well run them down before they crossed to the other side. A glance over his shoulder told Hanshee that this was true, as the guardsman now had his mount under control and was bearing down on them.

Urging Ray to keep running toward the wall, Hanshee pulled up and turned to face the fast-approaching horseman.

The scene seemed to unfold in slow motion for Hanshee as he weighed different options for dealing with this threat, even as death sped toward him. For his part, Drannon was happy that this one had decided to make his job easier. Drannon's plan was to simply run him over and then proceed to gut his companion who was between the hog pens and the wall and had nowhere to go. Imagine his surprise to see the first one suddenly raise his sword and, screaming a war cry that would chill the bones of the dead, spring foreword to meet him!

Hanshee, having noticed that the rider carried his sword in his left hand, angled his charge to the right side of the approaching rider, forcing him to have to strike across his skittish and unreliable mount in mid-stride. Unwilling to chance such a blow, Drannon pulled up on the reins and tried to turn the horse to the right so as to meet this fool with his left side and a clear path for his sword. But even as he turned the frightened beast, Hanshee changed directions, darting forward and to his right - the rider's left. This quickly brought him behind the wildly spinning horse and gave him a clear shot at Drannon's unprotected flank. Only by twisting halfway around in his seat did Drannon manage to parry the blade that he thought was meant for his back. But this came with a price, and that price was evident when Hanshee's hand closed about his left wrist and jerked him from his seat in the saddle. Drannon now found himself lying face down in the dirt and mud.

Hanshee could have ended it there and maybe he should have. But he did not. He stood back, still poised to strike, while the warrior struggled to his feet. He waited while Drannon wiped the mud from his eyes and even allowed him to locate and retrieve his sword. This done, the guard turned to face his adversary, but not with the same fire that he had when he was mounted and clean. No, the ease with which this man had managed to dismount him, fling him into the mud, and then the audacity he displayed by waiting while Drannon readied himself for combat, was demoralizing to say the least. Add to this the memory of his two companions, both better swordsmen than he and both having been laid low probably by this same man, and Drannon had little hope of surviving this encounter.

Hanshee could see it; this was a beaten man. Drannon held his sword aloft, standing his ground as a soldier should, but his eyes told everything that he tried so valiantly to hide. Hanshee met those eyes, met them with a fierce stare that spoke of a death as sure as the rising of the sun, and watched as the facade of bravery wilted. The muddy guardsman dropped his sword and fell to his knees in search of a quick and merciful end.

It was an end that Hanshee considered granting for all of a second, before sheathing his sword, scooping up the bow and arrows, and turning to sprint the remaining distance to the wall. He climbed it with ease. Upon reaching the top he turned to look down on the scene he had just left. The guardsman had not moved, still overcome either with fear at the closeness of his death or joy that his life was spared. Fifty yards behind him the old woman and her son continued to watch, glued to the exact spots they held when the horsemen first appeared. A few feet beyond them lay the still form of the first guardsman. Whether dead or just injured Hanshee could not tell, but either way he was no threat to their escape.

Dropping down on the outside of the walled city, Hanshee located Ray. He had watched from the top of the wall until the guard dropped to his knees. Thinking to spare himself the sight of Hanshee committing a murder, he had hastily turned away and scurried down the wall to the road beneath. When he saw Hanshee throw his leg over the wall and start down toward him, he somehow knew that the life of the city guard had been spared. He bowed his head and breathed a quick, "Thank God." Then he followed Hanshee as he sprinted off to the east, away from the city, but also away from the direction they had been traveling prior to deciding to visit this inhospitable place.

With Hanshee leading the way, they sprinted along the outside of the wall, quickly reaching the road they had first followed in from the forest. Expecting to turn left and retrace their steps north, Ray was surprised when Hanshee continued across the road and plunged into the thick brush on the other side.

Hanshee was quite reckless as he made his way through the vegetation, leaving a trail a child would be able to follow. In some instances Ray was sure that he deliberately broke twigs off of bushes, stamped down hard in soft earth, and generally gave the impression of a man in a panic, taken to headlong flight, concerned only with getting as far away as quickly as he could. After about a mile or so of this, Hanshee began to slow down. He took more care with how he moved through the brush, still leaving signs of his passage, but not so easy now to follow. This pattern continued for the next several miles, with Hanshee treading the last mile as carefully as Ray knew he could. Not wanting to deviate from the plan he knew was being executed, Ray had followed Hanshee's lead with respect to their headlong flight. Now, thanks to his weeks in the wilderness and Hanshee's expert tutelage, he trod the woods almost as carefully as his mentor.

"They will come for us at first light," Hanshee said. The pair had stopped to rest on the perimeter of a small natural clearing dominated by a huge oak almost in its center. These were the first words spoken since they left the city.

"They are sure to come," Hanshee continued, "for we leave their dead guardsmen behind us."

Ray wanted to scream. "What do you mean, 'we left dead guardsmen'? I didn't kill anybody!" He bit his tongue, realizing how ungrateful that would sound to the man who had, on several occasions now, saved his life. Besides, Hanshee was right. Those in the city wouldn't know which of the two the killer was. They would assume both were responsible.

"We will work our way back to where we earlier lay," Hanshee said as he started away from the tree, this time to the northwest. "Then we will leave this place."

"Amen," was Ray's reply.

CHAPTER 13

They found no sleep that night.

True to his word, Hanshee led them unerringly through the darkness and back to their earlier campsite. Once there, they did what they could to cover their trail, retrieved their water bags and walking sticks, and started west with hours still to pass before the sun would come up. When it finally broke the horizon they were several miles west of their campsite and farther still from the false trail that would lead the initial pursuit to the east.

Ray was still in somewhat of a state of shock from the events of the previous night which had led to Hanshee killing four, maybe five, men. His logical mind understood that, had Hanshee not acted as quickly and decisively as he had, they would most likely be dead. Unfortunately logical thoughts did little to help him deal with the four savage killings he had witnessed.

Ray was finding it a little uncomfortable to walk beside Hanshee now. He constantly cast sideways glances at him when he thought his companion was unaware. He wondered just what he was looking for. Maybe some sign of remorse from Hanshee for what he had done?

What he had been forced to do, Ray had to constantly remind himself.

Still he should show some sign of regret, Ray thought, but there was none. As far as Ray could tell, Hanshee never gave a second thought to the dead men he'd left lying in pools of their own blood back in the city. This thought shook Ray even more.

What kind of man have I thrown in with? Ray asked himself repeatedly as they continued on their way through the shadows of the early morning forest.

Hanshee kept them moving at a brisk pace. Even considering the terrain, which had now changed from the scrub oaks in sandy soil back to the deciduous forests they had grown accustomed to during the first weeks of their journey, they were making remarkable time. Speed was the goal now. While Hanshee always prided himself on stealthy movement, he was willing to risk leaving more signs of their passing than normal in an attempt to put as much distance between them and the city as possible

It was late in the day when Hanshee finally called a halt to their frenetic pace. They had just passed through a wash and over a shallow creek that Hanshee thought led to a river. They were now following a trail that was surprisingly wide though apparently not used by anything but wildlife. Since it ran east to west, Hanshee had decided to make use of its convenience. When they finally reached the river, it became clear why the trail was so wide.

The trail had at one time been a road. Many years ago it had served as the main road between the cities of Aggipoor, from which they had just escaped, and Thessilli, its sister city to the west. There was a third city, called Went by its inhabitants, which lay to the south and formed the tip of a southward-pointing triangle. Hanshee knew of the three cities, having passed between them on his initial travel eastward, but had not used this particular road during that part of his journey. He instantly realized the connection when they reached the river and saw that an ancient bridge spanned the swift, brackish waters.

There was no telling how long ago the bridge was built but, from the condition of the road they had been traveling, one could guess that it had not seen heavy use for decades. It was made from timbers which must have been thick and solid in their day. Some appeared to have stood the test of time admirably. Most appeared worse for wear, and some, along the rails and across the floor, were missing altogether. The bridge was built to provide a level crossing over the river, with the center supported by two once-mighty wooden pillars that had been secured to the riverbed. The pillars had seen better days and the constant push of the current, along with whatever debris had collided with them while flowing downstream, had produced a pronounced lean that made the whole structure seem but moments from collapsing into the water below.

The two travelers stood at its eastern end looking intently upon the span which they would soon ask to bear their weight.

"How long do you think it's been here?" asked Ray, eyeing the bridge with concern.

"Who can say?" replied Hanshee. "I crossed this river on my journey east, but not here."

Ray let his eyes wander to the banks upstream of the bridge. Both sides of the river were bordered with large trees: oak, gum, elm and more. They towered above the flow and, in some places, created a canopy of leaves that cast their shade well out over the water. The bases of the tree trunks were obscured from view by the thick undergrowth that surrounded them. The proximity of the vegetation to the water meant that there was no earthen bank visible. The water simply gave way to a solid wall of leaves and vines that appeared to rise up from them, or flow down to them, depending on one's perspective.

The water was of such a dark hue that anything moving more than a foot beneath its surface was invisible. This gave rise to all sorts of imaginings as to what could be lying in wait there. Ray would much rather try the bridge than have to swim across and then pull himself up into a tangle of bushes, roots, and vines that looked ominous in their own right.

"Do you think it will hold us?" Ray asked, as he continued to eye the bridge suspiciously.

Hanshee did not respond immediately. He struck several hard blows upon the wood directly before him with the base of his walking stick. The wood gave back a heavy *thunk* with each blow, giving Hanshee the confidence to step carefully onto the bridge and test it with his weight and further thrusts of his stick. After about fifteen feet of this, he turned to Ray and motioned for him to follow, first cautioning him not to stray from the path Hanshee had taken. Ray hesitated before taking a tentative step onto the very spot where he had seen Hanshee's sandaled foot touch down. He paused, expecting swaying or creaking or something that would signal the instability of the old wooden structure, but nothing happened. Looking up, he saw that Hanshee had traversed half the distance across the bridge. Aware that soon he would be on the span alone, Ray hurried to catch up. Moving swiftly but carefully he closed the distance between them. By the time Hanshee stepped upon solid ground Ray was practically at his side.

Hanshee stopped and looked about, trying to gauge the lay of the land through the trees and thick brush that surrounded them.

"To the south lies another city," he said. "It is larger than the one we fled. This road will turn south and lead us there. To the north begin the foothills of the mountains which lie before us." He pointed northwest. "These mountains are where we must go, but we have pushed ourselves hard for two days without sleep. We will begin at sunrise."

Ray readily agreed.

Until that moment he was unaware of how tired he was. The thoughts of the night before were still fresh in his mind. That, and thoughts of a possible pursuit, had served as a distraction to the fact that he had last slept two nights ago. He now realized that he was exhausted and would be more than happy to call a halt to the day's travel. Still, the pair managed to put some additional distance between themselves and the ancient bridge before Hanshee decided to halt for the coming night. With the little sunlight that was left they had just enough time to find a spot and, minus a fire, make it as comfortable as possible.

• • •

It was still very dark when Ray was shaken awake by Hanshee. Thinking at first that it was the continuation of a dream, he tried to settle back into sleep. As Hanshee continued to shake him, Ray recognized his companion but still had to fight to gain a semblance of consciousness. He was very tired and perplexed at being awakened so roughly in the middle of the night. Hanshee remained patient, allowing Ray time to gain his faculties. When he was sure that he would be understood, Hanshee spoke: "The smell of smoke comes on the night breeze."

Ray looked at his companion with a puzzled expression, his mind not yet where it needed to be to comprehend what he was being told.

"They are camped beyond the river," Hanshee continued. "Their tracker must be very skilled."

Ray's eyes grew wide with surprise as his powers of comprehension kicked in.

"Who...?" he began. "Who's camped? You mean... from the city?"

Hanshee answered him in low, even tones.

"They are fighting men, their horses tied nearby. I count twelve. They sleep now, but when they awaken, they will be less than half a day behind us. More if they cannot coax their horses to cross the bridge. They travel heavy."

Ray was wide awake now, and hanging on every word that Hanshee calmly spoke.

"What do we do?" he asked as his mind began to race. "We've got to move... now... fast!"

"Not fast, but with purpose," Hanshee spoke. "We have not tarried, still they are close behind us. We will not outdistance horses on this road. Gather your stick and the bow and quiver. Follow me."

Ray rose from his makeshift bed and turned to dismantle the sparse cushion he had made from grass and pine straw, but Hanshee stopped him.

"Stop!" Hanshee said. "Do not hide your bed. Kick it apart." He demonstrated on his own bedding. "They will think us panicked and careless, rushing to stay ahead of them."

"And they would be right," said Ray, as he imitated Hanshee and haphazardly kicked at his bedding.

"Right that we left hurriedly," Hanshee said, "...never panicked and careless. Now come!"

Again turning westward, Hanshee broke into a trot on the ancient road which was barely visible in the light of the half moon filtering through the trees. Ray fell in behind him, relieved that he had only to follow Hanshee and not have to read the trail. Fueled by adrenaline born of surprise and fear, he had no problem keeping pace with his rescuer. Occasionally Hanshee would back off the pace, allowing Ray to catch his breath. When he saw that Ray no longer labored to breathe, he was off again with an easy lope that ate up distance.

They ran this way, alternating between a lope and a fast walk, for what Ray thought to be about half an hour, maybe a little less. Hanshee was now spending more time examining the surface of the road they traversed. When they reached a particularly rocky section, he stopped.

Ray was glad for what he saw as another brief rest before they again picked up the pace, but this time Hanshee gave no signs of continuing westward. Instead he squatted down and began a closer examination of the road.

Here the road was paved. Stones of varying sizes had been chiseled or scraped to flatness then laid down to provide a hard surface. Ray looked up ahead, then turned and looked back in the direction from which they had come. Even in the darkness he could see that this part of the road was the low point at the center of a dip. The road behind them had a slight slope which had brought them downhill to his point. Farther up ahead he could barely make out an incline as the road gradually rose to higher ground. Ray guessed that the section of road where they stood was most probably a severely rutted and muddied part that had been inlaid with stones for several hundred feet in order to aid wagons, heavily laden with trade goods for the markets of one city or the other, in passing through.

Hanshee continued his examination of the stones, then he made his way over to the northern edge, or what used to be the northern edge before vegetation and small trees had taken root, displacing many of the flat stones and obscuring the place where they ended and the forest began. Carefully parting the brush, he reached down to the ground to feel where the stones continued into what was now the surrounding forest. Satisfied with what he found, he turned his attention to Ray.

"Remove your boots," Hanshee said.

Ray's reply was a blank stare.

"Quickly!" Hanshee snapped, and Ray found himself bent over and untying his boots before his conscious mind even registered the uncharacteristic impatience that Hanshee had displayed.

Hanshee watched Ray step out of one, then the other boot, then nodded as he picked them up.

"These boots," Ray began sheepishly, "they probably made it easier for them to track us, didn't they?"

"Yes," said Hanshee, stating fact but not belittling Ray. "You will carry them when we enter the forest," he said, gesturing to the place where he had discovered more stones. "This will be difficult but you must remember all you have learned and move through the wild without leaving any sign."

With those words Hanshee turned and melted between the trees and bushes, becoming one with the forest. Ray watched in awe, then treaded carefully over the stones and followed Hanshee into the darkness of the trees, thankful for the thick wool socks which miraculously had held up for these many weeks.

They had moved about fifty yards into the thick brush before Hanshee turned east and began to parallel the road back in the direction of where they had earlier lain. The going was much slower as they made their way over, under, and around the many obstacles that the forest placed before them. After a while they came upon a game trail that continued in the direction they were going and this made for swifter travel.

The sun was just rising when they reached a spot in the woods just north of their old camp. Hanshee proceeded beyond this point, to a piece of ground slightly higher than the rest but still protected from view by a thicket of trees and shrubbery. Here he sat, directing Ray to do the same, instructing him to assume a position of comfort from which he would feel no need to move. Hanshee sat cross-legged. Ray placed his back against a tree and sat with the soles of his feet together, knees out to the side. In this way he could raise or lower his knees, if he felt too uncomfortable, without making noise or attracting attention.

About an hour later Ray heard the faint, distant hoof beats of the party that was in pursuit. They did not move quietly, nor did they seem to care. *It's probably very hard for twelve men on horseback to move silently through the early morning quiet of the deep woods*, he thought.

The hoof beats grew steadily in volume until about half an hour after he first heard them, then they stopped. Ray now heard voices for the first time; voices gruff and deep, talking low among themselves but even so projecting to where he and Hanshee sat. *These were the type of men who filled a room with their whispers*, he thought, and his imagination began to move on its own, toward thoughts of huge, rough warriors, much like the first guard they had encountered in the city. Men whose first impulse was to lash out... to strike, thoughtful only after those before them had been subdued. *Not the kind of men you would want after you*, he thought to himself.

Ray gave an involuntary shudder and pushed those thoughts out of his mind. He had no idea of what kind of men pursued them, but even if they were demons on horseback, there was nothing to be gained by building them up as such before they proved it. He looked to Hanshee, who had remained motionless since assuming his position, showing neither fright nor fatigue. He simply sat and listened. Ray gathered his faculties and attempted to do the same.

Now there came the sound of shouting from down below. Ray, having miraculously and inexplicably picked up their language, understood what was being said. Leaning forward and striving not to make any undue noise, he whispered in Hanshee's direction.

"They have stopped at the bridge," he said, so softly that he doubted Hanshee had heard him. A quick nod from Hanshee assured him that he had and, with a slight gesture of his hand, Hanshee bade Ray to continue translating.

"Their leader is telling the others that the bridge looks unsteady," Ray said. "He is saying that, once they establish that it is safe to cross, they must unload their horses of all weapons and gear and lead the animals. Then they must return and carry all of their weapons and supplies across before reloading the horses and moving on."

Hanshee gave a slight smile and nodded understanding. Ray remembered Hanshee saying how much the bridge would slow them down. He had led Ray back to this very place, above the bridge, so as to take the measure of their pursuers while they were in disarray. It occurred to Ray that Hanshee was always several steps ahead of what he expected. He hoped they could stay several steps ahead of the men who were now attempting to cross the bridge.

Upon hearing the clopping of the first horse being led across, Hanshee moved. Very slowly and very carefully, he eased his body into a supine position and crawled forward through the tangle of brush. He used the morning breeze as cover, moving forward only when the wind created noise as it swirled through the trees and only when the motion it induced in the foliage at ground level would hide any disturbance he might cause. In this way Hanshee inched his way forward in hopes of gaining a line of sight on the men who were after them. Ray hung back, not trusting himself to be as stealthy as his companion, but trying to commit to memory everything that he heard. There was no telling what important information might be gained this way.

It became clear after a time that it would take the company of twelve a good while to coax their mounts across the leaning bridge. Some horses had to be blindfolded before being led across, and the discovery of more and more weak spots in the old timbers seemed to make each crossing even more of an ordeal. The fact that they had to proceed one at a time led to boredom and a lack of discipline among those waiting for their turn to cross. This sense of frivolity, so out of place among this group, continued as more men gathered on the far side of the bridge. Amid the teasing and loud banter, Ray picked out several choice bits of information that he was anxious to share with Hanshee.

Sometime during this boisterousness the commander, moving to again take control, sent two of the men forward to see if they could pick up the trail. After receiving their orders, one of them spoke up loudly.

"It shouldn't be hard, Captain," the guard said in a voice far less gruff than Ray expected. "Those prints the one leaves would stand out on a mountain slope!"

Some of the men laughed at this as the two who were chosen rode off down the old road in a westerly direction.

Ray would have turned red if he could have. The prints left by his boots, a novelty in this world, had led their pursuers past Hanshee's first attempt to throw them off and probably were responsible for the pursuit catching up to them so quickly. Ray looked down on the trail boots which had held up so well to the punishment of the outdoors. They had almost gotten him skewered in the city; now they had brought a group of armed men to within a few hours of riding them down.

After a while Ray heard a cry go up from down the road. Shortly after, the two who had been sent off came galloping back to the group still gathering on the western side of the bridge. More conversation was followed by more laughter as they waited for their comrades to cross, reload their mounts, and don their armor and weapons. Finally, after what must have been a two-hour delay, the group reassembled under the captain's command and proceeded down the road. Once the sound of hoof beats was gone, an unnatural quiet seemed to envelope the forest. With the slightest of sound, and the barest rustling of brush, Hanshee reappeared and took a position with his head close to Ray's.

Without being asked, Ray launched into his report.

"It was the boots," he said. "They found us so quickly because of my boots. I'm sorry, Hanshee."

Hanshee dismissed Ray's anguish with a wave of his hand.

"As I thought," he said. "And we have used this knowledge to our advantage. What else did you overhear?"

Ray continued. "One of them laughed and said they were running us right into the fellows moving northeast from Thessilli. It seems a message was sent the night we escaped from the city. One of them said the guards from Thessilli would be bringing dogs. They have the best tracking dogs this side of the Ursal Mountains, he said."

Ray watched Hanshee carefully as he relayed this information, searching for signs in his companion's face that would tell him how worried he should be, especially at the mention of tracking dogs. But Hanshee remained stoic as he continued his report.

"The captain replied that it was for the glory of… Aggipoor… to find the filth that had killed three citizens and one of their own," Ray said. "They would use the additional men, and the hounds, to run us down, but we would be taken by the men of Aggipoor. I guess Aggipoor is the name of the place we fled."

"And Thessilli is its sister city," Hanshee said. "The second of three cities between your river and the mountains we strive to reach."

"The Ursal Mountains," Ray said. "I think that means 'Bear Mountains,' or 'Mountains of the Bear,' or something like that." Even before he finished with his translation, he wished he had kept this bit of trivia to himself. Hanshee seemed to pay it no mind.

"Was there anything else worth our knowing?" Hanshee asked.

"No," Ray replied. "Not that I can remember."

"Good," said Hanshee with a smile of satisfaction. "Now we go to the foothills."

CHAPTER 14

They stayed to the thickest woods for the better part of the morning.

The going was considerably slower, but they were able to move in concealment. Hanshee had not let Ray put his boots back on yet. He made it clear that their priority was to leave as faint a trail as they could. They had come across several game trails, some of them running north-south, but Hanshee avoided them all for the first few hours.

When the sun was close to its zenith, they came upon another trail. This one was more substantial than the others they had passed. Hanshee called a stop a short distance away from it in part because he thought Ray might need a rest. He also wanted to consider their next moves.

There were questions that Ray had been holding in all morning so, while they were resting, he asked Hanshee what he had observed back at the hill above the ancient bridge.

"In truth," Hanshee began, "the city guard is determined. They saw past our false trail and were near upon us within a day. Their tracker is very skilled."

"Tell me about the men themselves," Ray said. He had a picture in his mind of a formidable band of killers on horseback, steadily closing the distance between them. He hoped his imagination was overactive.

Hanshee hesitated before he spoke. It was not his intent to frighten Ray, but he believed that a warrior should know what he faced.

"There are twelve on horseback," Hanshee began, "with three pack animals." Unsure whether Ray understood, he spelled out the implication. "They are a city guard, but some are not long from a warrior's life. They are well provisioned. They mean to have us. Their pursuit will not stop."

Hanshee saw the apprehension growing in Ray's eyes. He guessed that his companion was waiting to hear soothing words, reassuring words, telling him that there was no need to worry. Here Hanshee paused to consider how best to explain their situation.

When Hanshee failed to immediately dispel his growing fears, Ray's level of anxiety instantly doubled. *We're being pursued by twelve men on horseback,* he thought, panicked. *What are we going to do?* He searched Hanshee's face for some sign that he understood the depth of their plight. They couldn't outrun horses, and how much help could he be if Hanshee had to stand and fight twelve armed men?

Ray's thinking was that they should be in full flight in an attempt to get as far away as possible, as fast as possible, from men whom Hanshee had described as hardened killers. For the life of him he couldn't understand how Hanshee could keep such a calm demeanor in the face of almost certain capture and gruesome death.

Hanshee watched as Ray's expression continued to reflect the fear and the frustration of their situation. Finally, he spoke up.

It was not what Ray wanted to hear.

"I see your fear," Hanshee said leaning in closer to Ray. "That is good. Men such as these should be feared."

"What the fuck?" Ray was exasperated. "Is that all you have to tell me? Is that all you have to say?" His voice took on a pleading tone. "What are we going to do?"

"They will not have us," Hanshee pronounced confidently. "They have pushed their mounts too hard in making up this distance after first following our false trail. And the weight that each man carries! They boast heavy shields, broadswords and axes, bows, arrows, and armor. They give us much waah!" He smiled proudly, using a term in his language which meant "respect". He added, "But they could never move as swiftly as we through the bush."

"But they can rest their horses," Ray interrupted, "and then there will be no escape!"

Hanshee smiled. "Steady your heart, my friend. We will not be seen. When pursued by horses, flee to where horses cannot pursue."

Ray sat in stunned silence at this simplistic response. He didn't know if he should fear for his life, based on the description of their pursuers, or take heart at Hanshee's confidence.

Hanshee saw this and reached out a steadying hand to grip Ray's forearm.

"This is why we go north, to the foothills," Hanshee said. "There will be no paths to suit horses, much less horses weighed down with large men, their many weapons, and heavy armor. We will go where men on horseback find it hard to follow. That is my plan. But we must move swiftly. Their tracker is skilled and they could be on our trail soon."

The laying out of a plan, any plan, had the desired effect on Ray. Hanshee could see him begin to regain his composure as he thought about what he had just been told.

"How far are the foothills?" Ray finally asked.

"A day's journey," said Hanshee. "This trail that runs beside us may lead us there. We will leave the dense brush. You will wear your boots. Just as stealth was our companion since the rising of the sun, now speed will be our friend."

• • •

Ray thought back to the time they had first paused beside this trail they had now been traversing for the better part of the day. That was the last rest he had been afforded. Hanshee had pushed him hard, knowing that in his frightened state he would not only fail to complain, but would push himself beyond what he thought he was capable of. Just after noon a killer pace had been set and, to Ray's thinking, they had never slowed. Hanshee had kept quiet tabs on him and had adjusted his pace several times during the day when he saw his companion laboring.

It was twilight now and the trail was getting harder to see. They had been drinking from their water bags and taking quick bites of dried fruit and dried meat on the run and their bags were lighter for it. The game trail had been running alongside a clear stream for some time now and they crisscrossed it at several points, requiring Ray to leap from one bank to another, or splash through shallow water. Mostly they ran parallel to it and always to the north. Hanshee had been surveying the country as they ran, and as the light began to steadily decrease he slowed their pace.

"I believe us to be far ahead," he said, referring to their pursuers. He watched as Ray worked to catch his breath. "They will not come for us here in the dark. We will be safe tonight."

"Do you think we might have lost them?" Ray asked.

"Only for a while," replied Hanshee. "Their tracker is skilled. A search will reveal our trail to one who has eyes to see. If it is our fortune to have lost the men, we will have much less fortune when faced with dogs."

"Damn," Ray said, having forgotten about the hounds of Thessilli.

"Fear not," said Hanshee. "See how the ground rises to either side? We are almost among the hills. Soon they will face great difficulty. Soon we will have a chance."

Ray had not noticed the changes in the terrain. All of his focus and energy had been geared toward keeping pace with Hanshee. Now he looked to either side and, even in the failing light, could see how the ground rose on both sides of them, leaving them in a small valley of sorts.

"At first light," Hanshee said, "we will move farther up the trail and into the foothills. I may run ahead to scout. You must keep moving as swiftly as you can. I will leave a sign: a sapling broken at the level of your eye. It will be broken in the direction you should take. If you doubt the sign, stay near to it and hide. I will return."

With these words, Hanshee led them off of the trail and to a cluster of what Ray thought he recognized as cedar trees. They moved in between them and found a small hollow near their center with room enough for two to stretch out.

Ray was asleep almost before he touched the ground.

They were up and running as soon as the rising sun provided enough light to see the trail. Hanshee again set a killer pace, with Ray struggling but matching his stride as time and distance flew by.

Hanshee had been keeping tabs on Ray, slowing a bit to allow him to find a pace that he could settle into and hold for some time. It was mid-morning when he looked back over his shoulder and saw that Ray, though winded, appeared to be holding his own. He gave him a nod of his head and received a nod of understanding in return. Then he was off; sprinting ahead at a pace that caught Ray completely off guard. In no time at all Hanshee was beyond his sight and, soon after, could no longer be heard.

Now it was for Ray to look within and push himself to keep his pace, trust his eyes to keep the trail, and trust in Hanshee's word. It was much easier when all he had to do was follow the body in front of him. To a practiced hunter and woodsman such as Hanshee, the game trail stuck out like the center line on a city street. Ray was having a much harder time making it out but he continued to press forward, trusting in what he had learned in the last month of living in the wild to guide his steps. Twice he came upon an apparent fork in the trail and both times there was a sapling broken off at eye level, the broken end leaning toward one fork. Each time he took the designated fork, barely breaking stride.

While he ran, thoughts of his pursuers continued to find their way into his mind.

He wondered if the broken saplings would make it easier for the riders to follow them. *That's ridiculous*, he thought. *If they already tracked us this far, it wasn't because of some broken saplings.*

Hanshee had said he was impressed by their tracker. The thought ran through Ray's mind more than once. He must be good. Based on his earlier words, Hanshee was impressed with almost nothing that came from a city. Yet twice now he had laid a false trail then doubled back on it. *The first time they were on us right away*, Ray thought. *The second time…? Well, that remains to be seen.* These thoughts fanned the flames of his ever-present fear, and he found himself picking up his pace.

It was just before the noon hour when Ray ran past a bend in the trail as it curved around a large pine tree, and saw Hanshee waving to him from just a little farther ahead. Relief overtook him as he approached his companion. He had to force his legs, now locked it seemed, into the rhythm of running, to slow to a walk. He covered the last few feet to Hanshee in a kind of stiff-legged limp.

"Take your rest Way-Mon," Hanshee said when Ray came to a stop beside him. He watched while Ray leaned his back against a nearby tree, not wanting to kneel or sit for the moment because he knew that if he did if would be difficult to get up again. He untied his water bag and took a long pull, followed by several small sips. Hanshee reached into his pouch and produced some smoked rabbit meat from their last meal before entering the city. He took a piece for himself and offered some to Ray. When he saw that Ray was relaxing, he again spoke.

"We are close to the hills. They will provide cover and safety from capture," Hanshee said. "See the land... the steep hills to either side?" Hanshee motioned with his hand. "This is a good place to lose a pursuer on horseback."

Ray fought through his exhaustion to raise his head and look at the surrounding land. His focus had been on following the trail and keeping his legs moving. He had never even noticed as the hills had become higher, some towering above the game trail that, like flowing water, followed a path of least resistance.

"We will keep to this path," Hanshee said. "When the hills are highest we will turn to the setting sun, to the west."

Ray nodded his head and continued chewing. He was too tired to ask questions of Hanshee now. At this point, whatever plan he recommended, short of surrender, was fine by him.

CHAPTER 15

Because of the good time they had made that morning, Hanshee allowed Ray to take an extended rest.

Ray had finally succumbed to his weariness and sank to a seated position, his back still against the tree. He had feared at first that if he let himself sit down he might never rise again. What he found was that, after what he gauged to be about thirty minutes, he felt pretty good. In fact, he felt much better than he had expected to feel after running through the forest for half of yesterday and again this morning. After a period of rest and a drink from the water bag, he had managed to rise with only a little trouble and began pacing back and forth to loosen the tightness in his legs.

Once he felt certain that he was ready to continue, he gave Hanshee a nod and they moved off northward, up the game trail. This time their pace was a steady walk with a stride calculated to eat up distance while not being overly tiring. Ray took this as a sign that Hanshee was satisfied with their progress over the last two days. They had worked hard, laying down a false trail, changing direction, and putting a great deal of distance between them and their pursuers. In the land that surrounded them there were steep hills, hidden valleys, thick cover, and a hundred ways to evade pursuit. Ray was finally beginning to feel free of the dread that had hung over him for the past three nights.

About mid-afternoon they reached a river, the same one, Hanshee assured him, they had crossed on the rickety bridge three days ago. They were a good distance upstream from that bridge now and Ray thought it ironic that they had covered so many miles only to return to where they already were, in a manner of speaking.

Here they took their second rest of the day, drinking much of their water and eating the remainder of the rabbit. Hanshee had been pointing out to Ray edible plants along the way and the two of them had been grazing on certain leaves, roots, and mushrooms as they traveled. They had succeeded in keeping their energy up and, considering the distance they had covered the past two days, they both felt strong and in good spirits.

After this brief respite, they continued along the western bank of the river, following as it wound in and out among the steep hills that made up the landscape this far north. Moving at a more leisurely pace, they were able to spy much of the local fauna. They were still feeling the pressure of being pursued so there was no time to hunt. But just knowing that, when they felt comfortable enough to again make a campsite and build a fire, there was an abundance of game helped place their minds further at ease.

With a couple of hours of light remaining in the day, Hanshee paused atop an overhang supported by the massive roots of an ancient tree that had probably sprouted beside this river before his grandfather's grandfather was born. He took his time gazing up and down the part of the river he could see, then fixed his eyes on the far bank and the towering hills that were visible between and above the trees that grew there. In some places the hills seemed to break through the trees, with sheer rock walls partially covered by vegetation protruding until their base merged with the river itself

"We will cross the river." Hanshee said after a while. "It will further slow riders and dogs. On the eastern side are more slopes and valleys. It will be harder for the horses there."

Though Ray was willing to do whatever Hanshee said to evade capture, he was more than a little apprehensive about entering this expanse of water.

As a swimmer, Ray was adequate at best. He had done nearly all of his swimming in swimming pools, with a few trips to the lakes in the area where he grew up. He had no experience in swimming across a river such as this. But understanding what was at stake, he began steeling his nerves for the crossing.

"We will move upstream." said Hanshee. "There we will find a place to cross."

Ray felt a sense of relief, like a prisoner whose date with the hangman had been postponed. He happily followed as Hanshee led him up the paths that moved in and out along the banks of the river on their right, with the land rising steeply to their left. Ever northward, ever upstream, they covered another mile or so before he heard a rush of water in the distance. Hanshee had heard it too, probably well before Ray, and led the way to its source: a waterfall.

This was a place where the waters coming down from the mountains found room to spread out over a rocky ledge that must have been three times wider than the river above and below. Here the river lacked great depth, but the currents were swift as the waters wound their way over and between the rocks and the debris that had become lodged among them, before launching over the falls in a deluge that crashed violently some thirty feet below. Once over the falls, the waters again succumbed to the dominance of the riverbank, which funneled them into a narrower, deeper path.

Viewing the falls from below, Hanshee and Ray marveled at the beauty and power on display. After a while Hanshee turned away to seek a path that would take them up to the top of the falls for a view of the river beyond. What he found was a climb of at least twenty feet up a nearly vertical wall of vine-covered rock. A difficult but straightforward task for a man, it was impossible for a horse. This made it perfect for their purpose.

One more obstacle between us and them, thought Ray. He felt there must be a way for a man on horseback to circumvent the rocks, but that probably meant doubling back and blazing a new trail west, into the heart of the forest in order to find somewhat level and passable ground. That could be an ordeal unto itself.

Reaching the top of the rocky slope and pushing through the thick vegetation surrounding it, they again came to the river's edge. They stood on the western arm of a horseshoe-shaped patch of ground, the mist rising from the tumultuous waters below thick enough to almost block their view of the lower river.

Holding fast to a sturdy-looking limb of a tree growing on the bank, Hanshee leaned over the water and used his walking stick to test its depth. When he struck the river bed he raised his stick and checked it, seeing that roughly three feet of its length was wet. He passed his pouch and walking stick to Ray, gripped the limb with both hands and slowly lowered himself into the water. He was relieved when his feet touched bottom, confirming the dark water to be hip deep. Releasing his grip on the limb, Hanshee took his stick and his pouch from Ray. Holding the pouch above the water with his left hand, he used the stick in his right hand to aid his balance as he proceeded to move about in the water. After Hanshee's first few steps, Ray reluctantly took the plunge, joining him in the cool flow. Together they made their way farther upstream.

The water varied in depth as they traveled against the relatively weak current at the river's edge. They never ventured more than a few feet from the bank and the water was never more than waist deep. In some places it failed to reach their knees. They had gone about two hundred feet upstream when they came abreast of the curve in the horseshoe and stopped to assess their chances of crossing.

They could see that the waters above the falls were swifter-moving than those below, swirling between the rocks that were visible at irregular intervals all the way across to the opposite bank. Since the river was probably at its widest at this point, it stood to reason that it was also at its most shallow. Ray could envision them crossing by working their way from one rock outcropping to another, depending on how deep and swift the waters ran in between. Hanshee had similar thoughts.

"It is good that this is not the time of thaw," Hanshee said. "Then these waters would be treacherous indeed. Crossing here could mean death. But the water is low, with many dry rocks to be seen. We will be safe."

And they were.

In some places they could actually leap from one rock to another, avoiding the water completely. Other times they had to carefully lower themselves into a swift current, trusting that it was not too deep or too strong, and wade to the next outcropping of dry rock. In this way they made steady progress across the expanse and soon found themselves climbing out onto the eastern riverbank.

It was now close to dusk. As there was no trail to follow, Hanshee decided that they should make camp for the night. Moving a little farther upstream and a little inland from the river, he found a sandbar. It was probably deposited in the spring when the high floodwaters would have made this particular stretch of land part of the riverbed. Since it was now clean, dry sand and had little vegetation growing from it, he decided they would make camp there. He tested the wind, which was blowing from the west, and decided that it would be safe to build a small fire. Leaving the task of fire building to Ray, Hanshee returned to the river to gather what could be had for an evening meal.

Ray was more than happy to get to work building a fire. Even in only a shirt, shorts, boots, and socks, he wore substantially more than Hanshee. A fire would help them dry out and feel more comfortable. It also kept Ray busy and less prone to worry about their pursuit. There was plenty of dry driftwood, supplied by the same high water that had deposited the sand several months ago in the spring. In short order Ray found himself feeding twigs, then small sticks into the fire he had built at the center of the sandbar clearing.

Sitting back on his heels, he looked on the fire with the pride he always felt at being able to contribute in his small way to their comfort. The crackle of the dry wood, the sight and smell of smoke wafting slowly up to mingle with the twilight breeze, brought an unexpected sense of calm. He stripped off his wet clothes and propped them on sticks around the fire so that they could catch the heat and the breeze and dry out. Then he sat and waited for Hanshee.

Sitting naked in the sand, within earshot of the sounds of the water as it flowed between the rocks and over the falls, he could almost feel the tension draining from his body. In his wildest imaginings, he never thought that he would be here, in this situation, much less at peace with it. The mystery of his arrival here, the puzzle of where "here" was, the strain of survival in the wilderness, the tension of being pursued by dangerous men bent on catching and most likely killing them; all of these things were still present. But Ray had, for the first time, found a place within himself where he could temporarily hide from the confusion, the apprehension, and the fear. Ever so slowly a smile, the first real one in weeks, found its way to his face.

That is how Hanshee found him when he returned to the camp with a supper of freshwater clams, a few fat snails, two frogs, and a nice-sized turtle. Ray's eyes took in the bounty Hanshee had placed on a bed of leaves before the fire in preparation for cooking, and his smile broadened.

They cooked and ate in relative silence. Ray surprised himself by greedily eating every morsel that Hanshee placed before him. By the time he was finished, his clothes had dried out. He stood and brushed the sand from his body before getting dressed. A thin layer of leaves and grass, enough to separate them from the sand, was all that was needed for a bed, and soon they were sleeping soundly while the fire slowly burned down to ash.

• • • • •

Hanshee and Ray awakened well before sunrise. Ray re-stoked the fire as Hanshee again visited the riverbank. Ray was guessing that, in the pitch blackness prior to dawn, Hanshee would be unable to find anything else to eat. He was wrong. This time Hanshee returned with some cattails, and the remains of what must have been a good-size fish. They ate the cattail stalks raw while the meat of the fish cooked beside the hot coals of the re-stoked fire.

"The clams and snails I can understand," Ray said. "It's not like they could run away from you. The turtle, and even the frogs, you could see in the twilight and hit them with a stick or something. But how the hell did you catch a fish with your bare hands in the dark?"

"I was fortunate," was all Hanshee offered by way of an explanation.

Ray opened his mouth to press his companion, but thought better of it. Instead, he focused on enjoying his morning meal. They finished eating before dawn. Rather than try to blaze a trail in darkness, they chose to sit around the remains of the fire and prepare themselves for the day that lay before them.

"We've given them a hard trail to follow on horseback," Ray said, referring to the twelve men who had been following them for the last three days. "Do you think we're safe?"

Hanshee squatted by the fire, taking in its warmth. He heard Ray's question but didn't answer right away, leaving Ray to wait patiently until he was rewarded with a response.

"We have done what could be done," Hanshee said thoughtfully. "Our trail is faint, but they are determined and their tracker is skilled. We will continue to test their resolve. We will know in time."

The pair again fell into silence. Ray began to notice the darkness receding and the twinkling stars fading as the sky slowly changed from black to grey before the growing light of the soon-to-rise sun.

Knowing that the time to depart this camp was quickly approaching, Ray again queried his companion.

"What are your plans for the coming day?"

"As before," Hanshee replied. "We will move into the foothills and hope to lose our pursuit there. The hills are rugged. When we know we have lost them, we will turn west toward what they call the Ursal Mountains."

He turned questioning eyes to Ray.

"Are you ready for Mother's challenge this day?" Hanshee asked with a touch of humor in his voice.

"I think I'm ready," was Ray's reply, and he was surprised to find that he really meant it.

CHAPTER 16

They waited until the morning was fully upon them before breaking camp. Hanshee had done a bit of scouting while Ray continued to rest and he returned with the opinion that they should get below the falls before heading farther east. Since the vegetation here was particularly lush, the easiest path downstream lay close to, and sometimes in, the river. Luckily, they were able to use the many exposed rocks to keep relatively dry while they made their way downstream.

They were soon looking down into the misty gorge carved out by the falls, this time from the eastern bank. The way down wasn't as steep as on the other side but was just as treacherous. Holding tight to the vines and jutting rocks, they carefully made their way down until their feet touched the firm earth of the riverbank beside the falls.

Farther inland Hanshee found a faint trail, made by deer, or wild pigs, or maybe the bears for which the western mountains were named. It headed south, meandering in and out among the rocks, trees, and shrubs while maintaining a connection to the river. As they followed it downstream, the river narrowed from its widest point at the waterfalls, gaining depth but maintaining the strong currents that resulted from the same volume of water being funneled through a narrower bed. The steep hills that Hanshee sought were sometimes visible to their left through the trees but they chose to continue on, expecting that the trail they were on would at some point veer off to the east.

They had just emerged from a patch of brush onto a clear portion of riverbank that jutted out about three feet above the murky water below when a sound stopped them both in their tracks.

"THERE… ON THE OTHER BANK!"

Ray understood the shouted words, but the sight of the heavily armed man on horseback who was pointing at them from the opposite bank also made the meaning of the words crystal clear to Hanshee.

On either side of the river the two parties paused, as if unsure what to do now that they had finally openly lain eyes on the other. Then both parties were taken by surprise as one of the armed pursuers spurred his horse past his comrades till it leapt from the bank and into the river!

The splash was thunderous. Both man and beast momentarily disappeared from view before their heads reemerged just above the water, the wide-eyed mount fighting the depth and the current to get to the opposite bank. The struggle was made even more difficult by the additional weight of its rider and his weapons, armor, and supplies. It was a battle the horse seemed doomed to lose. One of the horseman's comrades, seeing the animal's distress, let loose with a cry.

"Get off his back, Leo! You're dragging him down!"

Others took up the cry as the horse was being carried downstream much faster than he could make headway toward the far bank. Finally Leo, who was spitting water and struggling to keep his head up, heeded the cries and threw himself off of the animal to the downstream side. As soon as the horse was free of his weight it turned its body upstream in an attempt to reach the bank where it could see Hanshee and Ray standing.

What happened next was a mystery to those on both sides of the river, as none could see below the water's surface.

Apparently Leo was no great swimmer. Due to the added weight of his mail, his sword, his axe, and his shield, he was pulled straight under. He still held the reins, but both they and his arms were stretched out beside his mount. Thus, when the horse turned in the water, Leo was perfectly positioned for a kick from the animal's churning right rear hoof. The iron-shod hoof caught the guardsmen in his hip just left of his groin. The pain that accompanied it caused Leo to double over in the water. This was not Leo's day, as his new position placed him in line for the horse's front hoof to crash into his helmeted head. The result was that Leo's horse was making a beeline for the opposite bank where Hanshee and Ray stood watching. The heavily weighted Leo, knocked unconscious by a kick to the head, slipped under the water and was never seen again.

Hanshee and Ray held their position on the far bank, fascinated with the events in the water even as the tired horse drew ever closer to them. Once it was in the water before them, they knew that there was no way the animal could climb the vertical bank which rose three feet above the waterline. Apparently the horse sensed it too and, aided by the roots of the trees that jutted out below the water's surface, and from the bank itself, it began kicking its way farther upstream.

Both parties kept their eyes glued on the animal as it fought valiantly against the current that fortunately was weaker near the bank. The beast kept churning its legs, fighting the current, until eventually it found stability about fifty feet farther upstream. First its entire head, then its neck, rose from the water. Standing on a portion of the river bed not as deep as it had been farther downstream, it remained motionless, except for the flaring of its nostrils as it took in much-needed air.

"The water must be shallower upstream!" cried the commander of the guards, freeing his men from the trance of watching the horse's struggle. "We can cross there. Hurry!"

This cry brought Hanshee and Ray back to the present. Ray pointed as he translated, "They're going to try to cross where the horse is, farther upstream, closer to the falls!"

"Quickly!" was Hanshee's shouted reply, as he turned and dashed into the brush behind them.

Ray followed close on his heels.

Tree limbs, vines, and thorns tore at their skin. At first neither seemed to feel it or care. Finally Hanshee drew his sword and began moving and hacking without pause. Ray brought up the rear, having enough sense to give Hanshee the distance needed to cut a path. How long they plowed through the bush neither knew but, just as Ray was starting to feel the pain inflicted upon him by the thick forest, they burst out into a clearing.

Hanshee, sword still in hand, never paused as he raced through what was now high grass, toward the steep hills which rose up on the opposite side of the treeless field. Ray had no choice but to put his discomfort aside and sprint behind him.

Hanshee was quickly making his way toward a gap between two high hills looming in the distance. About halfway across the meadow Ray saw his partner go airborne. In a few more steps he, too, had to leap to clear the twelve feet from one bank to the other of a stream that dissected the meadow. It appeared to flow from the gap they were approaching.

As the grass was thinning out, Ray watched Hanshee disappear behind a rock which jutted from the base of the hill to his right. In a few more steps he made the same turn, almost careening into Hanshee, who had stopped to sheath his sword and check his body for cuts. While Ray caught his breath, Hanshee made sure he still carried his knife and what Ray thought of as the "magic pouch". He then looked to see that Ray still carried his flask, the bow, and the quiver of arrows. Finding everything in place, he then turned his attention to their surroundings.

Ray raised his head to take a look too.

The space between the two steep hills opened up into a small valley or canyon of sorts. It was not a depression so much as a widening, leaving room for the small stream and a surprising amount of thick vegetation reminiscent of what they had just cut their way through. To their right, along the base of the hill, there was a path of sorts, made by the bottom five or so feet of hill that had weathered and crumbled into a mix of dust, shale, and rocks both large and small. This continued for as far as the two could see, with the thick brush and trees on their left filling the gap of about two hundred feet to the base of the other hill, a twin of the one rising before them.

The air here was still and in the silence both Ray and Hanshee could just make out the distant sounds of horses trying to fight their way through water and heavy brush.

"They will be upon us before long," said Hanshee. "Come!" and he started down the path at the base of the hill to their right.

The footing on the loose rocks was treacherous; forcing them to take their time and severely limiting the distance they could cover. The sound of the horses became ever louder. It looked like they would not be able to traverse the canyon before their pursuers were upon them. Ray found that the little ball of fear he had managed to put aside was back and was growing. What he didn't realize was that this was exactly the type of situation that had prompted Hanshee to lead him here.

Halfway through the valley Hanshee came to a stop.

"Pass the bow and the quiver!" he said, his hand outstretched.

Ray complied, and Hanshee pointed up the hill

"Now climb, Way-Mon! Use the bushes and vines to pull yourself up. Keep to cover as much as you can, but climb to a place of safety… to the very top if you must!"

Looking up Ray saw that the side of the hill, though indeed steep, was covered with vines, brush, and even some saplings that had managed to find a precarious purchase there.

"Climb!" Hanshee barked. Ray jumped up to grasp the lowest of the vines that he thought could hold his weight.

As he pulled himself up he felt Hanshee offer a brace for his feet to push against, and so he easily cleared the first few feet of broken and dislodged rock and pulled himself fully into the brush. Upward he climbed, fear propelling him through the obstacles much as it had pushed him through the brush at the river's edge. It was not until he had climbed over thirty feet - still only a fraction of the distance to the crest - that he chanced a glance over his shoulder to check on Hanshee's progress. There Ray froze on the side of that small mountain.

Hanshee was nowhere in sight!

Ray continued to hang there, holding onto the base of a prickly young cedar while staring down at the deserted path.

It was not deserted for long.

As Ray continued to stare down toward the path he first heard and then saw a horse and rider as they passed beneath him. The rider sat still upon his mount as it gingerly picked its way along the loose ground and between the stones. This picture was repeated with a second horse and rider, and then a third and a fourth. It was not until the fifth horse began to pass beneath him that the rider happened to glance up and meet his eyes.

"There they are!" the rider's cry rose up and instantly he vaulted from his horse and onto the side of the hill in pursuit of Ray.

The height of his horse allowed him to clear the shattered portion of the hill. In an instant he was working himself up the steep incline toward his prey. He was followed shortly by the guardsman who had been riding directly behind him, but Ray didn't notice. As soon as he saw the first guardsman leave his horse, Ray turned his face upward and began climbing for all he was worth.

If Ray had been looking he would have seen that the overly equipped guards were having a hard time matching his pace as he scaled the hillside. The first guard soon discovered that the broad shield which he wore strapped to his back made squeezing between trees and brush nearly impossible and he paused to rid himself of it. His partner saw his dilemma and did the same. Now, with their two shields sliding down the hill to land on the loose path below, the guardsmen again threw their will and sinew into climbing after the butchers who had recently left a trail of corpses in Aggipoor.

The first arrow seemed to appear from nowhere, striking the second guardsman low in his back, bringing forth a piercing cry of surprise and pain. Before the echo of his cry could die out the first guardsman, who had been the first to spot Ray, took an arrow low in his left buttock. He, too, cried out in pain. Holding onto an outcropping of rock with his right hand, he frantically reached back with his left to pull the arrow free. He learned quickly that the pain from trying to tear the arrow out was much worse than what he felt when it struck. Cutting short his attempt, he began to slowly lower himself down the hill.

The guardsman below him had yet to move. He held on to an outcropping of rock with one hand and a vine with the other. His eyes were scrunched tightly shut and his teeth gritted as his mind reeled, both from pain and the speed at which his situation had changed. This soon became problematic, as the guardsman above him continued lowering himself until he collided with his companion, whose head now became nestled in his crotch. Cursing and arguing ensued as the two seemed to merge into some type of giant, bloody insect hanging from the side of the steep hill; an eight-limbed marvel, unable to go up or down.

The guardsmen below had closely followed their fellows' progress and witnessed the first guardsmen take an arrow in his back. When he cried out, all eyes on the ground looked up in time to see the second arrow strike the higher guardsman. As a man, they turned toward the tangle of thick vegetation on their left from which the arrows came. Quickly dismounting with shields held high, the seven that remained swatted their horses away and formed up with their backs against the hill, eyes glued to the small, dense forest before them.

A voice called out: "How many have we been tracking?"

It was the captain of the group.

"There's sign for two of 'em," the reply came from the tracker, the only woman in the group, who stood beside him on the trail.

"Then one is climbing the hill," said the captain, "and one is in there." He motioned with his head toward the trees and brush that gave excellent cover to an archer whose aim was either very good or very bad, as a quick glance upward showed that neither of the wounded guardsmen appeared in fear of losing his life anytime soon. Looking to either side of his formation, the commander took stock of the men remaining. Pointing to the ones at either end, he gave his orders.

"You... and you," he said, pointing to each in turn. "Move down your side of the path until I signal to stop. Then enter the brush and flank the archer. Arrows are of little use in there. Draw your short sword. Kill him, or flush him out to us. We will spread out along the path so that he cannot pass. We will wait for your word and be ready when he comes out."

Without hesitation the two detached from the main body of guardsmen. Moving in a half-crouch behind their shields, they worked their way in opposite directions down the path. They continued until the commander raised a hand, bringing them to a halt.

Without lowering their shields, both men pulled their short swords, the perfect weapon for close-quarter combat. As silently as possible they slipped into the small, dense patch of forest.

As the remaining guardsmen began to spread out along the path, their attention was brought back to the two wounded men on the hill.

The lower man gave a gut-wrenching moan and began to slide down toward his comrades, unleashing a cascade of shale pebbles and larger rocks as he went. This became an ordeal as he repeatedly became stuck on the same rocks and vegetation that had provided hand and foot holds on his way up. With his lack of mobility, the pain in his back steadily increasing, and the continued loss of blood, he found it harder and harder to move his legs and dislodge himself when he got stuck.

The men on the ground were now motionless with indecision. Spread out and wait for the archer to be flushed from the woods or help their wounded comrades who were clinging to the hill above their heads? Their dilemma was soon solved as, with a scream of pain, the wounded guardsman managed to kick his way free of the last shrub. Amid a torrent of rocks and dirt, he slid the remainder of the way down the slope. He would have crashed heavily onto the path had not two of the remaining five detached themselves from the others and rushed forward just in time to catch him and ease him facedown onto the loose gravel of the path. More gravel and rocks rained down on them as the first guardsman, now free of the obstacle of the second, continued his controlled slide down the steep slope of the hill. Seeing this, the two that had caught him now scooped the second guardsman up and moved him farther down the path to clear a place for his partner's landing. The wounded man screamed again as the repositioning was none too delicate, but lay still while an examination of his wound was begun. Now another guardsman broke formation to help the first wounded man down, prompting the commander to assert himself.

"Get them stretched out and regroup!" he spat. "Their wounds will be tended later! First we deal with the archer in the brush!"

The positioning of the wounded took longer than planned, but the pair was eventually made as comfortable as possible, given the circumstances. The guardsmen then returned to their places on the line. Hunkering down behind their shields, they drew their swords and waited for a sign that the archer was about to be flushed.

CHAPTER 17

Hanshee was fortunate to have found a place that gave him adequate cover yet still allowed a view of the hill above the path. He had hoped that the pursuing men would bypass them. Then he would have climbed the hill and joined Ray. Of course he could have climbed the hill right behind Ray, except that would have left both exposed had they been spotted. This way, if Ray was discovered, Hanshee would be in position to cover his ascent

And cover he did.

Hanshee saw the two guardsmen leave their mounts in pursuit of what they believed were the two of them. He knew that, weighed down as they were, they could not hope to match the pace Ray had set. When they released the shields from their backs, Hanshee saw his opportunity.

Quickly stringing the bow, he let fly two arrows. Each found its mark. The guardsmen's cries of surprise and pain were sweet music to Hanshee. He could only guess at the reactions of the remaining men, as their positions were obscured by the thick brush. What he was sure of was that, for the moment anyway, he had their attention and Ray was safe.

Having revealed himself, Hanshee now expected an assault of some sort on his position. Silently he made his way farther into the thicket and the deeper shadows. There he would wait for whatever was to come.

He did not have to wait long.

Hanshee's hearing was keen. Even through the noise of the men sliding down the hillside, the clanging of shields and armor as their brethren moved to catch them, and the moaning of the wounded as they were laid out, he heard the sounds of men entering the thicket from both his left and his right. At first the sounds were faint and too far away for him to guess at numbers, but of the fact that he was presently under siege he had no doubt. He relaxed himself and settled in, content to listen to the sounds of advancement. Through the crunch of footfalls and the cracks of sticks and branches being bent and broken, Mother would reveal all in time.

And She did.

It did not take him long to decipher the sounds that came drifting to him through the brush. There were two men, he soon knew, one approaching from each side. Though they worked at being stealthy, their footfalls were heavy. They were either city dwellers or armored, and Hanshee knew them to be both. The man to his right was moving more swiftly than his comrade and would reach Hanshee's position well before the other.

He would be first.

As silently as the shadows that surrounded him, Hanshee moved through the brush toward the guardsman approaching from his right. He listened carefully to the sounds of his approach and deduced the path the guardsman would take. He then found a place amid the thick brush and the shadows where he could hide and wait.

Hanshee had long practice in the stalking of both man and beast. He willed himself to relax, causing a drop in both his breathing and his heartbeat. He willed himself to total stillness, letting nothing take his attention from the approaching guardsman. He became just another shadow amid shadows deep in the forest thicket.

Hanshee continued to listen for the sounds the oncoming guardsman made and when he heard the heavy footfall not ten feet to his right he did not move his head, or even his eyes, in that direction. He remained perfectly still even as the man approached close enough for Hanshee to hear his heavy breathing, tense with caution and excitement.

The guardsman carried his shield high as he stalked through the brush, keeping his gaze focused on the most distant trees. He was hoping to glimpse his quarry before he himself were spotted, and take him unawares. Hanshee did not move, but instead listened intently for any change in breath or gait that would signal that he had been detected. None came. The guardsman took yet another step, ever closer to Hanshee's position.

The guardsman's breath came in ragged bursts as adrenalin coursed through his body and his excitement grew with every step. He figured his quarry to be just a little farther up ahead, but still out of sight.

He took another tentative step.

If he kept to this path he felt he could take the archer by surprise. He brushed a low branch from his path with his shield before stepping past it, keeping his eyes focused on the distant trees, expecting the archer to reveal himself at any moment.

He took another step.

Like any young man, he had dreams and ambitions. The plan was to flush the archer out into the open if he could. But he also knew that, were he to close with the killer and deliver the deathblow, his own reputation would be assured.

He took another cautious step.

He hoped one day to become a leader in the guard of Aggipoor, maybe even its captain. Oh, he had great dreams, and he meant to see them take flight on this very hunt... perhaps on this very day!

He took yet another step.

The guardsman never saw the bush behind and to his left come to life. He never saw the arm that reached toward him, the hand that moved swiftly past his cheek. He never saw anything. What he felt was an iron grip around his mouth that cut off his cry of alarm before it could leave his throat. What he felt was his head and neck being wrenched back and down, pulling him off balance and almost bending him over backwards. It is doubtful that he felt the blade that slid quietly through the base of his skull and into his brainstem, where it was moved quickly back and forth, severing all connections. He assuredly did not feel his lifeless body being lowered quietly onto the carpet of decaying leaves, moss, and damp soil that made up the floor of this tiny piece of forest.

Hanshee looked down at the dead guardsman. He lay between two clumps of thick brush and should remain hidden as long as his comrade, approaching from the opposite direction, did not take a path to this exact spot. Pausing to consider his next move, Hanshee listened for the approaching footsteps of the other guardsman, marked his position, and then effortlessly became a part of the forest once more.

• • •

The sun was still low in the eastern sky, not yet above the many tall hills to the east that cast long shadows into the little valley where the captain of the guard of Aggipoor squatted with his command.

The captain was growing surlier by the minute.

The moans of his wounded were a constant assault on his ears, and he had heard nothing from the men he had sent into the brush after the archer. He kept his poise, as an example to his command and so as not to give away the positions of those on the hunt, but to his mind more than enough time had passed for them to flush out the coward. What was holding them up?

"Captain?"

The whisper came from one of his men down the line to his left. He looked over and saw the guardsman pointing farther down the path. He let his gaze follow the pointing hand and saw the man he had sent in from his right. Apparently he had traversed the entire patch of forest in a semicircle, emerging not far from where his partner had entered. The captain chanced a glance in the other direction to see if the other guardsman had emerged too.

Nothing yet.

Looking back to his left he saw the man approaching and rose to meet him.

"What did you find?" the captain asked in a clipped whisper.

"I saw no one, Captain."

"Did Hedro not see him too?" the captain asked.

"I never saw Hedro," was the guardsman's reply.

The captain stared at him for a moment before looking back over his shoulder to the far end of the path. There was still no sign of Hedro.

Now he fixed his gaze back onto the miniature slice of wilderness before him. One man might be able to hide in such a place for a short time. That could be explained. But for this tiny patch of woods to silently swallow up an experienced guardsman while his comrades waited nearby with not a sound to be heard?

He turned back to his men, trying to exude an air of confidence to cover his doubt and confusion.

"We started this day with ten. Now, at mid-morning, we are down to six able men," the captain said, counting the tracker in their number. Turning to the tracker he asked, "How long do you think before the others arrive with the hounds?"

The tracker, a small, wiry woman in light armor, scratched at her neck as she thought.

"If they met up with our boys when and where we thought they would," she said, "and moved at a good pace, I'd guess they should get this far a little before sundown, or early morning at the latest. The dogs would have to be walked on leashes, so the party can only go as fast as a man on foot. Unless they have cages for the horses to carry the dogs, they can't make the same time as a man on horseback."

The captain looked from the tracker to his still-crouching men. Then he looked to the wounded and lastly to the thick vegetation before them.

"Almost half of us are dead, wounded, or missing!" he spat. "We left two to meet the others, and guide them to us. I don't know how many men they will bring but we are in need of their numbers now."

"Get the wounded up," he told his men. "If they can't walk, they will have to be carried. Tracker, collect the horses. We will make camp close to the river and wait for the others to join us. If Hedro is still alive, maybe he will join us. If not, we will search for his body when we have greater numbers. As it now stands, I'll not take you five into that bush and risk losing you to whatever man or demon lurks within."

• • •

Neither of the two wounded guardsman were able to sit astride a horse. With arrowheads lodged in the lower back of one and the hip joint of another, they could not stand if helped to their feet. Litters had to be fashioned to carry them away from the hills to the campsite yet to be cleared at the riverbank. This was time-consuming. Along with the job of rounding up the horses that had strayed away, it meant that Hanshee had to wait several more hours before the members of the City Guard of Aggipoor finally gathered their wounded and trudged back across the field of tall grass to disappear among the trees and brush beside the river.

CHAPTER 18

Hanshee was patient, as he was with all things that required patience. It was Ray who was antsy.

After climbing up to a ledge about thirty feet shy of the crest of the steep hill, Ray had wedged himself in and listened. He had been so preoccupied with his escape that the clatter of the debris he had loosened while climbing and the blood rushing in his ears had drowned out the sounds of the assault on his pursuers. Peeping over the edge of the ledge he could see nothing through the brush that clung to the hillside, but as his pulse and breathing slowed he began to hear curses and moans coming from below him. Not from the very bottom of the hill, he thought. These sounds wouldn't carry that far. This was farther up the hill, closer to his last position. He figured that something must have happened to whoever was climbing after him.

After a while he heard the clatter of more debris falling, along with the errant clank of armor, but it appeared that there was no one trying to climb up to reach him. Relieved but wary, he allowed himself to relax a little more. He felt for his water bag, the only thing besides his walking stick that Hanshee insisted that he carry. It was still there, attached by a strong leather cord to his belt. Hanshee had not yet fashioned a strap so he could carry it over his shoulder. He untied the cord around the small leather bladder and took a long drink before carefully tying it back.

Slightly refreshed and sill alert, Ray thought back to the last commands of his protector. Hanshee had told him to climb, keeping to cover until he reached a place of safety. Well, this ledge seemed to satisfy the part about cover and safety for the moment. Hearing no sounds of pursuit, Ray settled in to wait for Hanshee.

The sun continued its journey across the sky as Ray continued his lonely vigil, unable to see or hear much of anything going on below him.

In this time of silent uncertainty that accompanied his wait, Ray was hard pressed to control his errant thoughts. His mind floated from one possible scenario to another, each one ending in tragedy for himself, Hanshee, or both. If Hanshee were captured or killed the result would be the same: Ray would be left on his own in the wilderness. That was a depressing thought. Or perhaps they'd both be captured and carted back to what these people called a city – Aggipoor – to be tortured and killed. He shivered as each new tragic ending occurred to him. His imagination was doing him no favors.

He judged it to be just before noon when he heard the sounds of wood being cut, orders being barked and, finally, the sound of the iron-shod hooves of horses being led across the loose rocks of the trail below. It was well past noon when he heard the sound of hooves again, this time receding into the distance, back toward the river. It was much later in the day, the sun having travelled to a point where the high hills again cast the narrow valley into shadow, before Hanshee showed himself.

He startled Ray by approaching almost noiselessly from above and to the side of the ledge on which he hid. By then Ray had become comfortable enough to nod off, and he nearly jumped from the ledge when he felt a hand prodding him awake. Ray didn't think he'd ever been happier to see anyone. There was enough room on the narrow ledge for both of them to sit, so he edged over and made space for Hanshee to join him.

Not yet aware of the situation below, Ray held his tongue. For the present he felt immensely relieved and secure just knowing that his guide and protector had rejoined him.

Hanshee broke the silence.

"They have returned to the river and cleared a campsite. They will not be back tonight."

"What happened?" Ray asked. "I was climbing, like you told me. Then I looked down and saw them passing under me. When they saw me one of them jumped from his horse and started after me. I kept climbing and by the time I reached this ledge they'd stopped."

"I was able to halt those that pursued you up the slope with arrows," Hanshee said calmly. "The others then had to turn, for they knew they had an archer to their back. To continue in pursuit of you was to be struck down from behind, like their brethren."

"You killed more of them!" Raymond nearly shouted, surprising himself with the emotion of his accusation, yet not turning away as Hanshee met his eyes with a steel hard gaze.

Hanshee looked hard at Ray and saw the concerns that had been present after they left the city. They had been pushed aside by the need to take flight, but had now resurfaced.

For the first time Hanshee felt himself losing patience with this *mulit,* this fool, who came here with no knowledge of life or survival in this land. For a fraction of a second his eyes flashed with anger and Ray instinctively recoiled at what he saw there. But just as quickly Hanshee regained his composure and turned away, looking off into the distance.

When Hanshee finally spoke, his thoughts were to use this as a teaching moment, but his words did little to hide his frustration.

"Way-Mon," he began slowly, "you are as a young child, lacking in knowledge, and so must be taught the ways of the world. But unlike a child, you are unaware of your ignorance."

These words were spoken slowly as Hanshee continued to gaze northward at the sky above the hill on the other side of the little valley below them.

"Know this," Hanshee said. "Of your world and your place in it, I know nothing. But in this world - my world - you are helpless. And as with the young of all creatures born helpless into the bounty of our Mother, you will learn or you will die."

Hanshee spoke these words with no undue emphasis. None was needed. He was not attempting to frighten Ray. He was simply stating a fact.

"You have shown a different face since our time in the city," Hanshee continued. "You have voiced distress at my actions, at my taking the lives of those who would have taken ours."

Now Hanshee turned to his companion. Ray had also been looking into the distance, simmering with frustration. Feeling Hanshee's eyes on him, Ray turned his face toward him and quickly found himself held captive by the intensity of his stare.

"Know that I am Hanshee of Clan Dula, and I am Maiyochi!" Hanshee said with all the fierce pride that it took to claim the title. "It is given to me to defend my people and no limit has been placed upon me save that I not fail! I will take life as the moment demands, with no hesitation or remorse, but only as the moment demands! It was I who halted your pursuers with my arrows, but I did not take their lives!"

Hanshee paused a moment to regain his composure. When he continued, it was with the intention of instructing Ray about the actions he had taken. Still, there was an undercurrent of anger in his words that Ray did not miss.

"Listen and learn, 'young one'," Hanshee said, mimicking the language used by the elders when instructing a child of his tribe, "for one day you may have lives besides your own to account for, and at such time you may have need of every lesson that fortune has taught you.

"Nine pursued us from the river," Hanshee explained. "Two pursued you up this slope. Had I killed those two, seven would be pursuing us even now. But I am Maiyochi. My aim is true! I placed arrows into those who pursued you, not to kill but to cripple; to wound them in such a way so as to bind their brethren with the need for their care. And now, because they cannot leave their wounded as they would their dead, because their number was once nine but is now six, they must return to the river. And because they are saddled with the care of their wounded, they cannot pursue us at speed. Now they are only as swift as the injured they must carry. By choosing injury instead of death, I have turned a swift pursuit of nine fighters on horseback into a slow pursuit of six fighters who must carry two wounded.

"They will wait by the river for others to join with them," Hanshee said, answering the question he knew would be coming. "If the others come, they will again have the numbers to pursue us. If others do not come, the pursuit ends."

Hanshee maintained eye contact with Ray as he imparted this lesson in strategy. Forced to consider the simple truth and beauty of Hanshee's actions, Ray bowed his head in shame for all but accusing his protector of being nothing more than a wanton killer.

But Hanshee was not yet finished.

"A warrior ever chooses the path that leads to victory. Sometimes the moment calls not for killing. Sometimes it does."

Hanshee leaned in so that Ray could see his resolve as he spoke his next words.

"If called for, I will kill every one of those now camped at the river's edge."

CHAPTER 19

The afternoon after their encounter with the archer between the hills saw the men of the Aggipoor garrison tending to their wounded. The arrowheads had struck deep and had to be cut out by those more accustomed to taking life than to saving it. The ensuing scene had been brutal. The loss of blood from the arrow wounds was dwarfed by that which was lost during the surgery, if it could be called surgery. The cries of the wounded were only minimally muffled by the sticks and rags they clenched between their teeth.

That evening the guardsmen had been joined at their river camp by the two men they had left behind to guide the riders and the fabled hounds of Thessilli.

Their sister city had contributed but an additional three men to the show of force. Two were well armed men of the Thessilli garrison, though neither appeared particularly formidable. The third was the handler of the two hounds. Since the hounds were in cages on the back of a mule, the small party was able to move quickly and had been less than a day behind the main group.

When they arrived at the camp beside the river, the Aggipoor guardsmen already there greeted them with disappointment at the sparse Thessillian contribution.

Cursing privately, the Captain welcomed them and offered the hospitality of his camp. The handler of the hounds moved off to see to the welfare of his dogs and the two men at arms settled around the evening fire, helping themselves to the contents of the stew pot. The guardsmen from Aggipoor closely watched these newcomers who ate so greedily from their provisions, wondering among themselves if Thessilli had sent two able fighters or its dregs.

When morning came the captain was eager to put the hounds to the test. He approached the handler with the contents of Hedro's saddle bag. He then led them through the brush and across the field of high grass to the small valley between the two steep hills. Here the handler allowed the two hounds to sniff at some of the clothing from the bag and, with curt commands, sent them into the brush. It seemed but a moment had passed before their baying told him that the missing man was found. Soon his dead body was lying on the path in front of the captain.

Well, the captain thought, *two questions have been answered; Hedro is indeed dead, and the fabled hounds of Thessilli can at least track a corpse.*

After a hurried burial, the company broke camp to continue the pursuit; a pursuit that was slowed considerably by the two litters that were required to carry the wounded. The head of each litter was tied to the saddle of a horse whose rider had to be particularly careful in how he handled his mount. A guardsman followed on foot. He was needed to lift the end that dragged the ground over any obstacles in the path. Sometimes he had to bear the weight of his injured fellow for a considerable distance, such as when they crossed the stream that ran through the center of the field of tall grass. Though these duties alternated, two men attached to each of these litters – one on foot and one on horseback - meant that four healthy guardsmen were always occupied with something other than searching for the 'Assassins of Aggipoor'. This new title given the killers, earned by the injury and death left in their wake, served to impress the newcomers from Thessilli with the gravity of the pursuit.

Slowed considerably by their wounded, the snail-like procession was led by the dog handler and his hounds. He held tightly to their leashes, giving them just enough line to cover the width of the trail with noses to the ground. Every so often he would remind them of their task by having them sniff at the robes the killers had worn while in the city. These had been obtained from the woman in the hog shack and were carried in the captain's saddlebags in anticipation of the fabled hounds of Thessilli taking up the hunt. So far the results had been utterly disappointing.

So much for the fabled hounds of Thessilli, thought the captain in disgust.

The sun was getting low in the western sky when the handler finally saw a reaction in his dogs that told him they had caught a scent. Both dogs became agitated and tried to turn into the brush to their left that lay at the base of yet another steep slope. The tracker came forward and took a considerable amount of time examining the trail and the brush on both sides, before approaching the captain.

"Them hounds are on to somethin' sir," she said. "It looks like one or two of 'em made their way straight across the trail ri'chere. They went from brush to brush. They wasn't on the trail but for a step or two."

"Which way were they going?" the captain asked.

"Appears they were heading in this direction," the tracker said, indicating the hill to the left.

The captain tilted his head back so as to survey the slope of the hill the tracker had pointed out. Although it appeared to become more horizontal about fifty or sixty feet up, the angle that greeted them until then looked to be just a few degrees short of vertical.

"Damn," the captain exclaimed under his breath as he considered how to climb up. He looked to the dogs, then back at the hill, quickly dismissing that idea. His frustration with this chase was growing greater by the minute.

"You two," he pointed to two of his men not occupied with the wounded, "and you," he pointed to the two from Thessilli. "You take the lead and you others go the opposite direction. Find me a way up this damned hill! The rest of us will wait here for your return."

The sun had signaled less than an hour's passing when the two that had circled to the rear returned with good news.

"We think we've found a trail up the side, Captain," said the Thessillian.

"You 'think', or you know?" barked the captain.

"We've found a way up, sir," the man said. "At least we think, uh...we *know* the horses without the litters can make it."

"Damn it!" the captain spat as he turned toward the remainder of his patrol. "You with the litters stay here and wait for the others. When they come, lead them around to where we started up the hill. We'll leave you signs. Then you make camp at the base of the hill until we return. Everyone else is with me."

The captain then turned back to the two soldiers from Thessilli. "Lead the way," he said.

• • •

They were now two days into the "foothills," as Hanshee had called them. To Ray they were more like mountains, but in miniature. Towering hills rose on all sides, with narrow trails winding between them at their base. As the trails allowed horses to move freely, Hanshee and Ray stayed in the hills, crossing the trails only to get from one hill to another. In this way they managed to stay hidden and always ahead of their pursuers.

Twice Ray had laid eyes on the pursuing party, and both times he silently praised the beauty of Hanshee's strategy. Seeing the hardened fighters who had once struck such fear in his heart with their dogged pursuit reduced to blindly plodding along the narrow trails between hills, searching for a sign of their quarry, gave him a renewed sense of hope.

Ray was at a point just below the summit of a hill that the guardsmen appeared to be bypassing. If things proceeded as he hoped, they could double back and head west to the Ursal Mountains while the guardsmen remained hopelessly lost in these foothills. He was primed to tell Hanshee of his wonderful idea when something caught his eye.

It looked like the pursuit had come to a stop as the dogs sniffed the trail and the brush on both sides.

Is that where we crossed the trail? Ray wondered, as he saw the woman step forward to examine the ground where the dogs had been sniffing. After a while she turned and spoke to the first man on horseback, who seemed to take in what she said before leaning back in his saddle and looking up the hill, straight into Ray's eyes if Ray believed his imagination. It was at this time that Hanshee eased up beside him.

He arrived noiselessly, as Hanshee always did, and silently took in the scene unfolding below them. He watched as the first horseman, obviously the leader, spoke to two pairs of riders and sent them off in opposite directions. Once they disappeared the remaining men dismounted and hunkered down, resting their mounts and themselves as they waited for the return of those that were sent out. Hanshee had a good idea what was happening below. He pulled Ray back behind the shrubs that concealed them and passed on what he had learned.

"This hill," Hanshee began, "is not so steep at its top as the others. There are many signs that men have been here."

Ray was puzzled.

"What do you mean?" he asked. "How can you tell?"

"There are markers and altars made of stone," said Hanshee. "They are very old. This place was used long ago. It was a place of worship. Sacrifices were made. Many dead are buried here."

"How could that have been?" asked Ray, still not comprehending.

"There are paths up the slopes, Hanshee said. "They are ancient, but horses may find a way. If so, the riders will pursue us here."

"And you think that's where the leader sent the riders," said Ray, the pieces clicking into place, "to look for these paths?"

"They will find them," said Hanshee. "We must move. We must be gone from this place when they reach its summit."

Before Ray could respond, Hanshee turned and, keeping low so as not to present a profile against the sky, began working his way up the remaining distance to the top of the hill. Mimicking his low profile, Ray followed behind and was amazed that although he could reach out and touch him he could barely hear Hanshee move. Once they reached the top Ray observed that the ground did indeed level out. They proceeded several feet farther before they were able to safely stand. From there Ray could see what Hanshee had referred to.

There were piles of stones of several sizes, scattered all over the hillside. Among them were slabs of stone almost whole and standing upright, but most were toppled and broken into pieces. Ray cast his glance on those closest to him and was surprised at how much they resembled headstones from the graveyards that dotted his home city. However, the ones before him were so old that he couldn't be sure there were ever any markings of any kind on them. In the center of these piles of crumbling stone were two slabs of white stone, one about eight feet long and not quite three feet wide. The other was slightly smaller.

Those must be the altars Hanshee mentioned, thought Ray, who immediately had visions of sacrifices - possibly even human sacrifices – having been made upon them.

As Hanshee led him through what now was little more than a field of debris, Ray noticed how different the summit of this hill was, not cone-shaped or ending in a peak, but like a shallow bowl turned upside down. It was as close to flat as one could imagine the top of a steep hill to be. Therein lay its danger. If there were indeed trails to be found, men on horseback could pursue them to the very top of this hill and the small piles of stone would provide little cover from swords, axes, and arrows.

"This way, Way-Mon!" Hanshee encouraged Ray to follow him as he quickly made his way through and between the crumbling monuments.

As they passed the largest altar Ray felt an urge and stretched out his hand, allowing his fingers to trace across the top of the smooth stone. A chill coursed through his body and he allowed his hand to slip from its edge. He quickened his pace to keep up with Hanshee.

Reaching the other side of the "graveyard," as Ray thought of it, they could see the path that approached from the left. It began, or ended, depending on one's perspective, at the edge of the hilltop and wound its way downward, disappearing around the curve of the hill.

"Their path," said Hanshee, as Ray took a step toward the path. "If you would not meet them head on, follow me." He started down toward the edge of the graveyard but away from the path. The side of the hill here was as steep as he had become accustomed to, with enough vegetation and jutting rocks to make it possible to descend. Hanshee carefully started down its side. Ray watched closely, noting the hand and footholds Hanshee used, before following him down.

Ray was never comfortable with heights, but it helped that the sides of these hills were not of a pitch that would cause a fall if he were to lose his grip. It could result in a painful slide down the hillside for a distance, which could be avoided if he kept his wits and managed to find another hand or foot hold as he slid.

Because of his uneasiness with heights, he refrained from looking to the bottom of the hill, scanning only the space immediately about him. Once, he looked over his shoulder at the hill beyond this one. He assumed they would scale it once they reached its base. He thought he saw a path leading to its top much like the one providing access to the horsemen on this hill. He knew if he saw it Hanshee must be aware of it also. This might complicate things even more, but for now, they had no other place to go but the adjacent hill. Once there they could hopefully come up with another path to avoid their pursuers.

Climbing down carefully but quickly, they descended to the place where the two hills adjoined and started up the second hill, the higher of the two. They were halfway to its summit when they heard, and then saw, the mounted guardsmen almost at the top of the first hill, near the graveyard. Hanshee's first instinct was to freeze and trust that their lack of movement would hide them against the rocks and the much thinner brush that covered this hill. The problem was that if they failed to move and were still spotted from the top of the other hill, they would be just at the edge of the range of a good archer. With that thought in mind, Hanshee made the decision to push for the top.

CHAPTER 20

The path up the hill was obviously ancient; its base overgrown with so much brush and debris as to be almost indistinguishable from the terrain that surrounded it. The men from Thessilli had earned a bit of respect from the members of the Aggipoor garrison for its discovery. It proved to be much wider than first expected, almost akin to a road, with the flat white stones used in its paving still visible in some places. Over time they had been displaced by the roots of vegetation and covered by debris falling from the hillside above. Along with the slope, these combined to make a difficult ride to the top. The captain bade the Thessillians to lead the way, and at many points the two men had to draw their swords and blaze a trail through brush that impeded their progress.

About three hundred feet along its way, and well out of sight of the bottom, the trail divided. The path to the left crossed a small patch of level ground before merging with and ascending a still higher hill. The captain kept his men on the path leading to the right and continued up the hill they were climbing. He wondered if he had made the correct decision in ordering them to climb to the top of this hill, but he had it on the word of his tracker, and of the noses of the fabled hounds of Thessilli, that this was the hill the killers had chosen to climb.

When they finally reached the top the horsemen had no stomach for exploring the sparse maze of ruins they saw there. Instead they dismounted while the hounds did their work. The men were hardly out of the saddle when the hounds caught the scent of the two that they sought. They followed it from the central monuments where they picked it up, to the edge of the hilltop opposite the path. The captain hurried over to inspect the ground where the two had apparently begun their descent. He stared down the steep hillside and then allowed his gaze to rise as he scanned the taller hill before him.

"There!" the captain cried out, pointing to a spot near the crest of the other hill.

The others looked and could just make out two figures patiently making their way upward. The captain estimated they were at least a hundred feet from the summit. As he continued to scan the hill he saw what appeared to be another trail leading up to its top. As he observed it, the trail seemed to wind its way upward before it forked halfway up the hillside. The fork that continued to the right, the easiest for his eye to follow, snaked its way upward and appeared to end very close to where the two would crest the summit. The fork that continued to the left disappeared around that side of the hill.

The captain considered all that was before him, and what he already knew, as he devised a strategy to contain and capture the killers. But his men must move quickly.

"Able," he called out to one of his men near the rear of the line.

One of the guardsmen sprang to his feet upon hearing his name.

"Hurry down to the base and assemble the four riders we left there. When they are ready, lead them up the trail to the first fork. There take the left fork. That should lead you to the next hill over there." The captain pointed at the hill the assassins were still climbing. "When you get there, again take the fork to the left. It should lead you to the other side of the hill.

"Be on your guard!" the captain continued. "I expect either you, or I leading these others, to run into those two. At the least, one of us will drive them into the other. Do not let them pass! I want them alive if possible, but they have proven themselves dangerous. If you cannot capture them alive, do not fail to collect their heads! Now hurry, man! We haven't much daylight left!"

Able sprinted to where he had left his mount, leaped upon its back, and urged the beast down the hill toward those who had been left to care for the wounded.

"Tracker, you stay here and watch that hill," the captain said. "If I am correct, their only escape will be in attempting to descend the same way they went up. If they do I want you to signal. Do you still carry your horn?

"I do," the tracker said.

"Give a blast if they start back down," said the captain. "Everyone else, follow me!

• • • •

Hanshee and Ray had reached the summit of the hill and both were showing signs of wear at the quick descent and hard climb they had just completed. Hanshee stood and scanned the layout of the hilltop which stretched before them while Ray took a little extra time to catch his breath and rest his aching muscles.

While this hilltop was not as level as the other, it was not an unblemished peak of raw stone either. Hanshee looked to his left for the trail that he knew breached the hilltop there and observed that it continued across several hundred feet, ending at what appeared to be a huge stone wall that faced east, toward where he now stood. This wall was not a construct, but rather appeared to have been carved to its present shape from one huge stone that had been imbedded on this hilltop for millennia. Before the wall was another altar of stone, not as dazzlingly white as were the two on the other hill. Hanshee first looked to Ray to make sure he was all right, and then began to walk toward the altar and the wall just beyond it. By the time Ray got to his feet, Hanshee was standing and staring at the wall as if in a trance

As Ray went to stand beside Hanshee, he saw what had captured his companion's attention.

The wall was covered from top to bottom and from side to side with drawings. Some were easily identified. There were representations of men, women, and children. There were also drawings of animals. Others were not so obvious. There was one that could be a symbol for water, and another that could be for mountains. Still others were symbols the meaning of which Ray had no clue. The whole thing resembled a large hieroglyphic mural but the story being told was a mystery to both Ray and Hanshee. Still Hanshee stared.

"These writings are old," he finally said, referring to them as if they were a language and not simply art. "I have seen many like them near the summit of the Blue Mountains where dwell the Elder Priests of the People of the Earth."

"Your people," Ray stated.

"Yes," replied Hanshee. "The Elders oversee the training of the Maiyochi. They make the choice and perform the holy ceremonies. They are by far the wisest of my people. I was taught to respect such as these," he waved a hand to encompass all that was on the wall before them, "no matter where it be found. It speaks of a people, and tells their story."

Ray was silent before this new, reverent side of Hanshee. As he continued to look at the wall and the various pictures and symbols drawn there, he thought he could feel some of what Hanshee must be feeling: a sense of curiosity, awe, and wonder. As he continued to study the drawings another strange feeling began to overtake him. It was the feeling that, given enough time, he would be able to understand what was being said here... the story that the people who made these drawings were trying to tell. He hardened his stare, trying to focus in on one figure, then another, but this did not help and the feeling of almost understanding diminished. This brought on feelings of frustration and with it the feeling of understanding disappeared entirely.

Ray turned his eyes away from the mural. Looking at the remainder of the hilltop and into the sky, he noticed the loss of daylight. The sun must already be behind the trees to the west. Soon it would be dark. He glanced back at Hanshee who was still entranced by the hieroglyphics, and turned a more relaxed gaze back to the wall.

Again the feeling of understanding was there.

He knew that if he were allowed to study this wall, and could maintain a calm mind, he would be able to interpret this for Hanshee. Why, in just a few moments...

The sound of hoof beats on hardened dirt and rocks brought them instantly from their stupor. Without hesitation Hanshee called for Ray and dashed to the other side of the wall. Here the ground sloped gently downward and away from the monument for a good distance until coming to an abrupt end at a drop much like others on these hills, one not so severe that a careful man could not make the climb but much too steep for a horse to manage. At the bottom of this sharp slope, about twelve feet down, was another trail. It was as wide as a road and wound around the hill from the left, ending just short of the hilltop in a wall of brush and rock off to their right. There was another sharp slope on the far side of the trail and far below, in the shadows of distant trees, Ray could see what looked like the flowing waters of a river.

"Go," said Hanshee as he pushed Ray toward the edge. "Soon they will be upon us. I will watch for them as you descend."

Ray's head was fairly spinning as the feeling of understanding the writing on the wall was snatched quickly away from him, but the present situation didn't allow for idle contemplation. This was a time for action. He immediately knelt, found a handhold, and began the short climb down the slope toward the road below.

The days of climbing steep hills had their effect. Ray now scampered down as if he had been doing it most of his life. He reached the road and looked up to Hanshee, waving his hand to signal that he had safely made it. Hanshee took another glance toward the stone wall before turning his attention to climbing down.

As Ray looked up at him, he saw Hanshee look to his left and watched as his eyes grew wide with surprise. Ray instinctively spun in that direction and he, too, was caught up in a wave of shock and surprise as he saw two men on horseback, no doubt two of the pursuing guardsmen, staring at him with the same look of surprise!

Without thinking, Ray took a step back from the slope, then another, placing himself in the center of the wide path that the horseman had been following. As he did so, the guardsman in the lead drew his sword and spurred his horse forward. His intent was clear. Ray had no doubt that the guardsman meant to kill him.

This is not my world, Ray thought, *or the kind of death I had imagined. I never thought I'd be killed by a guy with a sword, wearing armor and riding a horse.*

He wondered at the absurdity of these thoughts as he remained in the path of the oncoming guardsman, frozen both in fear and morbid fascination. He could see the sneer that curled the guardsman's lips. The bloodlust that consumed him at this unexpected opportunity was visible in his expression as he quickly closed the distance. Ray watched as the guardsman's right arm, his sword arm, drifted back in anticipation of delivering the killing stroke, but still he could not bring himself to move.

Ray continued watching as, only a moment from striking, the man was torn from his saddle by the force of the arrow that caught him high on the right side of his chest, sending him sprawling to the ground and over the edge of the path. Still frozen in place as he watched these events unfold before him, Ray suddenly found himself flying through the air after being grazed by the shoulder of the riderless horse as it barreled by him. He landed heavily, rolling after he hit the ground until he came to rest with the upper half of his body clinging to the path while his legs dangled over the edge of the slope.

Being thrown into this precarious position saved his life, as the second rider, closely following the first, leaned from his saddle and swung his sword downward toward where Ray had initially hit the ground. His sword missed by inches as Ray rolled toward the edge.

Fighting to catch his breath and clear his head, Ray now watched as the second rider pulled his horse up smartly and fairly leapt from the saddle. Ray thought the man would quickly finish him off, clinging as he was to the edge of a precipice, but instead the guardsman stepped briskly past him and toward Hanshee, who had made the climb down in record time and now stood astride the road with his own sword in hand.

Ray was poised to witness yet another demonstration of the savagery of this strange land.

The guardsman, sword in his right hand and buckler on his left forearm, approached Hanshee with long, swift strides. There was no hesitation as he stepped forward and into a vicious thrust aimed at the center of Hanshee's chest. Hanshee, gripping his sword in his right hand with the blade toward the ground, brought it swiftly across his body right to left, in a parry of the deadly thrust. Though successful, this left him exposed as the guardsman, never breaking stride, slammed into him with his shield and sent him stumbling backwards. As Hanshee struggled to regain his balance, the guardsman closed with another determined stride and thrust with all of his might toward Hanshee's exposed midsection. He was supreme in his confidence that the killer now stumbling before him, one of the now famed assassins of Aggipoor, would be spitted on the end of his blade.

What Ray saw was an apparently off-balance Hanshee instantly regain his footing and again use his sword to parry the blow, this time left to right, bringing him outside the guardsman's extended right arm as the fellow followed through on his thrust. Off of the same motion he used to parry the thrust, Hanshee then executed a lightning fast spin of three-hundred-sixty degrees that placed him slightly behind the guardsman whose body was still extended in his follow-through. Hanshee never even looked back as he came out of his spin with a backwards and downwards slash of his blade, laying open the back of the guardsman's left thigh, cleanly severing the tissue down to the bone.

The guardsman collapsed onto his right knee, unable to bend his injured left leg now extended behind him. No sooner did he go down than he felt the metal of Hanshee's blade at his neck.

Hanshee's words were unrecognizable to the downed warrior but Ray, brought sharply to his senses by the violence playing out before him, instantly translated.

"He says to drop your blade and your shield!" Ray shouted in the language of Aggipoor.

The guardsman instantly released his grip on his sword, casting it to his right as he continued to use that hand to prop himself up.

Hanshee spoke again and again Ray translated.

"And your shield!"

The guardsman had been using his shield to steady himself. Now he pushed it away and balanced himself on his two hands and one good knee, his bloody and useless left leg still extended behind him.

When the man was weaponless Hanshee grabbed him by his hair and, keeping his blade to his neck, half lifted and half dragged him over the path toward his downed, but still living, fellow. The guardsman struggled to get his good leg under him as he was roughly propelled across the distance. He finally sprawled down where he was thrown: in front of his comrade who still carried Hanshee's arrow protruding from his upper chest.

The guard with the injured leg looked up at Hanshee in pain and confusion. Hanshee motioned with his sword toward the other who was still clinging to the edge of the drop with his one good arm and digging in with his feet to keep from sliding down the slope. This time there was no need for a translator. The guardsman reached out his hand and grasped the other in an attempt to pull him up and onto the road.

While the guardsman was pulling at his partner, Hanshee quickly moved over to Ray and kneeled down beside him.

"Are you injured?" Hanshee asked, concern in his voice.

"No. I don't think so," Ray replied.

"Good." Hanshee said as he re-sheathed his sword into the scabbard on his back, slid the dropped medicine bag onto his shoulder, and retrieved the bow and the quiver of arrows.

"We must continue downward from here," he said. "Now," he said pointedly, when Ray hesitated. He turned and looked up toward the crest of the hill as Ray began to look for hand and foot holds in the quickly failing light. Satisfied that they had not yet been seen from above, Hanshee followed Ray over the edge. Together they carefully made their way downward toward the river.

It took them a while but, although they eventually heard a commotion from above as the other guardsmen arrived and found the two wounded men, there was no outcry that would indicate anyone had seen them as they made their descent.

As they approached the water Hanshee directed Ray to his right, where there was a small sandbank bordering an accumulation of driftwood. Once there, Hanshee set about freeing a large log with the remains of some branches still attached. The wood had been out of the water for some time and the heat of the sun had sufficiently dried it out until it weighed a fraction of what it had when it first fell. Nevertheless it took both Hanshee and Ray, pushing with all of their might, to get it back into the water. When they were sure it would float,

Ray watched as Hanshee tied his medicine bag to the stump of a limb that protruded high above the water. Then they both took a good hold of their makeshift raft, and began to float off into the darkness.

As they pushed past the river's edge they felt the current take over and begin to propel them downstream, away from the skillful tracker, away from the fabled hounds of Thessilli, and away from the stubborn guardsmen of Aggipoor who now had two more wounded to care for.

• • •

As the morning sun was cresting the eastern horizon, a tired and cold Ray looked downstream and took in the sight of the old bridge they had warily traversed only six days ago. It seemed like months, but the perfect timing of the rising sun to their arrival here was more than enough to bring smiles to the faces of the two soaked and weary fugitives.

Pushing, pulling, and kicking, they managed to guide the log close to the bank just upstream from the bridge. There Hanshee caught and held fast to a tree root while still holding onto an extended branch of the log, then he pulled until he had their makeshift vessel up against the bank. Ray climbed up first, but only after untying Hanshee's "magic pouch" and throwing it into the thick vegetation along the riverbank. Once he was out of the water, he turned and extended his hand to help Hanshee up onto the bank. Both travelers now safe on the bank of the river, Ray watched as Hanshee used his foot to re-launch their hasty conveyance back into the current to continue its voyage downstream into the unknown.

"We came this far in one night," said Ray. "How much time do you think we have before they find our trail?"

"Their horses cannot follow in the river," said Hanshee, searching for and finding his medicine pouch.

Ray heard in this statement a comment on his concerns when he first learned that mounted men pursued them. A half-smile found its way to his lips and he nodded at Hanshee in recognition of his chastisement.

"Horsemen must pursue us over land," continued Hanshee. "They must go back the way they came or find a new trail down the east bank. And now they have two more wounded to care for."

Hanshee turned to Ray with a broad smile of satisfaction on his face.

"They are many days behind us now," he said.

"Yeah," Ray agreed. "It took them five days to get up there. We've seen how they carry their wounded. Every man except the captain will be weighed down now."

The pair carefully waded through the thick vegetation of the riverbank and soon stepped once again upon the road at the spot where they first crossed the bridge. Ray thought it ironic that they walked the same ground they had tread earlier, stopping at the same place where they had briefly camped five nights ago. Here Hanshee freed himself of his bow and quiver, his pouch, and his weapon harness.

Ray waited patiently for Hanshee to finish before addressing him. He wanted to watch Hanshee's eyes as he asked his next question.

"Did you wound those last two on purpose?"

"When I released the arrow," Hanshee said, straightening up and looking Ray in the eyes, "it was meant to kill. The guardsman was fortunate."

"What about the swordsman?" Ray pressed.

"Wounded," Hanshee replied, "to further burden them."

Ray considered this response for a moment before responding. "So, you're really that good?"

"I am Maiyochi," Hanshee said blandly, as if informing Ray that water was wet.

"Okay," said Ray. "One more question. Do you think we can risk a fire? I need to warm up and dry off."

"Yes," said Hanshee, as he reclined with his back against a sweet gum tree. "Make us a fire."

CHAPTER 21

Ray struggled to climb the few remaining feet to the ledge where Hanshee stood. This was his hardest climb of the last several days. Though not as steep, this slope was much higher than any they had encountered in the foothills.

There were, however, short sections that were almost vertical.

A fall from one of these vertical sections usually only meant a drop of eight or nine feet onto a wide, stable shelf. The average climber hanging from the ledge could let go and drop neatly to his feet with no fear of injury. But a series of these vertical walls, set between thirty to forty-foot spans of steep slopes with inclines of varying degrees, added up to a continuous climb that was long and grueling.

Hanshee had been deliberate in his choice of this spot to climb. The rock face here did not support as much vegetation as the earlier foothills, so the climb was more difficult. This feature, along with its height, meant that men armed and provisioned as their pursuers had been would think twice and maybe three times before attempting to follow them up here. For men thus armed and provisioned, and on horseback, pursuit up these slopes would be impossible.

Hanshee led the way and had blazed a trail, so Ray knew which hand and foot holds were secure. Still his muscles, especially those in his forearms, ached from the strain of such a long and arduous climb.

Ray was now on the verge of topping a fifteen-foot wall of rock, the last and tallest of the vertical walls

As he held on with the ends of his fingers, his left boot sought the foothold that he knew was there. His forearms throbbed and his frustration grew as his foot found only the rough surface of the cliff side with nothing to brace against. Ray hugged the rock wall much harder than was needed and didn't dare to look down. He knew that if he saw how high he was above the ledge below he might lose his nerve and call out for Hanshee to help him up. It would be a shame after having come so close to reaching the top unaided.

There!

He found the foothold and, with a sigh of relief, relaxed his death grip on the rocks to either side of his head. After a moment's rest he braced against the new foothold and pushed up far enough to grasp the edge of the ledge on which Hanshee stood. Using what he imagined to be his last ounce of strength he hauled himself onto the ledge, rolled his body away from the edge, and lay there gasping for breath, proud of himself but still staring an indictment at his companion who had offered no help.

Hanshee continued to scan the forest spread out to the east below them. Then, as if feeling Ray's accusing eyes upon him, he spoke.

"You did well," he said, without turning from his survey of the forest.

Ray had to smile and shake his head. He had just received about the nicest compliment to escape Hanshee's lips in all their time together. He hoped this meant that his stoic host was finally warming up to him. He figured it also meant that Hanshee felt at ease with the distance they had put between themselves and their pursuers.

As he pushed himself to a sitting position against the back wall of the broad ledge, Ray allowed his mind to wander back to the days following their hasty exit from the city of Aggipoor and the chase that had ensued.

Zigzagging through the forest, laying false trails, placing every obstacle between themselves and the pursuing guardsmen, they had made their way to the rugged foothills which lay to the northeast. Once there they dared to hope, but never really believed, that they had done enough to have finally lost those who followed.

Twice during the pursuit they had spied the armed men before they themselves were confronted. Twice there had been a confrontation and twice more Hanshee had saved his life.

The last three days had been a mad dash, a straight line to the northwest, toward the cliffs they had just climbed. They had started the climb a little after first light and now, in the glorious light of a sun halfway to its peak, they looked out onto the forest that had become the prison of those who had sought to hunt them down and end their lives.

Ray let his head turn from shoulder to shoulder, taking in the entire view, and realized that, after days of hardship, stress, and conflict, they were finally free.

"Even if they were to find our trail, it could take many days just to find a path up here for their horses," he said.

"Is there a path?" Hanshee asked with a sly grin, as he turned and led the way from the rocky ledge, across the upper face of the cliff and onto the wooded slopes that awaited them. There was no rush now, no need to watch every step. And though they were accustomed to moving stealthily through the forest, it no longer felt like a matter of life and death.

The trail they traversed still led upwards but the slopes were now more like gentle hills and the going was much easier. They made good time and traveled deeper into the woods than they had to before finding a suitable spot beside a mountain stream to make camp. They were on the edge of a grove of pines that grew far enough apart to let a generous amount of sunshine reach the thick layer of needles covering the ground.

Here they took stock of their persons and supplies. Feeling the dirt and grime of several days on the trail without time for hygiene, both men relished an opportunity to bathe in the cold, clear water.

Ray had been left with the impression that Hanshee's people, though forest dwellers, cared deeply about cleanliness. As they had traveled, he noticed that Hanshee often took time to clean his teeth with a twig or leaf. He never let the dust and dirt of the forest accumulate on his person, bathing whenever water and opportunity were available. He had also rubbed the oils of certain plants into his skin, which had taken on a deep brown glow and, except for the scars of battles past, was unblemished. Ray had picked up some of Hanshee's practices and had found early on that the oils of the plants which they rubbed into their skin were natural repellents to the hordes of insects that would otherwise feast on them.

Despite Ray's careful observation some of Hanshee's secrets were still just that: secrets.

He had never seen Hanshee shave, yet his face remained hairless. Even his head, except for the single braid, was as bald today as when he first laid eyes upon him at the riverbank. Whatever Hanshee's secret, Ray wished he had it. His own hair, both on his face and his head, was now into its second month without attention. The itching had been terrible when the beard was first growing in, but this settled down after a while. Now his facial hair was full, as was his 'fro,' and he was startled and amused when he saw his reflection on the surface of the water.

After a good scrubbing with the sand and gravel at the bottom of the stream, he approached Hanshee for a solution to his problem. Hanshee examined his face and head before drawing his knife from its scabbard. In no time at all he had reduced the pile of hair on Ray's head to so much fuzz. Then he started in on the facial hair, a much more delicate undertaking. Ray survived with only a few cuts, but in the end his beard and mustache were no more.

Then Hanshee reached into his medicine pouch and pulled out a smaller leather pouch containing a brown powdery substance. He mixed a small portion of this with some water until it had attained the consistency of a paste, which he then spread on Ray's face and neck. The cool, creamy compound felt good on his freshly shaved skin, but the cooling relief soon gave way to a fire the likes of which Ray had never felt. Unsure of whether it was supposed to burn like that Ray's first instinct was to stoically "take it like a man." Then the pain truly kicked in and he realized that exercising his manhood was not an option.

Chest heaving in breath after deep breath, eyes wide with alarm, he looked wildly around to find Hanshee for instructions on what to do next. He found him, doubled up on the ground, laughing as he had never seen him laugh before. Ray wanted to ask him what was so damn funny, and what he should do about this horrible burning paste on his face; wanted to... *HOLY SHIT, THIS STUFF IS HOT!*

Without consciously willing it, Raymond found himself sprinting for the water where he dove into the deepest part of the stream face first. His hands flailed at his head, cheeks and neck until the terrible paste was gone, and still he flailed as if trying to push the cold water into his skin. After a while the burning subsided and with it the thrashing. Ray stood chest-deep in the water, gulping down huge breaths of air. His relief was palpable as he stood there, with goose bumps forming on his skin.

Now he was cold, but he didn't care.

Gently he reached up to touch the sensitive skin that had been exposed to the paste. He was a little surprised when his hand came away bloodless. Then he felt again, and this time the smoothness was what startled him. The paste had removed all traces of hair and, despite the vicious burning, had left his skin undamaged.

As he turned toward the bank, Ray found Hanshee still lying on the ground, an amused look on his face, chuckling every now and then.

Hanshee, the practical joker.

This was a new side to him, one Ray wouldn't have thought possible a few days ago. The laughter was contagious, as all lighthearted laughter is, and Ray found himself chuckling along as he waded to the bank and stepped out of the stream.

"How does it feel now?" Hanshee asked.

"That burned like the fires of hell!" was Ray's reply.

"But your skin, it is smooth?"

"I admit," said Ray, "it's as smooth as it's ever been."

"It will not begin to grow back for three moons," said Hanshee, holding up three fingers for emphasis.

"Three months?" said Ray incredulously. "If I were home I could make a fortune off of this stuff. Of course I'd dilute it first."

The quizzical look on Hanshee's face told Ray that this last comment was wasted on him. He shook off the water and sat down on a rock in the sun, letting the bright rays warm and dry his skin. He glanced back at Hanshee, who had busied himself cleaning and sharpening his knife, then turned inward to the thoughts that had come to the surface again.

Home.

He hadn't thought of it for a while, which was surprising now that he realized it. As bizarre as his current situation was, and "bizarre" was an understatement, he found himself acclimating at a rate well beyond what he thought he was capable of. The sudden change of environment, of reality really, should have driven him mad. When he reflected on all he had done and seen since waking up in this strange place, Ray could only shake his head in wonder.

He looked to Hanshee, to prove to himself that it wasn't all a dream, and found his companion readying himself to rest.

They had escaped death in Aggipoor and escaped capture in the forest beyond, but there had been little time for rest while eluding their pursuers. They had snatched bits of sleep when and where they could and, by Ray's reckoning, had not slept soundly in at least forty-eight hours. They had finally scaled the cliff walls and found these quiet woods and this peaceful mountain stream. It was time to rest.

Ray stretched out on his rock, in his little patch of sunlight, and felt the warmth seep into his body as he slipped into unconsciousness.

They camped at the mountain stream for the next several days, building their strength and replenishing their supplies. Hanshee had found a fertile pool a few hundred feet upstream and they had fresh fish as often as they liked. Game was plentiful too, and if this had been a hunting trip they could have departed loaded down with skins and fresh meat. But they were traveling swiftly and therefore had to pack as light as possible. Hanshee took the time to prepare a few of the best skins and dried the meat that they did not eat. Then he made a bundle of them for Ray to carry when the time came to leave.

* * *

They had now been in these mountains, known as the Ursal Mountains in the sister cities of Aggipoor and Thessilli, for a few weeks. In that time there had been a noticeable change in the weather. The warm days and slightly cooler nights of late summer were quickly coming to an end. The days were still warm enough, but the nights were growing steadily colder. The leaves of the trees were in the midst of turning from the deep green of summer to their vivid fall colors and Ray sometimes woke up expecting to find the foliage covered with frost.

For some time now he had to endure whatever nature sent his way, clothed in only his cargo shorts, khaki shirt, wool socks, and hiking boots. This had not been much of a problem initially, as the temperatures had been mild and the rains had been few and mostly light. Now, after more than two months in the wild, his clothes, or what was left of them, were getting threadbare. They were still adequate for coverage, not so much for comfort. Hanshee should have really been suffering, dressed as he was in little more than a loincloth and sandals, but he seemed not to be bothered by the variances in the weather. Neither the heat of the plateau above the city, nor the cool mornings of these mountains, seemed to matter much to him. He simply endured, without complaint, anything that nature served up.

Ray had noticed that their journey had taken a southern turn, following the slope of the mountain range rather than the up and over route.

Hanshee was keenly aware of the coming change of season and their requirements in this environment. He had originally crossed these mountains in the early summer, "four moons ago" by his reckoning. He had been alone then and could move swiftly, as much as twenty miles in a day, depending on the terrain. And these forests were much like those of his home, though not as dense. It had been no problem for someone of his upbringing. Ray knew he was slowing Hanshee down. He suspected that the change of direction, hopefully toward a more temperate climate, was mostly for his benefit. For this reason he was determined to keep pace, no matter how hard Hanshee pushed, and to never complain.

Hanshee took note of the new resolve he saw in Ray's eyes, taking it as a good sign. It meant Ray had made some sort of peace with his present situation and was ready to take seriously the struggles that lay ahead. Hanshee did not want to disappoint, so he increased the tempo of their journey. The faster they moved, the sooner they would escape these highlands. And escape they must, before the full force of winter came down upon them.

Hanshee took every opportunity to teach Ray more about his surroundings and how to best make use of them. Ray's new receptive frame of mind made him a willing vessel into which Hanshee poured knowledge about nature and the different challenges it had to offer, about his people and their long and storied history, even a little about himself.

Ray had seen Hanshee as a stoic warrior, a dealer of death both swift and awful. He'd seen Hanshee as a leader, a master of strategy and tactics. Then there was Hanshee the wise, a healer and teacher; even Hanshee the joker, as he had been by the stream. Now he began to put these different facets of his companion into focus. This revealed a much more competent and complicated individual than Ray had initially considered him to be. A man who, though immersed in the trials of survival, was capable of experiencing the simple pleasures to the fullest: the beauty of a wild orchid, the rejuvenating warmth of the morning sun, a hearty laugh at the expense of some butt of a joke, even if it is Hanshee himself.

This contrasted greatly with the practical Hanshee, the survivor, who could analyze a situation, formulate a plan and implement it with deadly precision, all at a moment's notice. These different sides of him seemed to strike a balance. It made Ray think of the samurai of feudal Japan, those fabled warriors who could appreciate the delicacy of stroke needed to create fine art equally as well as the skill and strength needed for a single-stroke decapitation.

Hanshee, the samurai.

CHAPTER 22

The first arrow whistled through the air and imbedded itself into the tree trunk with a loud THWACK!

Hanshee froze in his tracks, correctly surmising that an archer who could put an arrow into a tree two feet before his face at a distance great enough to remain concealed could just as easily have put it through his head.

Ray's reaction was entirely different.

The sound of the arrow striking the tree shocked him away from his idle contemplation and straight into the here and now. The sight of the arrow still quivering in the tree up ahead brought his fight-or-flight instinct to the fore. Before he even realized it, Ray had spun on his heels to run back the way they had just come. He was pulled up short by a second arrow, which was sent into the trunk of a tree about three feet in front of him. Quickly he turned again, his eyes frantically seeking Hanshee for some idea of what to do. Hanshee had turned to examine the placement of the second arrow. It confirmed his first estimate of the skill of the archer. Satisfied that there was no immediate danger, he stood his ground and waited.

Ray was dumbfounded and was about to protest, but Hanshee cut him off with a raised hand.

"The archer did not miss," Hanshee said.

After a brief consideration Ray concluded that this was true, but he still crouched low to cover the few steps that separated him from Hanshee to wait for whoever it was who had chosen to make their presence known in this way. They did not wait long.

Hanshee and Raymond had been walking a narrow game path when the arrows struck, and now before and behind them on the path stood a pair of archers.

They were dressed in dull grey tunics that fell to just above their knees. Their leggings were like sandals, but with laces which wound up the calf. The laces held furs in place around their lower legs. These were worn for either protection, warmth, or both. Also for warmth, each man wore a greenish-grey cloak of woven cloth. On their heads were helmets of leather-lined metal, and at their sides were scabbards holding short swords. Each pair also held bows with arrows notched but not yet drawn.

Their faces were those of competent men who know their duty and would not shirk it. They were lean and hard, and their piercing eyes never left the persons of Hanshee and Raymond, looking for strengths, or weaknesses, or an excuse to send their next arrows whistling into warm targets.

Hanshee took all of this in with a glance. He understood that these four were here to ensure the safety of, and command respect for, whoever had ordered their detainment.

As the moments grew longer, Hanshee turned to face the dense foliage to the left of the foreword pair and watched as another man emerged and regarded him.

He was dressed similarly to the archers, but carried no bow. Instead, his wide belt provided room for a short sword, a hand axe, and three or four knives of varying types. He was noticeably shorter than the others. Nevertheless, he carried himself with a confident air that left no doubt that it was he who was in charge here. He approached to within ten feet of Raymond and Hanshee, followed closely by the two archers. He took his time looking the travelers up and down. Then he barked out orders to the two archers behind him.

"Take their weapons, and bring them along," he said.

Upon hearing their speech, Hanshee was slightly taken aback. He was not sure, but thought that their language seemed to have some elements similar to his own.

Three of the archers trained their notched arrows on the captives, while the fourth stepped forward, motioning to Hanshee in a way that communicated his wishes. Hanshee did not need to understand the words spoken to know what was expected. The situation spoke for itself. Seemingly without concern he passed his bow and quiver, as well as his harness, which held sword and knife, and his pouch into the archer's outstretched hand. The archer then searched Ray and his bundle for weapons. Finding none, he dismissed him with a look of contempt.

Hanshee's weapons now secured, the other archers parted to let their leader step between them, then closed rank and followed, motioning for Hanshee and Ray to fall in. This was done as one of the archers fell in behind them, while the fourth used his knife to remove the two arrows from the trees before joining his brethren in a rear guard.

They stayed on the game trail for about another hour before the leader led them off and to the right. Here was an incline of about sixty feet to the ridgeline above. The two captives were made to wait at the bottom until the leader and the two archers had reached the top. Then, with arrows again notched and at the ready, they motioned for the four who remained to make their ascent. This was all done without a word, and spoke of a high degree of training and discipline.

This was not lost on Hanshee, who had placed these five as soldiers from the uniformity of their dress. He now revised his opinion: these were *well-trained* soldiers.

At the top of the ridgeline Hanshee could see that the land again fell away, this time at a gentler angle. This appeared to be a small valley, with fewer trees around the slopes and more dense forest toward its center. The six stood their ground and, from the floor of the valley, were silhouetted against the sky and the treetops. The leader kept an eye peeled toward the dense trees below and, when satisfied, led the group down toward the valley floor.

Ray and Hanshee had been silent since their capture. Ray's silence was born of fear and uncertainty. Hanshee's was of concentration. He was observing their captors and everything he could about their situation, making mental notes of the way they had come, and checking the forest for signs of other people. He was not alarmed when, as they approached the trees, he saw the figures of others dressed similar to those who escorted them awaiting their arrival.

Hanshee stole a quick glance at Ray. Though he seemed calm enough considering the situation, Hanshee knew that panic was just below the surface. As they descended the slope, Hanshee inched closer and spoke in a soft voice. "We are safe for now. Remain calm and do as I do."

Ray had been taken aback by the five that had captured them, and his apprehension had risen when he saw others among the trees they were approaching. The lack of fear in Hanshee's eyes and the confidence in his voice were welcome and served to steady him. He saw how Hanshee walked tall and proud, head held high, eyes piercing, and lips pulled back in what was almost a sneer. He was showing his captors that, though currently captured, he was not a captive. Ray took heart from this display and, knowing he could not match it, he still managed to lift his head a bit higher, set his jaw, and harden his gaze. Whatever happened, he would try his best to face it as did Hanshee: like a warrior.

They passed through an outer ring of trees and found themselves approaching a military encampment. Before and around them were many soldiers involved in the various duties necessary to sustain a large armed force. Some were cleaning and sharpening their weapons. These were many and varied, but consisted mostly of different styles of swords and axes, along with knives and arrows. Others were repairing equipment or clothing. There were those who were busy preparing the skins of game which had been taken earlier. Still others had formed small groups to talk and some were simply resting, having recently been relieved of guard or reconnaissance duty.

All eyes turned to the captives as they were led into the midst of the soldiers. Most were gazes of curiosity, while a few looked on with undisguised hostility. As they approached, a particularly surly-looking fellow cleared his nose and let fly with a healthy wad of phlegm which landed in the dust of Hanshee's approaching feet. He grinned wickedly as Hanshee gave him a nasty glare. It was a look that said the insult was noted and would not be forgotten.

Moving farther along, they approached the center of the encampment where there were three large tents.

The first tent consisted of a high, peaked roof, its highest point an opening to let the smoke from the cooking fires beneath escape. Open on all sides, Ray could see several men inside busily butchering meat and cutting up vegetables for the stew pots that were atop the fires. There was food aplenty, as others used what must be portable ovens to bake breads, and still others roasted meat on open flames.

Beside this tent was another, this one enclosed. What went on inside was anyone's guess, but as Ray watched, two men with what appeared to be large scrolls under their arms approached and entered.

The third, and largest, could only be the command tent. It stood at the very center of the encampment, its peaked roof rising high into the trees above, with its center pole supporting a banner of emerald and gold beneath a slightly larger banner of crimson and gold. Here they were brought to a halt.

The leader stepped forward and spoke briefly with one of the two armed guards who stood to either side of the entrance flap. The sentries looked the captives up and down before one of them ducked inside the flap, leaving Ray and Hanshee to soak up the stares of the curious while they waited for whoever was within. Moments later the sentry reappeared and resumed his post just outside the entrance. Ray expected that he would be followed closely by someone in command but as the minutes passed it became clear that whatever was going on inside the tent was of more importance than the capture of two strangers.

Both captives and captors were showing signs of impatience when a rustle of the tent flap announced the end of their wait. As they watched, two figures emerged. They were tall men who, by their proud carriage, appeared accustomed to commanding respect.

One was a warrior; that much was obvious.

He was dressed as were the others around him, in a tunic of heavy greenish-gray cloth bound at the waist by a thick leather belt. Two things set him apart from the other warriors present. The first was his feet. Instead of the sandals of the common soldiers, he wore fine boots of good leather, the turned-down tops of which stopped just below his powerful calves.

The second clue to his position of authority was his weapon: a short sword which hung in the scabbard suspended from his belt. He wore this on his left hip with the handle protruding slightly to the front, giving him room to grasp and remove it quickly and efficiently with either hand. Though it hung in a scabbard which had obviously seen much use, the weapon itself was unusually ornate. It sported a handle of fine polished wood darkened from years of handling. The richness of the wood was the perfect background for the gold and precious stones that had been expertly worked into the hilt. The gold was laid in strips which encircled the handle. There were seven that could be seen, with room remaining for about three more, given the same spacing as the others. At the very end of the hilt was a cluster of clear, sparkling stones, most probably diamonds, encircled with blood-red rubies, each with an individual setting of gold.

Hanshee took all this in with a glance, satisfied himself that this was the person of authority here, and shifted his attention from the clothes to the man.

He was tall, maybe half a head taller than Hanshee, with a broad, meaty face topped by tight curls of jet-black hair. His neck was thick with muscle and tapered down to broad shoulders that were equally well-muscled. The slight paunch above his belt was the result of years, not a lack of activity, as the obvious fitness of the man was further spelled out in the hardness of his burnished arms.

He assumed a wide stance, resting his left hand on the hilt of his short sword, and studied the two captives with hard eyes. He seemed to pay particular attention to their strange clothing as he listened to the report of the squad leader who had taken up a position beside the commander as soon as he stepped from the tent. A look of disinterest began to creep onto the commander's face after he determined that the two were not of a people that he knew. He started to give orders to the squad leader as to how he wanted them dealt with, only to be stopped short by the man beside him.

"Commander?"

The commander, unused to being interrupted, spun quickly toward the speaker, only to catch himself before issuing a rebuke. He could not treat a priest as he would a common foot soldier. Relaxing his demeanor, he acquiesced as the priest motioned him to step aside for a private consultation.

The priest was of equal height as the commander, but there the similarity ended.

Though he wore a dagger, its hilt bejeweled elaborately enough to rival the commander's short sword, it appeared to be more for ceremony than for practical use. It hung by a braided leather cord encircling the priest's neck, dangling down such that the equally ornate sheath came to rest against a belly protruding almost grotesquely from an otherwise slim frame. He was adorned in a long, flowing robe of the finest wool, dyed a pale yellow and richly embroidered in red, green, and purple patterns which gave it a festive yet dignified appearance. From beneath the hem of his robes the toes of soft leather slippers could be seen, footwear completely out of place in his present location.

He was bald, his head shaven as clean as his face. It was a narrow face in comparison with the commander's, with full lips and a nose which would be dominant if not for his eyes. Heavily lidded, they seemed custom made for expressing many of the darker emotions such as outrage, suspicion, condescension, and contempt.

Just for a moment they had shone with open surprise, even awe, as he first took in the sight of the two captives. Quickly hiding his initial reaction, the priest led the commander a few paces to one side and began to whisper insistently into his ear.

The commander glowered in irritation. He was a man unused to speaking in whispers before his officers and unused to deferring to anyone in this, his domain. But he was far from a fool, and he knew when it was best to listen. Once the priest had finished, he turned to his aide-de-camp officer and spoke.

"I hope our guests have suffered no mistreatment?"

The officer stiffened. "No, M'lord. They appear before you as they were found, but without their weapons."

"Good. They should remain unharmed," the commander said with a slight nod of his head toward the priest. "Make them comfortable," the commander continued. "See to their needs. Bring them to me at sundown."

"M'lord." the officer gave a curt nod and turned to give orders to a pair of soldiers, who led Hanshee and Ray toward a tree where water bags hung.

The commander and the priest watched them depart.

"They will be under guard until I say otherwise," the commander told the priest. "Now what could the priesthood find so intriguing about those two?"

The priest smiled slightly as he watched a soldier offer the captives water from one of the bags.

"We are grateful for your indulgence, Galin," he replied, "but please don't try to understand our motives or our methods. Our knowledge is vast. Be assured that, in the end, we all strive toward the same goal."

That is questionable, thought the commander, but he kept this thought to himself. No sense inflaming the priesthood when such a trivial request was so easily granted. He gave a curt nod and proceeded to the other tent where the men with the scrolls had entered. He disappeared into the darkness beyond its folds, followed closely by the priest.

• • •

Jusaan was the picture of calm as he sat in a corner of the tent of the map makers. His eyes were half shut and he appeared to be ready to drift away into a deep sleep at any moment. He sat away from the surveyors and the soldiers, who were busy going over several maps that documented the peaks and valleys which made up the southern portion of the mountain range where they currently camped. The soldiers argued among themselves about the lay of the land they had traversed, while the surveyors consulted their notes and measurements. This would continue until an agreement had been reached, only then would the map makers begin to reconcile the parchments with the prevailing view. Updating the maps was the purpose of this expedition, or so the naive would think.

Jusaan knew differently.

A mapping expedition would hardly require this many soldiers; almost one hundred and fifty if his count was correct. These were not just regulars but the closest to an elite group that Galin could put together. All were highly trained, battle hardened, and loyal to their commander. No, this expedition was more about scouting out the southern borders for expansion, for locating and exploiting potential southern trade routes, for identifying a probable base from which to launch an invasion of their neighbors to the southeast. It was for any, or all, of these things.

All of which was fine with Jusaan.

He bore no love for anyone in the surrounding lands. His was a priesthood much like the other aspects of his society, holding conquest to be one of the highest goals to which a civilized nation could aspire. His people were, after all, born to rule.

And rule they had, long ago…on a grand scale!

His people were born of a house that had at one time cast its shadow over all the lands they had known to exist. Of course those were ancient times. They had eventually learned, much to their consternation and woe, that there was much more to the world than they had been aware.

But even further back in his people's history, before the time of conquest and self-anointed nobility, the priesthood had been one of warriors. Who else to minister to warriors than warrior-priests, who could divine the will of The One on the left hand, and deal out his justice mercilessly with the right? His shaven head was a testament to those first of his ilk, as was the blade which was always on his person. He had little, if any, skill with it. His order had long ago given up the warrior's way for the influence and intrigues of a priesthood which held itself aloof from the concerns of the common people. Instead they had cultivated mysteries and ceremonies which assured them a revered status without being directly exposed to martial training and bloodshed, holding on to the hollow echo of their past with their shaved pates and ornate daggers.

But what he had seen this day had chilled him to the very core.

Before him had stood a vision of his past, of the priesthood from which he had evolved. Before him had stood, as if somehow the images on the ancient scrolls had been given flesh, a warrior-priest of old! It had taken all of his skill, every ounce of his considerable self-control, to stand before him without betraying the shock that he had felt.

Even as he sat calmly, feigning disinterest at the activity around him, his mind recreated the picture that had, only hours before, presented itself.

Here was a man of the wild, of nature, a man at home with natural things. His body was the carved image of strength and stamina, of muscle and sinew. His posture, even in his captive state, spoke nothing of subservience. His eyes were alert and confident, the windows to a nimble mind which was accessing all the variables of his situation. His demeanor was stoic as he calmly waited to see how he would be received and treated by these strangers.

Jusaan wondered what would have happened had he not interrupted Galin. The commander probably would have given the order to dispose of these two. The stranger's unflinching eyes, his proud carriage, his obvious unwillingness to be humbled, these were things that a man such as Galin could not abide.

Jusaan smiled as the thought came to him. *Sometimes Galin was so easy to read, so uncomplicated. But sometimes...*

Jusaan allowed his mind to wander to the other, the companion.

On the periphery of all that was happening, his image was just beginning to come into focus. A hair taller than the warrior-priest, lean and well-muscled as should be any who submitted to the life that they had chosen, he lacked the confident air that his companion possessed. He was a follower, not a leader. Probably an acolyte to the other, devoted to following his footsteps and learning his way.

His mind returned to the warrior-priest.

He must be brought before the Council!

Jusaan had no idea how and why these two were here, but oh, what good fortune that he had been present when they were found! If this one truly was what he appeared to be, and Jusaan had little doubt that he was, it could be seen as nothing less than an omen, a message from The One! Maybe it was time for the priesthood to take a more active role in the overall ambitions of their people, and for him to assume a position of real leadership within the priesthood.

A lazy smile spread across Jusaan's face at this thought.

Oh, The One… he does move in mysterious ways!

CHAPTER 23

As the sun sank low on the western horizon, Hanshee and Ray were approached by one of the soldiers who motioned them to follow him. Both cautious and curious, they rose from their positions under the spreading oak and followed.

Hanshee had not failed to notice that, though not directly guarded, there had been soldiers positioned in various locations around them who had always found a reason for keeping at least one eye on the pair. A few of these followed in their wake as they were led toward the command tent.

They were brought to a halt before a small pit containing a fire which provided some warmth against the cool of the evening. Before the fire sat the commander with what must have been his senior officers spread out to his right. To his left sat the other - *a priest maybe? He has the look,* thought Hanshee - along with two others similarly adorned in rich robes and soft leather slippers. As Hanshee and Ray watched, these two, most likely servants of the priest, rose from their positions on his left and motioned for Hanshee and Ray to take their places. They did, completing a semi-circle around the fire that placed Ray at the three o'clock position to Galin's twelve.

Galin beckoned with his hand and soldiers appeared with goblets of wine matching the ones that the others enjoyed. Ray eyed his warily, while Hanshee brandished his and drank with gusto. As more junior officers joined the gathering, Galin again motioned and platters of meats and breads appeared. The officers, and even the priest, threw themselves into unabashed feasting in the loud and raucous way men so often do. As they ate and drank, stories and jokes began to flow. Men recited the doing of deeds, each more fantastic than the last, until the brazen lies brought forth a chorus of belly laughs from all within earshot.

As had happened before, Ray was quickly adapting to the language being spoken. He had ceased to question how this was possible, but now he understood almost every word that was said. He had to stifle a laugh at some of the more incredible proclamations. This went largely unnoticed, laughter being contagious in any society. Even Hanshee, who surprisingly was able to pick out some words and phrases from the conversation, found himself laughing for no other reason than that everyone else was.

But Ray knew better.

He had kept one eye on Hanshee, as instructed, through this whole ordeal and he saw the light behind Hanshee's eyes that never seemed to go off. Though he ate, and laughed, and appeared to greedily drink wine till it spilled from his chin, a part of him was always alert and wary. Hanshee was assessing the situation, sizing up the men around him, always preparing to survive.

There was another at the fire who saw this for what it was. Galin knew that Hanshee only pretended to let his guard down. He knew it instinctively. He knew it because he had often used such tactics to fathom the secrets of friend, rival, and enemy alike.

This one may bear watching, Galin thought, as he took a deep drought of his wine which had, on his order, been watered down and served only to him.

During a lull in the feasting, Jusaan leaned over to Hanshee and spoke a phrase of a different language. Instantly Hanshee's eyes went wide and his head snapped toward the priest. Jusaan met his eyes and smiled as Hanshee replied in the same tongue. Jusaan then went back to his meal, having now confirmed what before he had only suspected.

Ray saw the exchange and leaned toward Hanshee with a question.

"What was that about?"

Hanshee, having regained his composure, replied. "He spoke to me in my own tongue."

Ray's brow furrowed in surprise and he glanced over at the priest, who was smiling benevolently at the two of them.

When the platters of food had been removed and the feasting was over, Jusaan turned to Galin and spoke.

"I would ask your leave so that I may speak privately with our two guests," he said.

"They speak our language?" Galin asked, surprised.

"We of the priesthood are trained in many languages," Jusaan replied smoothly. "I believe I have found one in which we may converse on a limited basis."

Intensely curious but not wanting to alert the priest, Galin twisted his lips in a drunken smile, raised his goblet, and shouted, "Off with you then! My men have important drinking to do!"

This brought forth a chorus of laughs and cheers, to which Jusaan rose and took his leave, bidding Hanshee and Ray to follow.

Galin waited till they had left the clearing before discreetly making eye contact with one of his sergeants on the periphery of the group. A slight nod of his head and the man began to move in the same direction that the priest had taken, laughing and slapping backs as he went so that none were the wiser of his true intentions.

With his spy now moving into position to fulfill his duty, Galin again turned his attention to those still surrounding the fire. He could wait a few more hours to find out what interest the priest had in the strangers.

. . .

Jusaan led the small party behind the command tent. Hidden from view by the much larger tent was a smaller tent, the temporary dwelling of the priest. Jusaan stopped before the door flap and gave orders for his acolytes to wait outside and make sure that those within were not disturbed. One of them then stepped forward to hold back the flap, allowing the priest to lead Hanshee and Raymond into the dimly lit confines.

The interior smelled of rich oils and pungent incense, which blended in such a way as to bring to mind a pastry shop, or so

Raymond thought. Though not very broad, the dwelling was deep, and much larger than it appeared from outside. Jusaan led his two guests to the rear of the tent where there was a divan and several low stools. He motioned Hanshee to one end of the divan, taking the other end for himself. He motioned to the rug on the floor as a place for Raymond to sit. A look from Hanshee froze Raymond before he could make his displeasure known and he sank down onto the carpet, figuring that to follow Hanshee's lead was best for now.

Jusaan reached over to a table beside his bed and produced another flask of wine and two small goblets. He filled these with the contents of the flask, passing one to Hanshee and keeping the other for himself. He took a small sip and smiled, waiting for Hanshee to sample the contents of his cup. Hanshee smiled also, a half-drunken smile, as if feeling the effects of the feasting and the strong wine that he'd imbibed outside. He drained the small goblet with one swallow and then handed the empty cup to Ray without glancing in his direction, as he would to a servant. Ray, to his credit, took the cup without hesitation and placed it beside the flask on the table.

Jusaan then spoke to Hanshee, in Hanshee's own tongue.

"I am Jusaan," he said, "anointed priest of The One Spirit, sitting among the Council of Nine, of the nation of Pith."

Jusaan spoke these words with considerable pomp and authority. When Hanshee failed to look impressed he asked in a more subdued tone, "You…you have heard of us?"

"I have heard stories…" Hanshee said, his voice slightly slurred, "…vague tales of long ago, which spoke of the Pithians… those of the clan and tribe of Pith. But these were ancient tales, and none alive could speak to their truth," he lied.

"Then you are what I gather you to be, a warrior priest from my people's past. We are of a kind, you and I," said Jusaan.

When Hanshee did not respond, Jusaan went on.

"Where did you arrive from? Where are your people?"

"I am from afar," said Hanshee vaguely, swaying slightly. "I have not seen my people for seasons without end. I was sent into the World to wander, to learn, and to atone."

Jusaan pressed.

"How long have you wandered?" he asked. "Can you not say in what state your, or should I say 'our' people exist?"

Hanshee's eyes appeared to go dim, then sprang back to focus only to go dim again. He swayed, seeming to be forcing himself to sit upright, giving the appearance of having succumbed to the strong wine.

"You must be tired," said Jusaan, figuring he would get little from Hanshee in his current state. "My servants will show you where you can sleep. We will talk again tomorrow."

Hanshee let his eyes droop as he nodded consent. He swayed as he tried to stand and Ray, now attuned to his role, quickly moved to steady him. Jusaan clapped his hands and a servant appeared.

"Lead them back to the tree," he said. "See that they have bedding if none has been provided."

The servant bowed, motioned for Ray to follow, and again held the flap as they passed from the tent.

Jusaan was now alone and much less impressed with his find than he imagined he would be. This was not the vision of his order's glorious past that he had expected, and what began as reverent awe was quickly turning to schemes of how he could best utilize the heathen priest for his gain. He would return to the city with his prize and present him to the Council, not for what he was but for what he represented. This would bring certain prophesy to the fore of his people's consciousness. If he could ride this wave of prophesy to the position of High Priest, so much the better.

CHAPTER 24

Hanshee and Ray were led from Jusaan's tent by one of his retainers.

The cool night breeze was refreshing to Ray's lungs after the heavy perfumes within the tent. It was a clear night and the stars shone brightly, much more so than Ray remembered from another life. That was how he was beginning to think of his previous existence.

In the city.

In the United States, with a job and friends and...

It all seemed like a dream now and again he marveled at how he had managed to put it all behind him, or at least come to grips with the fact that he appeared to be in another time, another world.

I should be insane, Ray thought. *You might be insane,* he thought in reply.

They were led past the campfire which had warmed them while they ate. It still burned dimly, but warmed only common soldiers now. Those who had been there must have left shortly after they had, to pursue their drinking elsewhere or maybe to rest.

The pair was led back to the same tree under which they had been kept since their arrival and were given blankets to ward off the chill of the mountain night. They managed to make themselves comfortable, Hanshee still playing the drunken guest and Ray hovering and fussing over him, ready to catch him should his awkward lurching lead to a fall. After a while they managed to arrange their blankets and settle down to what appeared to be the sleep of the exhausted, their feet pointing in opposite directions and their heads not more than a foot apart.

While they had been fumbling with their blankets Hanshee had been cautiously scanning the area, picking out the sentries positioned to watch them. These were stationed at a comfortable distance, allowing Hanshee and Ray to talk quietly without being noticed.

"What was that about in the tent?" Ray whispered.

Hanshee did not respond right away. He appeared to be lost in thought, considering what he had learned and how he would present it to his companion. After a while he felt comfortable enough with this situation to speak.

"My people are of the earth, our Mother," he began. "We dwell close to her bosom. We will always be this way, be it the will of The One, but we have not always *been* this way. There was a time in our past when we forsook the mountains and the rivers, the valleys and the prairies, and lived as many others do: in a city. We did not seek this life, but rather had it thrust upon us."

He paused, and Ray sensed he was gathering his thoughts before continuing.

"During this time long ago we lived as we live now, but over a great many lands. We called the plains our land, but we were not strangers to the forest and the foothills and the mountain passes. We were free to roam as far as we could see. We hunted the field and the forest, raised our young and passed on our knowledge to each generation within our clans and our tribes, for though we knew who we were and of our kinship, we were not one people.

"One day word came from the west of a great people, with a great army. They were fierce and mighty, and had conquered all before them. We heard of them from the people of the small cities with which we traded. They were a curiosity but not our concern, though the city dwellers seemed fearful when they spoke of them. We laughed at their weakness. This enemy was far to the west! Why should they be afraid? Clearly we were not!"

Again there was a pause.

"We knew little of the ways of city men."

"Seasons came and went. My people were born, lived, and died. The lands we always claimed remained with us. Then one day word came, brought to us by a woman and a young boy. They were the only survivors of a clan of the far plains, they who dwelled closest to the cities. The tale told that day was one of mayhem, bloodshed, and evil.

"Through the passing years, all of the cities of the west had been conquered. They had fallen one at a time, until there had been only one remaining between the conquerors and our lands. We saw this happen but realized not how it could change us. We cared not for the city dwellers. If they were driven out, we would trade with whoever was left. We did not understand the bloodlust, the cruelty, and the hunger for conquest that consumed these others."

"The day came when the last of the cities fell and when the far plains' clan approached the conquerors for trade, then did the conquerors learn of us. They traded with us on that day, small things; cloth and beads and sweets, but no tools… no weapons. The warriors were puzzled, but returned to their clan with what they had. They knew not why they were denied useful things. And they knew not that their path was followed."

"These soldiers from the city followed our traders, who led them to the camp of their clan. Their clan numbered barely sixty, a quarter of them children. The men of fighting prime made up another quarter. The rest were women and the aged. The soldiers did not care. They numbered nearly fifty strong and were hardened warriors who had burned and pillaged their way across the cities of the west. But they saved their most savage assault for this small clan, setting upon them with a ferocity my people reserve only for their most hated foes.

"The legends say that our warriors fought bravely, but the enemy came from all sides and quickly cut them down. They meant to take the women for slaves and concubines but when they lowered their weapons to savor the fruits of their quick victory, they were set upon by the women of the clan. Taken aback by the suddenness of the attack, the invaders lost seven men before again raising their arms and joining the battle with equal, if not greater, fury than before. They cut down the women and the children, some of whom fought beside their mothers, with such brutality that she who told the story thought her clan attacked by demons and not men.

"But men they were, though whatever spawned such must have been of demon's blood. These conquerors from the west slew an entire clan. Only one woman and one boy, who were away to the east gathering grass for making baskets, were spared the merciless attack.

"But they were witnesses unto it.

"Hiding in the tall grass, they beheld the slaughter of their clansmen. And when it was finished and the men from the city had gone, they walked among the corpses of their families and mourned.

"Leaving behind their dead they walked east until they found another clan of their tribe. There they told all of what they had seen, and the story they told to the elders of that clan changed our people.

"Never before had we gathered as one, but after that day runners were sent. Those nearest were made aware, and from there others were sent to spread the story to the other clans of other tribes that lived on the prairies, and to those in the forest and the foothills and the mountains. To all the Peoples of the Earth, wherever they made their homes, the story was told. And along with the story went a message, a call for all the clans from all the tribes to come together on the prairie so that we could face this enemy that we now understood to be a threat to all clans everywhere.

"For a full season the clans gathered. None knew their number, nor needed to know, nor cared to know. The legends say that on the last day, when all clans from all tribes had joined the gathering, the warriors stood as blades of grass on a hillside, their number beyond counting.

"We were different but we were the same.

"And then Usaid, the priest of the house of Pith, rose before the gathering and repeated the story of how the woman and her child had come to them and of the massacre they described. Usaid told of how the warriors of his clan had been sent to view this with their own eyes, returning with descriptions of death and butchery and of driving the scavengers from the half-eaten remains of the women and children.

"And when his words touched the gathering, for the first time the People of the Earth became as one."

For a while Hanshee was silent, and the stillness of the night seemed even more so as he wrestled with the stories, the legends, and the history of his people. Ray could tell that this meant a great deal to him, as if it marked a turning point for Hanshee's people. There was a reverence in his telling which spoke to the significance of this event. Not wanting to break the spell, Ray waited in silence for Hanshee to resume. After a while he did.

"Oh, the songs that were sung of that day! We still sing them to our children around the evening fires. Every warrior knows them by heart.

"The warriors of the united clans were many, and all were true. They swept across the plains that night under a moonless sky. Swiftly they moved, to the scene of the massacre and beyond, until greeted by the sight of the city wherein those killers of the innocent dwelled. It was the last bit of civilized land before descending to the prairies and so the butchers had been content to stop there. They gave no thought to the prairie. They had not ventured forth since the slaughter of my people, the slaughter that for them had been only sport!

"Early that morn, before the sun rose, we had our sport."

Ray noticed the "they" of the gathered clans had now become "we."

"Our warriors fell upon them like locusts, sweeping over and around and utterly destroying them. Not stopping there, they continued on to the next outpost, and the next. We moved so swiftly and silently that we were upon them before they were aware. Our warriors' eagerness for revenge ensured that the fighting never lasted long enough to slake our bloodlust, a bloodlust which drove us ever deeper into the civilized lands. Our speed, our stealth, and our savagery, ensured that none ever escaped to sound the alarm. For six days we pressed forward, unopposed by any of consequence."

Ray could see that Hanshee's thoughts were there now, swept up in the fierce battles of retribution that shaped the future of his people, and thus himself. His eyes were slits of concentration, the light of suppressed hatred and rage burning brightly within before he caught himself and realized the degree to which his spirit was immersed in the lesson. His eyes opened wider and he took several deep breaths, exhaling slowly. This seemed to calm him. After a minute or so, he returned to the story.

"We took our revenge, my friend. We killed every soldier in our path for six days. And when we were finally met by an army, they too were slain.

"What drove us, what fueled this march of destiny, we did not know. Some say it was our righteous anger, some our distrust of those who lived in cities. Others say that we marched to the will of The One Spirit, our cause just and our purpose divine. Whatever the truth, we did not stop though army after army opposed us.

"We did not stop!

"One day, on the blood-muddied field before the city they called Sesen, we cornered their retreating forces and it was finished. After that battle, none remained to oppose us. Our enemies, either fallen or fled, were no more. And when we opened our eyes we saw we had conquered an empire!"

CHAPTER 25

The chill of the night was now upon them and Ray pulled his blanket more tightly around his shoulders. The camp was silent, with only the occasional crackling of the hot coals intermingling with the natural night sounds. Ray and Hanshee remained as they had been, with their heads close so they could converse without alerting any prying ears. But they were silent now.

Ray watched as the condensed breath escaping Hanshee's nose rose and dissipated on the gentle night breeze. The steady rhythm told him that Hanshee had found sleep, and that it was time he found it also.

But he could not sleep.

He lay awake, thinking about the things he had seen and heard as well as the story that Hanshee had told. Much was still missing, and the questions swirling around in his head would not let him find rest.

"At first there was much confusion," Hanshee spoke again, as if he had never paused in his telling. His voice was quiet but strong, and Ray had no trouble hearing every word.

"We had risen up, as one, to lay waste to our enemy. Our holy anger had been satiated, and now we could return to our way of life. But some among us looked about and saw what we had done, and what we had conquered, and what we had won, and they spoke:

Look, brethren! Look around you! These lands! These cities! Our people have fought and died for this! We have won this! It belongs to us now! By blood and fire it is ours!

"Others spoke up, replying: *What use does a people such as we have for cities? Would we forsake the bounty of our Mother to dwell among these wounds upon her back? Our purpose was not to conquer, but to avenge. We have exacted our vengeance. We have feasted on the corpse of our enemies! These lands had their peoples and our peoples have our lands. Let us return to them so that all can be as it was before.*

"It was then that Usaid, the priest of the house of Pith, spoke. It had been his summons that had brought the tribes together, his pleas that had forged us into a weapon of vengeance, and his voice that had sent that weapon hurtling toward this end. He had much waah and the warriors of every clan paused to hear his words.

"He spoke of a vision sent him by The One Spirit: a vision from his youth, before he became a priest. The warriors grew quiet as he told of sitting close to the evening fire with those of his clan as the sun set, and of staring into the flames, and of his mind being swept away by The One Spirit.

"Where once he sat with his familiars by the evening fire, he now stood alone on the open prairie, the fierce winds blowing unchecked and bringing tears to his young eyes. All about him was the flatness of the earth but in the distance, beneath the vastness of the heavens, stood towering mountain peaks. His mind raced as he wondered: Where am I? How did I get here? How do I get home? The boy spun around, casting his gaze ever outward in search of something familiar, something to mark the path home. But all was desolate except for the distant mountains which rose to every side of him.

"As he stood there, lost in confusion, he felt the ground beneath his feet begin to tremble. When he looked down he saw the very earth open up! His despair was now complete and he waited for his Mother to swallow him up. Instead he found himself rising… rising… high into the air, as beneath his feet a new mountain formed and grew, bursting up through the crevice in the earth and reaching toward the heavens.

"The boy was taken higher and higher. He felt the coolness of the high breezes. He looked down to see the land falling ever farther away beneath him. He looked outward and his vision increased many fold. It seemed the mountain would never stop rising as it bore him higher still, until the peaks of the other mountains lay beneath him and his gaze fell upon distant lands that were revealed to him. When finally he stood above all, the mountain stopped rising.

"As the boy looked out from atop the world he saw the other mountains, those which had earlier surrounded him, being swallowed up by the earth. And when it was done, there stood but one mountain, and in its cracks and crevices, its slopes and peaks and valleys, he saw faces. They were the faces of his people. As he marveled at this wondrous sight, the faces in the mountain became the faces around the evening fire... and the vision was gone.

"The priest Usaid told of his vision and the warriors heard his voice when he said that the meaning of his vision, many years old and ever a mystery, was now clear: that his people would become as one, would rise up and become as a mountain the likes of which had never been seen! All other peoples would be as the earth under their feet, and his people would rule all the earth.

"Many were swayed by this tale of vision, by the thought that the war of vengeance was a holy war, ordained by The One Spirit to bring his chosen people to their rightful place as masters of the earth. Though there were those who resisted, when the elders of all the tribes met, it was decided that they would indeed rule what they had won.

"The clan and tribe of the Pith led the way, stoked by those with dreams of power and greed. The elder of the clan became like unto an emperor, while Usaid became the high priest of an empire. Many lesser clans renounced their names and joined with Pith, making them the largest and the strongest of all the tribes. Other clans, though keeping their names, aligned themselves with the great house, increasing their number until all other tribes were dwarfed. They joined with the Pith hoping for the boons and favors granted those most closely aligned with the seat of power.

"And so began the ruling of an empire," Hanshee's mouth twisted in disgust and he seemed to spit this last out.

"What knew the People of the Earth of 'civilized' ways? What knew we of empire? Our people lived in clans and tribes, ruled by elders in accordance with laws and customs passed down from times long past.

"What we knew of the cities and their people was of their greed, their selfishness, their wanton destruction of their Mother, the many ways which they found to mistreat one another. These were the things we claimed to despise, yet rushed to emulate once it was we who ruled.

The tribe of Pith and their followers spread over the lands, laying claim to all that they saw, laying waste to all that they claimed. The people who belonged to these lands even before the first conquest were treated as dogs. No, worse than dogs! The warriors entered their homes as they pleased; taking whatever they wished of the little that had been left them after their years of hardship.

"There was no rule, only chaos.

"Buildings and roads fell to ruin. My people knew nothing of these things! The locals suffered such harassment as to have been rendered paralyzed. Few crops were planted, and what was harvested was taken, along with the livestock, by those who now called themselves 'Pithians'. It was a reign of brutality and terror, the like of which we had not known ourselves capable.

"Not all of my people behaved thus. Many clan elders held their ground. They camped outside the cities, holding on to the old ways as much as they could without condemning this new empire. From their encampments they witnessed their kinsmen's deeds. They witnessed the destruction, the misuse, the pillaging, the raping, and the degradation of all that surrounded them. And as they witnessed these sins, it grew among them that this was not part of some divine plan to raise them up over the peoples of the earth. It was the ambition and greed of a few infecting the many, and leading to an orgy of abuse. Some found their voices and spoke against what they witnessed. Others gave what aid they could to those whose lives had become a hellish existence.

"But the Pith would not suffer their divine rule to be questioned for long. A council was held and they called upon the other tribes to cease in their aid to the 'natives', as they were called, to cease in their questioning and be obedient to the will of The One Spirit and the tribe of Pith. The elders of the clans opposed to empire stood their ground, saying that it was not the will of The One Spirit to so abuse a land and its people; that they would not allow their warriors to commit such a sacrilege. Two of the largest clans, Kaneesh and Dula, stated that they would return to their ancestral lands, foregoing the spoils of war to which the Pithians so gladly helped themselves.

"The emperor of the Pith would have none of this!

"He saw clearly what his people had subjected the city dwellers to. He knew it was wrong and that they would one day rise up against his rule. But as long as he controlled a united people, any uprising would be futile. If these clans were allowed to speak against him and withdraw to the lands of their fathers, others would follow. His empire would weaken. The expected uprising, now far off in the future, could well begin before the new moon.

"But what could he do?

"This was not a concern for the elder of a clan. This was a concern of empire!

"The High Priest Usaid saw all before him. He saw the resolve of Kaneesh and Dula. He saw the weakness in his emperor; his 'emperor', who was but the leader of a successful clan and who could never lead a true empire; his 'emperor', who had been following Usaid's lead from the very beginning.

And so when, in the face of this righteous rebellion, his emperor turned helpless questioning eyes toward him, Usaid took this as submission to his power.

"T'was a power on which he was already drunk.

"Knowing that the emperor was his so long as he would put an end to descent, Usaid embraced the influence and control being offered. He arose from his seat and called to the loyal Pithians to seize those who would not stand as one with their brethren! At these words, the entire assemblage froze and eyes went wide with alarm. Not believing their ears, though understanding the meaning of the words, the elders of Dula and Kaneesh made for the door only to be cut down by the bowmen who stood at either side of the leaders of Pith."

"The throng could hardly believe what had happened. A member loyal to the fallen drew his bow, launching an arrow into the chest of one of the bowmen. When he, too, was cut down by a volley of arrows, those assembled erupted into battle and flight!

"Many aligned with the Pith were now accustomed to their place atop the order and, lest they lose it, fell upon the seceding clans. For others still with questions in their hearts, this caused them to come awake. They took up arms in defense of those first slain and the ensuing battle spilled first into the streets, then to the fields beyond.

"Thus were my people, newly united, immersed in civil war!"

CHAPTER 26

Though the hour was late, Ray was not tired. He had listened to Hanshee recite only a portion of the troubled history of his people thus far, and was eager to hear even more. Hanshee had been moved by his telling of the stories, and now continued to whisper into the cool night air.

"What followed was the near destruction, by their own hand, of an entire race of people. Having the advantage of rule, the Pithians quickly gathered their warriors and launched a vicious attack upon those who would be the most dangerous. Thinking that to destroy clans Kaneesh and Dula would quickly end the conflict, they marched toward those encampments which were still in the grip of chaos and confusion. When they reached the clan of Kaneesh they found a people milling about as would ants in a troubled nest.

Word had reached the Kaneesh camp of the happenings of the day but, though the messengers bore the wounds of battle, the story was too outlandish for any to believe. Their leader… their father… slain by the Pith for speaking his mind; the Pith then falling upon others who opposed the brutality of their rule? They were cruel and vicious, yes, but only to those whose conquered lands they held. They would never turn on their brethren, whom they beseeched to join them in holy war."

Hanshee's pause here only served to make his next statement more chilling.

"The Kaneesh were not prepared when the Pithians arrived. Most could only stare in horror and disbelief at the savage killing before they, too, were cut down. Those few who resisted stood no chance. To a man, those in the encampment were slain. The older male children were also cut down and the warriors of the Pith claimed what women remained as their own, against their will, as they had claimed everything in the land of the city dwellers.

"It was lost on them that they had become exactly like the enemy they had sought to slay when first the clans had gathered.

"Heady is the wine of victory and the Pithians marched toward the encampment of the Dula with the certain knowledge that they, too, would prove no match.

"They were wrong.

"The Dula were now led by Junee, the son of the fallen elder. Though he had gone with his father to the council meeting he had remained without, having no patience for the endless words of the wizened old men. He and his fellows were engaged in knife throwing when they heard raised voices coming from inside the great building. Curiosity led him to the door where he witnessed his father's last words and watched him wheel toward the door as he called to his clansmen to join him outside. Junee saw the first arrow tear through the back of his father's neck and out from his throat, cutting off the words before they were formed. He saw his father go down, saw the elder of the Kaneesh fall beside him, and saw those loyal to him rise up only to be felled just as quickly. Instantly, as in a vision from The One Spirit, he saw the carnage on the horizon.

Junee knew that for the righteous to prevail he must fight the urge to rush into the growing fray. Leaving two of his friends to watch, and bring word to him later, he hurried to the camp of the Dula to make ready for the battle to come.

"Upon reaching the encampment, Junee gathered the warriors, telling them of his father's death but not who bore the blood. He instructed them to gather all warriors of Clan Dula, and from the tribe of Dula. Most were camped nearby.

"Only when he had gathered around him a thousand warriors did Junee take to the high ground and speak. He spoke as a leader, an Elder, and told his people what he had witnessed. There was disbelief, just as there had been at the camp of the Kaneesh, but Junee knew that he had the time and the means to convince them of what must be done.

"The warriors cried out for more proof than just his words, and it was then that Junee's companions arrived. They told the same tale and more, of the battle that ensued in the streets before the great hall and how the victors then marched for the campfires of the Kaneesh. These words could not be ignored, but still a few voiced their doubt. Junee called some of the doubters forward and asked that they go to the camp of the Kaneesh. They would go as runners, weaponless, with only sandals and loincloth so as to make the journey there and back swiftly. If all was well they would return with the news and on his oath Junee would take to the wilds forever, without a clan, as befits one who spoke such vile lies to his kinsmen. But if his words were true, the remaining warriors would, as he put it, 'prepare for a battle such that you have never witnessed or taken part before.'

"With these words the runners were off.

"The moon was low in the sky when the runners returned. They were exhausted, having covered the distance of a day's march in half a night, but they had to bear witness to what they had seen. Rest could wait.

"As the warriors once again came together at the high ground, the passage of time allowing for even more to gather, all could see that the mood was different. Word had spread quickly among them and most knew what to expect. Still, to hear the words from the lips of those who had seen, to confirm as truth what all had feared, chilled the blood of even the most hardened of the throng.

"*Junee spoke the truth! The warriors of the Pith fell upon their brethren, the Kaneesh! All were slain and even now they march for the tents of Dula!*

"The gathered throng erupted in shouts of anger and outrage. There had been clan warfare in days past, with many valiant warriors having fallen before equally valiant foes, but never had there been mass slaughter such as had occurred this night. The depths to which the Pith had sunk was now apparent. If allowed to prevail they would give their own reasons, vilifying the Dula and Kaneesh to justify their slaughter. Few would be left who could speak the truth, and none who would dare. More of the undecided clans would join with the Pith, inspired by their strength and fearful of the fate awaiting them should they be seen as enemies. No clan would dare oppose the wrongs they witnessed throughout the land. The victory of Pith would be complete.

"Junee saw this from the first, and now it dawned on the faces of the warriors before him. Swiftly he seized the moment.

"Warriors...!

"The throng grew silent as Junee gazed upon their number. There were fighting men of every age, many whose blades tasted their first blood in the war of conquest, and women, too, who had come to fight. Their skill with the bow proven in the hunt, they now prepared to hunt the Pith.

"Junee looked out upon them and felt the awesome weight of this moment. He gladly shouldered that weight as he spoke:

"Warriors! You know now that Junee of Dula speaks truth! That the words of my father and Solbat of Kaneesh were words of prophesy! As we speak this night the warriors of the Pith, awash in the evil that has consumed them, prepare for our death!

"He paused once more to allow his words to be felt.

"They march four thousand strong, while we gathered here are but a third their number. But this night we shall meet them. WE WILL MEET THEM! We will smite them with the strength of the righteous and we will stop them where they stand! Nay, we will turn them back! We will rout them and show the way to follow for all who would rise up and trample this evil!

"Junee looked hard into the eyes of those closest to him and saw that they were with him and would follow him. He gazed out onto the gathering of warriors before him so that all could see the strength of his spirit soar, and add to their own from his.

"Then he spoke his final words:

"Three to one," he said, and his eyes blazed as his lips curled into the grin of the wolf. *"Follow me... to the slaughter!"*

CHAPTER 27

"And a slaughter it was," Hanshee continued.

"The Pith, flush from their easy victory over the Kaneesh, passing between them pilfered Kaneesh wine as they marched, were expecting another easy victory. They would encircle the Dula encampment while they still slept. Catching them unawares, they would fall upon the Dula before a blade could be drawn in defense and be guzzling Dula wine by morning's light.

"They never knew what hit them.

"Rather than await the coming attack, Junee led the Dula out to meet the Pith. There were heavy woods that lay between the oncoming Pith and the encampment of the Dula. It was here that Junee and his captains chose to make their stand. It was a strategy which caught the Pithian warriors completely unawares.

"A wide trail led through the darkness, with thick woods rising gently to both sides. This was the trail that the Pithians, fresh from the earlier slaughter of their brethren, strode boldly and without fear. By torchlight they marched, their torches giving ample light by which their ranks could pass through the forest. These same torches told their intended victims of their coming, and threw light onto their number so that, still a ways from the Dula camp, they were greeted by a volley of arrows that struck deep at their number. Another volley followed... and another... and the screams of pain and groans of the dying and injured Pithian warriors filled the night air.

"Not knowing where the arrows came from, the setting moon having darkened the remaining night, the Pith scrambled for a defensive position, often directly into the path of the archers of Dula. Despite the anguish they felt at having to fire upon their brethren, the archers shot true, taking a frightful toll upon the Pith.

"With death seeming to be coming from every direction and no visible enemy to fight, the Pithian warriors surged back against their own number, causing even greater disarray. Wounded and confused, their warriors reduced by almost a third from arrows of the deadly accurate archers, the column finally turned in wholesale retreat, only to be greeted by the bulk of the Dula. They stood only eight hundred strong, but with death in their eyes, iron in their hands, and a purpose: the total destruction of the Pith!

While arrows continued to rain down on the center of the confused Pith, the Dula tore into their flanks like ravenous wolves, their blades drinking deeply of the blood of their foes. Small pockets of disciplined warriors sprang up among the Pith, but these found themselves fighting the confusion of their own men as much as the blades and arrows of their opponents. Though they took their toll, each was overcome by the savage attack of the Dula warriors.

"By now the Pithians were in full, panicked retreat, many taking to the surrounding forest to escape the butchery their campaign had become. Now some of the archers, men and women alike, lay down their bows and took up their blades. Silently they hunted down the frightened warriors of Pith, killing each of them quickly before moving on to the next, and then the next.

"When morning's sun broke through the forest mists, the width and breath of the carnage was there for all to see. The ground was littered with the dead, their blood turning the earth in places to ankle-deep mud. The Dula lost but a tenth of their number, while it is said that less than a third of the Pithian warriors survived the night."

Despite the cool night air, Hanshee's face glistened with a light sheen of perspiration. The telling of this saga, no doubt required learning for the young of his people, had brought a quickened pace to his heart along with the anticipation of battle. Ray waited him out, watching as his excited breathing became more and more regular. After a while, Hanshee was ready to complete the tale.

"These were the beginnings of war, my friend, a war that pitted clan against clan, tribe against tribe, friend against friend.

"Hearing of what had happened, Usaid called for all who were loyal to what he called 'the vision' to rally to the Tribe of Pith and wipe out the betrayers. Those who were close to the Dula and Kaneesh, and those who now recognized the evil of the Pith, rallied to those banners. When their numbers were counted, greed and evil had its sway. The forces of the Pith outnumbered that of the remaining clans, not so much as to crush them, but enough to ensure their defeat had they not found the aid they needed."

"But there were none there to aide them," Ray found himself speaking for the first time since Hanshee began the tale. "How were they delivered?"

Hanshee smiled.

"By the people of the city," he said, "the very ones who had been trampled for so long, first by the invaders from the west, then by my people, led by the Pith. The two factions at each other's throats gave the city dwellers the time, the opportunity, nay the courage, to come together and revolt. At their darkest hour, the clans were joined by the rebels and the two together were enough to finally crush the bulk of the forces of Pith.

"After much bloodshed and great loss of life, Pith was driven from the lands of cities and back to the open prairie that had been their homeland for generations. Most of the clans that had joined with them were prairie dwellers also, and would have again been at home had they been allowed to stay.

"Having pooled their forces and driven off the remainder of the Pith, the city dwellers now turned their attention to their allies. After all, were those led by the Dula not also savages and brethren to the Pith? As some would say, were not the only good savage's dead savages? Ha!" Hanshee smiled. "They could not see that we fought not to conquer our brethren, but to put an end to evil, the very evil whose foot had been on their neck! But there was no need for further bloodshed. The remaining clans were happy to leave the cities to the city dwellers and returned to the wooded hills, the rivers, and the forest which had been their homes before this folly of conquest had begun. To this day the dwellers of the cities, those blisters of the earth, look askew at us, and we at them. We trade with some few of them, but any hospitality is merely a gesture. We are enemies," Hanshee stated almost casually. "That we both understand."

His curiosity prompted Ray to ask, "But what of the Pith?"

Again Hanshee allowed a sneer to cross his face.

"'The clan of the jackal'," Hanshee said. "The evil that sought to drag the whole of the clans into the pit in which it dwelled? The Pith? They were indeed 'tween the ram's horns and the cliff's edge!

"The ancestral lands of the Pith lay between the cities and forests, and neither the city dwellers nor the forest clans would allow them peace. So it was that the Pith were ever on the move, travelling ever southward, farther south than any had gone before.

The clans continued to send raiding parties against them for as long as they could be found. After many seasons a party of young warriors returned, having been unable to find them. Either they had traveled beyond our will to reach, or they had found a passage through the mountains toward the rising sun. My people thought it was the former, but now have I learned t'was the latter."

"How so?" asked Ray.

"The warriors that now surround us... they are descended of the Pith!"

CHAPTER 28

Ray was awakened by the rough hand of one of Galin's sergeants shaking his shoulder.

The late night spent listening to Hanshee, the thoughts that his story had spawned and the dreams that followed, had left little time for sound sleep. Now he struggled to open his eyes and focus on his current whereabouts. By now he had become used to awakening in this strange world. Indeed, he rarely ever dreamed of the life he had prior to awakening beside the river and finding Hanshee there. As he struggled to sit up he saw that Hanshee had already shed his blanket and was standing apart, eyeing the sergeant cautiously as he reached out to shake Ray again.

"Enough!" Ray shouted in English as he gave the warrior an angry stare.

This brought a smile to the sergeant's face, and he stepped back in mock fear to allow Ray room to stand.

"Please don't hurt me, ya heathen bastard," he said. "I was only following orders!" At this he leaned back and gave a belly laugh, assured that his insult had fallen on uncomprehending ears.

Ray understood him perfectly, though he and Hanshee had agreed that he would not let on that he did. Hanshee could pick out only a few words. After almost a thousand years the language of the Pith was now a blend of their early speech and the speech of every other people they had come into sustained contact with.

Still laughing, the soldier turned and waved for them to follow as he headed for the cook fires. Meat, probably the remains of last night's feast, was torn from a carcass roasting on a spit while bread was provided from a loaf resting on a wooden board on a nearby table. Once these were in hand, the sergeant again motioned for the two of them to follow as he led them away from the camp.

After hungrily devouring the breakfast that was provided, and wiping his greasy hands with leaves, Ray took notice of that which Hanshee had been aware of since awakening: There were almost no soldiers in the camp. As he turned this over in his mind, they were led down a trail which was well and recently worn. Rounding a turn and brushing back a low tree limb, Ray could see the back of Galin's head up ahead. It towered above those around him as he stood atop a broad, flat rock nestled in the earth above a natural hollow.

The hollow had been a lake bed in the distant past and had currently been useful as a place to keep the horses and other animals that a military force needed. Now the animals had been moved to the side and been replaced with close to one hundred and fifty eager soldiers.

Galin turned in greeting, having heard them making their way down the path.

"Hail, the morning!" he said, smiling arrogantly as the sergeant directed them to approach him. Turning back to one of his aides, he inquired, "Do these savages understand any of what we say? Oh, here comes the esteemed representative of our priesthood." Galin turned again, this time to face the approaching priest, who had taken a different path to the rock. "He can translate for us."

Jusaan, escorted by his acolytes, was being hurried along toward the rock by another of Galin's sergeants. It was obvious the priest was not used to receiving such urgent summons from one he considered beneath his status. His feelings were evidenced in his indignant expression.

"For what have I been called from my tent at this hour? I was at my morning prayers when this soldier appeared, pressed me to follow, and then herded us here like so many cattle. I take no orders from you, Galin, and if your men believe they can accost the priesthood without showing the proper respect..."

"Please, please, Jusaan," Galin held up his hand, cutting him off. "If one of my men failed to show you the respect which is your due, be assured that I will deal with him as a commander should." He smiled at the sergeant before nodding his dismissal.

This was not lost on Jusaan, who again took up his questioning.

"What is this about that it cannot wait until after the morning's prayer?"

"Our soldiers were fortunate last night in spying out the camp of what appeared to be a scout party from our neighbors to the southeast," Galin said. "We took them just before dawn... some of them anyway. The others, putting up more of a fight than we anticipated, had to be killed in order to be pacified. But these three," he pointed to three roped and kneeling figures at the far end of the line of soldiers, "they were kind enough to come along and answer some of our questions.

"If you believe them," he said, pointing to the bruised and bleeding bound captives, "this party of twenty hardened warriors was sent to track down two men. These were two outlaws who entered their city, robbed and murdered several of its citizens, killed a few of its militia who were unfortunate enough to come upon them, and danced away as nice as you please. Their description of the two desperate criminals put me in mind of our guests."

Galin waived a hand toward Hanshee and Ray.

"Since you've taken such an interest in them," Galin continued, "I thought you might want to question the prisoners yourself before my men have their fun."

Jusaan craned his neck to inspect the bound prisoners.

They knelt at the far end of the clearing and faced the rising sun. Galin, standing on his rock on the bank of the dry lake bed, was to their right, with the throng of warriors to their left. The prisoners looked to be ordinary soldiers, a bit battered due to their forceful capture, but for the most part physically sound. There were two who seemed a bit more seasoned than the third. They held their heads aloft and tried not to show the fear which all knew was there. The third hid behind hunched shoulders and a bowed head. Even from this distance his eyes clearly showed the fear which he was unable to hide.

The soldiers gathered to their left were taunting them, some throwing rocks and sticks in their direction. Those that landed close caused the first of the prisoners to tuck his head down between hunched shoulders, but he in the middle would have none of it. He stared straight ahead, with chin held high and chest flung out, even as a sharp stone struck his head and sent a trickle of blood running past his left eye and down his cheek. His bound hands prevented him from deflecting the missiles or wiping the blood from his face so he continued to stare straight ahead, occasionally turning his eyes contemptuously to his tormentors, to assure them of his continued defiance.

Jusaan took this in with a mirthless half-smile before turning back to Galin.

"I have no desire to interrogate these prisoners," he said.

"Then perhaps you would translate for me while I question our guests?" Galin said. "You seem to have developed a rapport with them."

With a disgusted sniff Jusaan approached Hanshee and Ray, who stood on the other side of Galin. Directing himself to Hanshee, whom he greeted with a smile and a slight bow, he began to speak haltingly in something close to Hanshee's native tongue.

"Hail the morning, my brother," he began. "I trust that you slept well and gave thought to the words we shared last night. Forgive these around you," he waived his hand to encompass all the soldiers that stood around, "but it seems you and I have been brought here to witness the ritual barbarism of our warriors.

"I have been told," Jusaan continued, "that the three prisoners yonder were captured early this morning. Our commander thinks that they are somehow connected to you. As I am the only one present who can speak with you, I must ask if you have had any dealings with these men."

Hanshee had taken in the entire scene upon his arrival, noting the three prisoners tied up and kneeling at the far end of the depression. Even from this far, he recognized the city guard whose life he had spared in the mud beside the hog pins. He now regretted that act of mercy for, without the guard's bruised pride and his ability to identify them, pursuit may not have been launched. Now it appeared that this one was heading for a death more harsh than Hanshee's sword would have brought.

The one certainty of this situation was that these three were considered enemies by the Pith. The fact that there remained only three of the many who had been in pursuit of them bore witness to that.

At first there had been fifteen in pursuit, twelve from Aggipoor and three from Thessilli. Having been thwarted in the northeastern foothills, their captain must have turned back for fresh reinforcements and resumed the search for them. His pride and persistence had led his men to this fate. Who knew how many were slaughtered in the capture?

To be seen as having injured these men would in no way jeopardize his and Ray's current situation. Hanshee saw no danger in answering Jusaan's question.

"If these three come from a city toward the rising sun," Hanshee said, "we were there."

Jusaan smiled his acknowledgment before turning to Galin and flatly stating, "He knows nothing of these three."

Sensing that he had been told a lie, Galin's suspicious eyes went from one to the other. Then he smiled brightly and nodded to his sergeant, who went hastily down to the men and began barking orders. Turning back to Jusaan, he spoke.

"Good!" Galin said cheerfully. "Since there is no connection between them, we may begin our sport. Perhaps your friends would be interested in observing."

Galin motioned for Hanshee and Ray to step forward for a better view. Not wanting to leave them entirely to Galin, Jusaan too stepped forward to share the high rock but Galin blocked him from standing next to Hanshee and he took his place on the commander's opposite side.

Ray and Hanshee surveyed the open depression before them.

From their position on the rock, there was a fall of about eight feet to the ground below. Another eighty to one hundred feet separated the line of soldiers gathered on the left boundary of the depression from the raised bank. The soldiers formed a line over one hundred feet long, its center being directly in front of Galin.

As all assembled watched, three archers who had been standing behind the prisoners moved forward and prodded them to their feet. This was made more difficult since the third prisoner, the young one, could not gain his feet on his first few attempts, fear having robbed him of some bodily control. Once he had risen, the three were prodded down to the center of the area formed by the bank on their right and the line of men on their left. There they were turned to face the rock. Galin addressed them, smiling apologetically.

"I have spoken with my men and it seems there has been an unfortunate mistake," he began. "Your capture, and the slaughter of your comrades, was not really necessary at all."

A snickering rose from the ranks, causing Galin to pause and fix his eyes on his men in mock anger, drawing an even louder chorus of snickering and snorting as the men fought back their laughter.

Playing to the crowd, Galin again dropped his eyes to the prisoners.

"But now I fear that, if we allow you to leave, you would go about spreading wild tales of a military force encamped in the mountains to the west of your cities, and the citizenry could get the mistaken idea that we were... mmm... I don't know... um... scouting and mapping the terrain in preparation for moving an army through and laying siege to your valley, perhaps?"

The snickering had become loud snorts and guffaws. Galin waited for the merriment to subside before he continued.

"We wouldn't want such misinformation to spread. It could damage the peaceful relationship our two peoples enjoy."

Galin propped an elbow in his hand, using the other hand to methodically stoke his lowered chin. He was making a show of giving this problem deep thought, to the delight and laughter of his men. Again he waited for the laughter to end before raising his head as if the solution had suddenly presented itself.

"I know!" he said happily. "As a show of good faith and fellowship, we will cut you loose and allow you to return to your people as living proof of our good intentions!"

This pronouncement brought down the house, with some of the soldiers clutching their sides and laughing until tears ran from their eyes.

Galin motioned to an archer who ran forward to cut the prisoners' bonds. The archer stepped back as the ropes were shed and the prisoners rubbed the places where the tightness had cut off their circulation. The youngest - it was obvious that he was in his teens and on his very first military patrol - had a look of profound relief on his face. He turned to his comrades and smiled, but the joyous smile was instantly wiped from his face when he saw their grim demeanor. The sound of Galin's voice brought his head snapping back toward the rock.

"You may leave on one condition: if you are able to best one of my men."

At these words one of the soldiers stepped forward carrying a rolled-up blanket, which he set down on the ground before the prisoners. From a kneeling position, he unrolled the bundle. Inside were knives and short swords. The knives, mostly of the cooking variety, were old and worn. The swords too were old, dull weapons, probably used to cut firewood when a hatchet or axe could not be found. All in all they were poor substitutes for true weapons of war.

The prisoners looked down at the weapons spread at their feet as if not comprehending what was expected of them. Galin quickly put an end to whatever doubts they had about what was coming next.

"My men have long been in the field and, having served me well, deserve some entertainment," he said. "Your comrades, may The One rest their souls, fought bravely but fell much too quickly. Some of my men had no chance to join the fray. They feel they missed out on the fun. So I propose a contest.

"You there!" Galin pointed down to the guard whose life Hanshee had spared. "Heft a blade... quickly now!"

The man stared up at Galin, then down at the pile of dull weapons, but he did not move.

"What ails you, man?" Galin asked, before nodding at the same archer who cut their bonds. The archer sprinted forward, this time with a leather lash. He struck the man across his naked back, pointed down to the weapons and barked, "Choose!"

The prisoner flinched at the crack of the leather on his bare skin and turned hateful eyes to his tormentor, but he did not move.

Crack!

Another blow fell, then another, and another. Finally, pained and angered, the prisoner knelt down and grabbed a kitchen knife, turned, and prepared to make a lunge for the whip-wielding Pithian.

Fffffth!

The two arrows struck as one, quivering as they jutted up from the earth two feet in front of the prisoner. Whatever thoughts he had of attacking the whip wielding soldier were immediately driven from his mind as he stared at the feathers fletching the arrows as they trembled before his face. Eyes wide with surprise, the captive slowly stood, almost unaware that he still held the knife in his hand.

"Now that is more like it," said the jovial Galin. "It's best to join willingly in the festivities. You'll feel better in the end."

Now there was movement among the gathered warriors as one of their number stepped forward. Ray recognized him as the man who had, upon their arrival at camp, insulted Hanshee by hawking a wad of phlegm at him. He was still surly looking, and much bigger than Ray remembered. He strode forward confidently, stopping within ten feet of the now-armed prisoner but showing little concern for his safety. Looking up at his commander, he gave a formal salute, clenched fist driven palm upward into the center of his chest as if driving a knife into his own heart.

"My life I pledge for Pith!" The formal words were shouted as the salute was made.

"And Pith accepts, Botha," Galin said graciously, inclining his head in acknowledgement and addressing the warrior by name.

With a parting glance of contempt in the direction of Hanshee and Ray, Botha turned his attention to the prisoner before him.

No words had to be spoken now. When the huge warrior reached behind him and withdrew from its sheath a real knife, a warrior's blade that was large, sharp, and edged on both sides, the captives all knew what was expected of them.

Gathering his courage, crouching low, and moving to his right, the captured guard tried to circle his bigger and stronger opponent, but Botha matched his movements so that he was kept with his back against the rock. Knowing that his only hope lay in keeping his distance and not letting the warrior trap him, the captured guard lunged, feinted, and spun away. Now he had room to maneuver and...

Moving quicker than it seemed possible for a man so large, Botha was upon him.

He held his knife tightly in his right hand, the blade running down the length of his forearm, his left hand extended as both a guard and a distraction. He used it to parry his opponent's panicked stab while drawing his own blade sharply up, slicing open the left side of the prisoner's face. Finishing his maneuver, he stepped away with a flourish, putting Ray in mind of a bullfighter who, after the first pass, moves off to acknowledge the applause of the crowd.

The stunned prisoner stood there, his hand to his face, feeling the warm wetness as blood oozed between his fingers. The first flashes of white-hot pain were beginning to reach his brain and, amidst a sudden burst of anger, he charged the exposed back of his taunting opponent.

Botha wore a heavy leather tunic, more than thick enough to turn the dull blade wielded by the injured guard, but still he remained alert. He knew, or at least expected, that exposing his back for so long would draw an attack. And a clumsy one it was. The guard, obviously unused to knife fighting, moved straight forward in an attempt to stab Botha in the lower back. Botha merely spun to his right, causing the kitchen utensil to roll off of his tunic and allowing him to complete a three-hundred-and-sixty-degree turn, bringing his blade down in a wicked slice that opened up the right side of the poor guard's face from his ear to the corner of his mouth as the momentum of his charge carried him past.

This brought a shout of appreciation from the gathered warriors.

Botha, awash in the glow of his comrades' favor, had already decided that he would take his time and slice this one up slowly. He loved fighting, loved killing, especially with a knife but really with anything at all. He wanted his brethren and his commander to have a good show. He turned to survey his work and await the next clumsy attack this lamb would make.

The guard's face was streaming blood from both sides now, the right side so severely cut that his teeth and gums were visible through the wound. Botha's blade having sliced into muscle, the guard found that he could not fully close his mouth and now resembled a grinning death's head when viewed from that side. Unable to hold his face together, and sensing what Botha meant to do, his only thought now was to draw his tormenter's blood before he himself was slain.

Again he charged but, though bleeding and in pain, less wildly this time. Aiming a thrust for the behemoth's stomach, he changed direction at the last instant and stabbed towards the throat.

Botha caught the change and parried the blow with his empty left hand, but was not quite quick enough and took a shallow cut across the right side of his neck. Enraged that the prisoner had managed to wound him, and still holding his outstretched right arm, Botha brought his blade straight up into the armpit, severing muscle and connective tissue, leaving a limp and lifeless limb dangling from the right side of the captive's now heavily bleeding body. Then he brought his blade swiftly across the guard's chest, slicing deep into the pectoral muscles and down to the ribs beneath.

The guard stood still, unable to do anything save stare at the blood spurting from his armpit, the blood streaming down his torso, the blood dripping from his face to the ground below. He stared for what seemed to him a long while, unable to tear his eyes away from the spectacle of his own death, until a meaty hand grabbed the hair at the back of his head and yanked his face upward and back.

Now he stood almost on tiptoe, staring up into the eyes of his killer.

Not one foot away the eyes of Botha sought and held those of his victim, not allowing him to look away. Botha gripped his hair tightly, knowing he was powerless to pull himself free or fight back. As Botha stared into his eyes, he brought his right hand up until the blade of his knife was touching the guard's lower abdomen. And then he slowly, ever so slowly, pushed the blade in until the hilt alone kept it from penetrating farther. The guard's eyes grew wide as he felt the blade's slow penetration. His mouth opened, trying to form words, but the only sound he made was a croak. Then, with the throng of warriors watching, Botha began to work the blade within his victim, moving and slicing, working it ever upward, all the while staring into the eyes of the dying man. Cutting upward on the guard's torso, Botha did not stop until the blade made contact with the sternum. Only then did he yank his blade free.

Botha released his hold and allowed his victim to drop, as would a puppet whose strings have been cut, into a heap upon the ground.

Botha now turned to receive the cheers of his comrades, which they gladly bestowed on him, while Galin looked closely to gage the effect of this bloody spectacle on his guests.

Ray stared in stunned disbelief. Never had he imagined anything like this - people killing other people in the most barbaric ways – simply for their amusement.

He felt the bile rise in his throat but somehow managed to fight it down. He saw Galin's eyes on him, measuring him and noting his reaction. Galin then looked to Hanshee. Ray did the same.

Hanshee stood motionless, expressionless, watching the bloody spectacle as if it were the cleaning of a fowl, or the gutting of a fish. He betrayed no sense of his feelings, pro or con, about the fate of the captive guard.

Galin smiled thinly and turned back to the bloody scene.

Botha had wiped his blade and now stepped forward to await his commander's pleasure. Galin nodded and another prisoner, the seasoned warrior, was pushed forward to stand before the pile of useless weapons. Immediately he stooped and grabbed a short sword, which he tested in his grip. The weapon was pathetic. He looked at Botha who let his knife fall from his hand and was smiling in anticipation as he awaited a similar, but sturdier, weapon to be brought to him. Their eyes met and the prisoner threw the sword to the side, stepping forward with his hands bare. Seeing this, Botha too shunned the weapon which was being thrust into his hand and prepared to meet his adversary in like fashion.

Taking one step, then two, the prisoner moved toward the larger Botha. Then he burst into a run, launching his body at the bloodthirsty giant with startling speed. Botha was unprepared as he was struck full in the abdomen by the prisoner's lowered shoulder. The two of them fell over in a pile of limbs, the smaller man digging and clawing at his larger opponent, searching desperately for some way to hurt him, some way to gain an advantage. His hands flew to the eyes, but Botha deftly twisted his face this way and that, allowing the seeking fingers to gain no purchase. Then down to the groin they went. Botha's groin was protected by his leather tunic but the prisoner managed to reach underneath, groping for the giant's testicles. Somehow Botha gained a grip with both hands under his opponent's torso and heaved. The prisoner was flung through the air, landing several feet beyond the point where Botha was now arising.

Slightly disoriented from the toss, the prisoner did not rise quickly enough. This was his undoing. Botha was on him in a flash, bringing a heavy fist, with his full weight behind it, down on the back of the prisoner's neck and smashing him back onto the ground. The prisoner was stunned and momentarily helpless.

Botha sneered down on his handiwork, allowing himself a brief respite, before reaching down and closing an iron grip around the back of the captured guard's neck. He then snatched the guard to his feet, where he teetered unsteadily. After twisting the man's left arm behind him, Botha ran the prisoner straight at the boulder on which Ray and Hanshee stood.

The sickening sound of the captive's face striking unyielding rock was somewhere between a thud and a crack.

That was the first time.

The second was definitely more of a crack but, as Botha continued to drive the prisoner's face into the rock again and again, the sound changed to more of a slapping squish, like the sound of a bundle of wet clothes dropped onto a floor. At the point of impact there appeared a red splotch roughly the size of a human head.

And still Botha drove the captive's face into the rock.

Only Botha held him up now, the captive's legs having long since deserted him. But Botha was up to the task, slamming his face again and again into the rock until the blood ran down the stone to pool in the dust below. When Botha finally tired, and let the limp body fall to the earth, the face that was left looked nothing like a face. It was just a disfigured mass of bloody chopped meat and bone.

Not awaiting a nod from his commander this time, Botha turned to the last and youngest of the three prisoners. The look on his face was terrible to behold and the lad, already traumatized by the bloody deaths of his comrades, felt the full weight of his terror come crashing down upon him.

As Botha approached, the boy bolted, running past Botha toward the protection of the distant trees.

He was running as fast as his traumatized mind could will his legs to move but, swift as he was, the three arrows were swifter still. They struck almost simultaneously, almost in the same spot in the young prisoner's upper back. They struck so hard that they lifted him off of the ground, flinging him ten feet through the air before he landed facedown upon the dusty earth, sliding an additional six or seven feet before coming to rest. His body spasmed violently, one hand clawing desperately at the dirt, as he instinctively fought for what little life remained.

Thankfully his fight did not last long.

As the gathered soldiers watched, the boy's torso slowly relaxed and submitted to the inevitable. His last breath hissed through twisted lips before his face settled to the dust in stillness.

Ray raised his head from retching the breakfast he had eaten so quickly, and the sight that greeted him was somewhat of a relief. He viewed the still body of the boy with one thought echoing in his mind: *Thank God, a quick death.*

This was cut short by the voice of Galin.

"Jusaan," the commander pouted, "I don't think our guests fully appreciated our display."

He motioned toward Ray and the puddle of vomit as he spoke, but his eyes never left Hanshee. Hanshee must have somehow betrayed his distaste for the slaughter to the sharp-eyed Galin, but Ray saw only a blank stare of indifference.

"I don't think they approve," Galin continued sadly. "Jusaan, tell this one," he nodded toward Hanshee, "that he may minister to the corpses if he so wishes."

Jusaan was silent.

"TELL HIM!" Galin shouted, glaring at Hanshee. Jusaan was so taken aback by the change in tone and mood that he felt compelled to do as he had been ordered.

"Galin… the commander… says that you may inspect the corpses… if you wish," Jusaan stammered.

Without hesitation or so much as a backward glance, Hanshee launched himself from the rock upon which he stood, landing deftly beside the faceless prisoner who lay at its base. A quick glance confirmed what he already knew: the man was dead. He turned to the youngster, face down in the dirt with three arrows protruding from his back, and knew that death had come for him also.

Hanshee then turned his attention to the first prisoner who had received the attention of Botha's blade. There was a slight quiver in his limbs that could be seen even from where Hanshee stood. As he moved closer, he could see an almost imperceptible rise and fall of the chest. As badly butchered as this man was, he still clung to life.

Walking over to where the guard lay, Hanshee stood above him for a moment, looking down into eyes that were wide open but oblivious. Kneeling down, he took the dying man's head into his hands, resting its weight on his left palm while cupping the chin in his right hand. With a quick twist he snapped the neck, putting and end to the poor man's suffering. Closing the lifeless eyes, Hanshee gently laid the head onto the ground before scooping up a handful of dust to clean the blood from his hands.

He then stood and fixed his gaze upon Botha.

CHAPTER 29

Botha took in Hanshee's accusing stare. He knew, along with everyone else in the camp, that this half-naked stranger was thought to be some kind of priest. But the glare that he found fixed upon him now came not from a holy man.

It came from a warrior.

Botha remembered seeing this one when he was first brought in. He had thought then that he would get the chance to deal with him as he had the three that now lay lifeless in the dirt. The priest Jusaan had put an end to that when he claimed them as guests of his tent, but now things had changed. They stood upon a field of battle and this stranger's accusing stare was a challenge as surely as if it had been shouted at the top of his lungs. Botha met that stare with a wolfish grin of anticipation and lust in his heart for even more blood.

Galin had been hoping for this.

For Galin, one of life's true pleasures came from baiting Jusaan. Since the priest had taken a liking to this stranger what better way to get his goat than to arrange a messy death for the man? As Botha glanced his way Galin inclined his head slightly, giving permission to proceed. He then turned smiling eyes on the shocked and speechless Jusaan. This could be fun!

Hanshee started toward Botha with a purposeful stride. Botha waited, the model of calm, his excitement betrayed only by the rhythmic clench and release of his fingers. He was eager for more killing to commence.

As Hanshee closed to ten feet he sucked in hard through his nose, cleared his throat, and spit a wad of phlegm at the ground before Botha, mimicking the sadist's earlier insult. Botha glanced down at the thick puddle of fluid which had hit his sandaled foot and raised his face to the oncoming Hanshee with a smile of anticipation. He raised it just in time to catch a second wad of phlegm that Hanshee had launched at his face. The thick glob struck just above Botha's right eye and quickly ran from his brow to his cheek, leaving a thin line between the two.

Botha was momentarily stunned by the suddenness, and the gall, of this gesture. His anticipation blossomed to anger, then to fury, and he lunged for Hanshee, swinging his fist with all his considerable strength at the fool's taunting face.

Though surprisingly fast for his size Botha could not match Hanshee's quickness. He leaned to his left as he parried Botha's vicious blow with his right hand. Forcing Botha's extended right arm into his body to keep him off balance, Hanshee used his left shin to fire three vicious kicks to the outside-rear of Botha's right thigh. The effects were readily seen on Botha's face, as the first of the three brought a grimace of pain, the second a vocal accompaniment and the third caused the leg to give way as Botha went down on his right knee. He immediately sprang up and turned to face the retreating Hanshee. Wary now, Botha circled to his left to cut off Hanshee's retreat, favoring his right leg as he moved.

Wearing a taunting smile which he knew would further enrage Botha, Hanshee moved fluidly to his left before pretending to stumble, a move designed to draw Botha in.

Eager to redeem himself after their initial clash, Botha moved in and drove his left fist into the side of Hanshee's head. But Hanshee's head was no longer there, having moved under and to the right of the blow. At the same time Hanshee parried the blow away from him but, instead of pushing in as he had before, he let his open left hand slide down Botha's arm until it closed on his left wrist. Then, with a twist of his hips, he pulled backwards and downward, bringing the already off-balanced Botha into a right forearm launched with the same hip-twist motion that had destabilized him. The blow struck Botha's left temple. Though it had the potential to be lethal, Hanshee pulled its force at the last second.

Fighting through his ringing head and sluggish thoughts, Botha was still able to strike back. He swung wildly at Hanshee with his free right hand, missing badly before bringing the same hand around in a back-fisted blow. Hanshee ducked the first but met the second with a hard block, really more of a strike, to the wrist. Botha felt something give but before he could withdraw his wounded wrist, Hanshee closed his fingers around it in a grip of iron. Then, twisting his torso to his right, he brought his left forearm into his opponent's still-extended right elbow.

Botha let out a bellow of pure agony as he felt the joint cleanly dislocate, but this was cut short as, with a twist of his hips back to the left, Hanshee raked his left hand, fingers extended like claws, across his victim's face, followed almost simultaneously by the heel of his right palm, driven with the same torso motion, into the giant's nose.

Botha fell heavily onto his rear and landed in a sitting position, the blood flowing freely from his shattered nose. Having never been in this position before, as he had always crushed any who opposed him, he sat frozen in confusion and pain.

Then he heard through the blood and the pain and the anger the shocked silence of the usually rowdy warriors. It was a silence born of disbelief at what they were witnessing. It lasted one heartbeat... two... then was broken by a single voice.

"He's kicking Botha's arse!"

The gathered warriors erupted in laughter.

Men such as Botha seldom had friends. Botha was both sadistic and natural in his bullying of nearly all about him. Many in the throng had felt his blows and insults, though he was strongly discouraged from injuring his comrades in arms. Truth be told, there were not many present who shared Botha's, and apparently Galin's, thirst for slaughter.

Heated battle? Yes. Fair combat between equals? Of course.

But the massacres set up as entertainment by their commander were a far cry from these. It wasn't right, and some secretly hoped to be present the day Botha got his comeuppance.

This was that day.

Botha could not see the soldiers, the blow to his nose having temporarily brought tears to his eyes, but he heard their mocking laughter and the taunts that followed.

They dare? Botha thought incredulously. *THEY DARE?!*

Pain and confusion driven out by renewed anger, Botha struggled to his feet, only to be met by Hanshee who again drove his shin into the rear of Botha's right thigh. Unable to keep his balance on the limb both numbed and painful, Botha again toppled into the dirt, but this time facedown. He could hear the laughter and the taunting, much bolder now, as he struggled to a kneeling position. There he stayed, on his knees, balanced on his still-good left arm but head down, and with the blood from his nose making a pool of red mud in the dust below.

Ray watched in silent fascination all that had transpired and now, with Botha clearly beaten, he watched Hanshee turn on his heel and walk away. It was over... but no!

Hanshee walked toward Botha's first victim and, bending down beside him, retrieved something from the dust. He then approached Botha again but the large man never made an attempt to rise, never moved. It seemed he was no longer a threat. As Hanshee drew nearer to Botha, Ray saw his right arm swiftly rise and fall, and then he knew what had been there in the dirt.

Botha strained to focus on the object that had imbedded itself in the center of the puddle of blood that drained from his broken nose. He gingerly reached out his throbbing right arm and felt new life as his hand closed around the hilt of his knife! He had dropped it when the second prisoner had first opted to face him with a short sword. Now he had it back and there would be hell to pay.

Slowly Botha struggled to his feet to again face Hanshee, the blood so thick on his lips and teeth that only someone as close as Hanshee could see that the smile of the killer had returned.

Hanshee stood weaponless and unconcerned. He had done his work well.

Though Botha held it in the accustomed right hand, Hanshee knew he would not be able to wield the blade. He had watched carefully as Botha had taken such pleasure in slaying the two captives, and he had noted many important things. Among them was the fact that Botha was right-handed and, like many who were naturally formidable, he had failed to train himself to use both hands. He depended on his good right arm and Hanshee had made sure to take that away from him before giving him back his blade.

Botha did not seem to notice as he made an awkward lunge toward his adversary, trying to inflict any damage he could but failing miserably. Again he flailed with his damaged arm and again Hanshee easily avoided the attack. On the third try Hanshee stepped in to parry the hapless stroke, grabbing and twisting the arm until, with a shriek of pain, Botha let the blade fall. With the speed of a striking serpent, Hanshee plucked the falling blade from the air and, still holding Botha's ruined right arm high, drove his left foot into Botha's right knee, dislocating it. The pain and shock drove Botha down on his left knee, his right leg extended somewhat behind him, his right arm still in Hanshee's grasp and extended above his head.

Botha reached for Hanshee with his left hand, hoping to rake his eyes or grasp his neck or to do something to make this demon let him go! Hanshee saw the fight still in Botha's eyes as he extended his hand toward Hanshee's face, saw the hope that the day could still be won.

Then, with a flick of the blade, Hanshee opened a deep gash across Botha's left arm. As Botha instinctively snatched the arm back, Hanshee was already raising his right arm to bring his right fist, and the knife hilt in it, down in a hammer blow that shattered Botha's left collarbone. The bleeding left arm now hung impotent at Botha's side as he looked up into the face of his tormentor.

Hanshee now saw that the look of the killer was gone from the giant's eyes. No longer did his lips curl in a sneer, his features distort in anger. Now there was room for only one emotion, one he had hardly ever felt before.

Fear.

And at the end, his body broken and all vestiges of pride having deserted him, Botha begged for mercy. He begged with his eyes, with the trembling of his mouth, and with the slack body that spoke of total and utter submission. With these, he asked to be spared.

This was what Hanshee had been waiting to see.

He was swift in bringing the blade to Botha's neck, but he was slow as he dragged it across. He did not want this one to die too quickly. He wanted the realization to sink in that he was moments away from death with absolutely no hope of surviving. He wanted Botha to feel his death long before death itself could erase the feeling. It was the most appropriate punishment he could give at this time, and he watched as the fear in Botha's eyes expanded until it consumed him before it slowly began to fade.

Hanshee continued to hold Botha's right arm aloft as the blood from the open neck cascaded down the heavy torso, not allowing the body to crumple to the ground until almost all life had been drained from it.

Ray was transfixed by the sight and, when Hanshee finally let Botha's corpse topple into the ocean of blood that had run from the opened veins, he felt no pity and whispered no prayers. No, this one deserved worse. If he could be resurrected, only to be destroyed in the same humiliating way, it would still be too kind.

And there, standing above his work, was Hanshee, dealer of death, the right hand of justice, swift and sure.

Hanshee… the avenger.

Hanshee raised his eyes from the slain brute and cast them upon the gathered warriors. Deliberately, he let his gaze sweep from one end of the throng to the other and any remaining questions found their answer in that ice-cold stare. Then, without a backward glance, he turned on his heel and strode toward the rock on which stood Galin, Jusaan, and Ray.

All eyes followed him as he climbed the embankment and approached the three. His bearing was proud, his manner restrained, and he paused before Galin just long enough to meet his hard, hot gaze. Then he approached Jusaan and, as if returning from a long hunt, a hard ride, or a day of work in the fields, he spoke.

"Is there water near?" he asked matter-of-factly. "I must wash."

Jusaan's strained features now broke into a smile and he answered as Hanshee had spoken, in the ancient tongue.

"Of course, my brother!" Jusaan said. "I will have one of the acolytes show you to a stream not far from here."

He motioned for one of his attendants to approach and gave him instructions to see to every need of his guests. Then he turned his still-smiling face to Galin.

"May I now take my leave, or has there not been enough bloodletting for one morning?" he asked.

Without waiting for a response Jusaan turned and followed Hanshee, Ray, and the others down the path toward the camp, leaving Galin to stew in his barely concealed anger and embarrassment.

Catching up to the group, Jusaan spoke again to one of the acolytes.

"When they have cleansed themselves, see that they are given proper attire," he said.

"But, M'lord, where will I find attire for the likes of these?" the priestling asked with undisguised contempt.

Jusaan turned an arched eyebrow upon him and proceeded to put him in his place.

"Look to your own bags, man!" he spat. "I'm sure you brought enough to outfit yourself many times over!"

Pushing past the stunned acolyte, Jusaan continued on before stopping short, turning, and adding, "Give them your tent also. It *is* the closest to mine, is it not?"

Wheeling away without waiting for a response, Jusaan could not restrain the smile that played upon his lips as he thought: *This has not been a wasted morning, after all!*

CHAPTER 30

Ray traveled with the main party, which included Galin and his officers, Jusaan and the priesthood, and the others whose presence made this more than an ordinary expedition, among them cooks, surveyors, and mapmakers. They were accompanied by the remainder of the military force, with Galin having ordered the others into advance and flanking positions until they were clearly established to be in Pithian territory. This was not necessary. No known enemy would think of attacking them here, but Galin, ever the diligent commander, left nothing to chance. Besides, a soldier could never train too hard.

The trail was not difficult and the soldiers set a leisurely pace, aware that there were those among them unused to the rigors of crossing open country. For Ray and Hanshee, who set themselves a grueling pace even when not being pursued, this was little more than a stroll in the woods. That was fine by them. It gave them time to think and to consider their position. Time Ray sorely needed to hash out his peculiar situation.

It had been a long time since he had given any deep thought to the whys and how's of his being here. Things had begun to move so fast, situations became so precarious so quickly, it had taken all of his physical and mental energy just to keep up. By his reckoning he had been with Hanshee, living wild, for almost three months now. The fact that he had not seen the slightest sign of life as he had known it had ceased to concern him as much as it once had. He had somehow come to terms, though not consciously, with the fact that he was in some type of medieval world, a world of ancient cities, armored warriors on horseback, clashing iron, and death both cruel and indifferent.

The butchery - there was no other way to describe it - that he had witnessed since his arrival had shocked him like nothing he could have imagined. He had actually seen men hacking, bludgeoning, disemboweling, and otherwise killing their fellows with no remorse and, in some cases, with glee! Of all he had seen, this struck him the hardest. Yet, on some level he could not quite understand, the ease with which death came in this land, the swiftness and the savagery, forced him away from endless speculation on his puzzling circumstances. One can hardly dwell on riddles when every ounce of one's focus was needed just to stay alive.

Maybe this was why he had not gone insane, as he had every right to.

Ray looked to his left, slightly ahead, and saw that Hanshee was still there. After watching him move swiftly and quietly through the forest for so long, he seemed now to be plodding. He turned his head to look at Ray, having sensed the eyes on him, and smiled the smile of one who knew, at least for the moment, that they were secure. Ray smiled in return, conveying to Hanshee the message that he was fine, that he was holding up and dealing with it all.

Throughout their time together Hanshee had been many things: a healer and provider, a guide, a teacher, and a confidant, a protector and a pillar from which he could draw strength. This man, who had shown him the only real kindness that he had known here, had also shown himself able to match, and surpass, the savagery of all who had revealed themselves as threats. To embody that much compassion and that much ferocity, and be ready to apply whichever was needed at a given moment; Ray could only shake his head in wonder. His life had been saved three, four, maybe five times now, all because this warrior who claimed the mantle of "Maiyochi" had found him floating almost lifeless in a river.

Ray's thoughts wandered back over the last few days. After Hanshee had dispatched the sadist Botha, things had changed. Though the commander, Galin, showed more open dislike for them than before, he could not move against them due to the protection of the priest, Jusaan. And Jusaan was simply in love with them!

Well, with Hanshee at least. And Hanshee was taking Ray along for the ride.

They had been given clothes to wear, robes from the priesthood by the looks of them. It was none too soon for Ray, whose cargo shorts and khaki shirt had been hanging on him like rags. The Nikes were holding up, though. He still wore them underneath the robe. Every now and then he would lift the hem of his garment and glance down to see the familiar "swoosh" on the outside of the hiking boots. This was all he had to let him know that he was not mad and this was not a dream.

They had been given a tent also.

It was a small one, compared to that of Jusaan, but it provided some degree of privacy and thoroughly infuriated at least one of Jusaan's underlings. Ray guessed that this was the fellow who had occupied the tent before. Inside, he and Hanshee had formulated further strategy for dealing with their situation. It was decided that they would continue with the ruse of "wandering priest and acolyte." This, after all, was what had saved their lives when they were first led into the encampment of the soldiers of Pith.

Hanshee remained limited in his understanding of the language of their captors turned hosts. Having been exposed to so many influences over the last millennium, there was little that resembled the language that lay at its foundation. He could converse only with Jusaan, whose priesthood had kept alive a form of the old tongue as their special domain.

Much like Latin in the Catholic Church, thought Ray.

For his part, he understood not only the core language, but the different dialects heard round the camp. He never let on; a task that became difficult when overhearing a bit of juicy gossip or a particularly funny story. When addressed by any of the Pith he would simply smile and nod his head, laughing if the other laughed, all the while fully aware of the base insults being jovially hurled his way.

Once he and Hanshee were in the secretive folds of their tent, he would explain all the intelligence he had gathered for the day. So that they could speak without fear of spies, they used a language none here would be familiar with. It was the language of one of the cities with which Hanshee's people sometimes traded. Knowing of Ray's special gift, Hanshee made a habit of speaking this tongue only to him and within a day Ray was almost as fluent as he. It was during one of these sessions, when Ray was relaying the day's overheard conversations to Hanshee, that he was surprised by a piece of intelligence from his companion.

"Jusaan says that the soldiers will be finished soon. He has suggested that we accompany him to the Pithian capital."

Ray studied Hanshee for a while before responding.

"And you think we should."

It was a statement, not a question, for he could see by studying Hanshee's face that he had accepted the idea.

Hanshee sat up on the small cot on which he had been reclining, another of the perks that accompanied the gift of the tent.

"The seasons are turning," Hanshee said, "and the high mountain passes have already felt their first snows. To travel them now, we lack the provisions for such a journey. Had we not met the Pith, even then it would have been difficult. We would beckon death were we to leave here now. Soon these low mountains too will feel winter snows. If we go with the Pith we will be sheltered from the cold. They will provide for us, their honored guests, until the spring. Then we will leave this place."

"That may not be easily done," Ray replied. "The priest, Jusaan, he seems to want something from us, or rather from you. We don't know what his plans for us may be. It may not be as safe for us as you think."

Hanshee regarded Ray with a look of pride.

"You suspect treachery," he said. "Now you think as you should."

"Of course the priest has schemes... schemes within schemes," Hanshee continued. "Most city priests do. We must remain wary, never letting our guard down. If we are to survive this hostile place, we must not be above schemes of our own. Whatever his plans for us, they have kept us alive until now. Perhaps they will keep us alive until the spring."

That had been several days ago, and then there had come the first snow. It was only a dusting but it was a harbinger of more to come. Hanshee was right, of course. They were now on the eastern face of a high mountain range. They could not travel south fast enough to avoid the cold to come. To travel farther up into the mountains, the only other way to the western face, was certain death. For better or worse, their fate rested with the Pith, at least for now.

And who knows? Maybe somewhere ahead, maybe inside the walls of this new city, maybe from the utterances of someone as yet unmet, he would at last find something to tell him where he was, why he was here, and how to get back home.

He pushed these thoughts to the back of his mind.

One thing at a time, Ray told himself. *For now let's worry about staying alive.*

END BOOK ONE

ABOUT THE AUTHOR

Phillip L. Johnson is a retired analyst living in Columbia, South Carolina. A graduate of the University of South Carolina, he and his wife Louise have raised two sons and are surrounded by family and friends. After spending a career in the Insurance industry, he now has the time to do what he really wanted to be doing all those years behind a desk, writing stories of excitement and adventure.

NOTE FROM THE AUTHOR

Word-of-mouth is crucial for any author to succeed. If you enjoyed *Awakening*, please leave a review online—anywhere you are able. Even if it's just a sentence or two. It would make all the difference and would be very much appreciated.

Thanks!
Phillip L. Johnson

Thank you so much for checking out
one of our **Fantasy** novels.
If you enjoy this book, please check out
our recommended title for your next
great read!

War of the Staffs by Steve Stephenson & K.M. Tedrick

"Offers an enjoyable romp for high fantasy fans."
-KIRKUS REVIEWS

View other Black Rose Writing titles at
www.blackrosewriting.com/books and use promo code
PRINT to receive a **20% discount** when purchasing.